# Boyfriend

# # 2

### A Novel

### By

## Caleb Alexander
## And
## Erick S. Gray

Copyright 2012

This book is a work of fiction. Any resemblance to real people, living or dead, actual events, establishments, organizations, and/or locales are intended to give the fiction a sense of reality and authenticity. Other names, characters, places, and incidents, are either products of the author's imagination, or are used fictitiously, as are those fictionalized events and incidents that involve real persons and did not occur or are set in the future.

# Boyfriend # 2

This book is licensed for your personal enjoyment only. This book may not be re-sold or given away to other people. If you would like to share this book with another person, please purchase an additional copy for each recipient. If you're reading this book and did not purchase it, or it was not purchased for your use only, then please return to your vendor of choice and purchase your own copy. Thank you for respecting the hard work of these authors.

Published By; **Golden Ink Media**

Cover By; Oddball Designs

ISBN: 978-0-9826499-5-4

# Boyfriend # 2

# Chapter One

"I am a boss bitch!" Tameka shouted as she threw herself onto her platform bed. She rolled over onto her back and peered up at her bedroom ceiling. She was beyond happy; she was in a state of giddiness. Tameka pounded her fists on the bed. "I can't believe that this is mine! All mine!"

She peered around her Asian themed bedroom, taking in her Feng Shui decor. She admired her black, low slung platform bed, and her white, silk wall paper with an enormous black Japanese cherry tree sprawled across it. She gazed admiringly at her black and white kimonos that were mounted in glass frames and hanging on her wall. She had created the bedroom of her dreams. In fact, her entire apartment was the apartment of her dreams. Everything had come together for her. Everything that she had worked for, everything that she had planned for, everything that she had longed for, was now falling into place. Her Harlem brownstone was the latest item that she was able to check off of her extensive bucket list.

Tameka sat up in her bed and began to sniffle in order to keep her tears from falling. She had worked so hard to get where she was. She had scratched and saved and danced her way through college. NYU had not been cheap. And yet, she had managed to find ways to pay for her education. She had done things that she wasn't proud of. Dancing at Big Al's strip club four nights a week was one of them. Her two abortions were another. And those didn't even include the number of 'morning after' pills that she taken. She had done what she had to do, to get

5

where she needed to be. That was her life story. Always had been, and perhaps, always would be. She was from the hood. And getting up out of the hood in one piece was not for the weak of heart. Sometimes the decisions you made had to be cold-hearted ones. Sometimes, they even had to be straight up ruthless. But she had learned to cope with her decisions, even if they sometimes crept back into her memory every now and then. But she learned to put those thoughts aside and keep moving.

Tameka rose from her bed and peered out the window of her newly remodeled brownstone. Children were on the sidewalk jumping rope and playing. The neighborhood was alive and vibrant and moving in all the right directions. Real estate prices in Harlem had steadily been rising through the years, and so she was extremely happy to be able to get the place of her dreams. Her home reminded her so much of the Cosby Show of the Eighties. It was why she always wanted one. The love that she saw on the television screen was the love and the type of home that she wanted to re-create. While growing up, people would tell her that she was stupid. That it was only a T.V. show. But what was the difference in her fairy tale of a Cosby like brownstone, and their fairy tales of a Prince Charming that would come and rescue them from the hood? They believed in a modern day Prince Charming rolling up in a black Range Rover sitting on twenty-four inch rims, with a fine ass baller sitting behind the steering wheel. She wanted to be Claire Huxtable, so what the fuck was the difference? A fairy tale was a fairy tale, right? The difference was, she thought, was that she was going to make hers come true. She was going to have the type of home that was denied to her while she was growing up.

Staring out of the window, Tameka thought about the next part of her plan. She had the brownstone, and now, she just needed to find her very own Cliff Huxtable to share it with. A doctor was out of her reach, she thought. She was from the hood,

6

and she was a hood chick through and through. She had grown up in Brooklyn, and she had a less than stellar reputation around the hood. She was known for being a 'gold digger' as some called it, while others called her a 'hood rat'. A hood rat, she thought. What the hell exactly was a 'hood rat'? Especially when she could count the hood niggas that had been up in her shit on one hand. How had that made her a hood rat? In college, yes, but in the hood, no. But nevertheless, that was her past. A past that she had scrapped and clawed to climbed up and away from. So she had to be a realist. She was not foolish enough to believe that black doctors grew on trees, or that one would want to scoop up a girl from projects of BK. So her Cliff Huxtable would have a different job, of that much she was certain. And she was pretty sure that she had found the perfect man to fulfill that role. His name was Caleb, and he was a stock broker with Goldman Saks. He was perfect to fill the role in her life that she needed him too. He was the perfect, respectable husband, the man that she could take to her office parties, the man she could take to weddings, the man who she could have babies with. The only problem with Caleb, was that he was too perfect. He had no fire, no passion, no sense of adventure. And that's where Eric came in. Eric was from the hood, like her. He was the one who put a smile on her face. He was the one who made her laugh, who gave her the adventure, and that thug love that a girl from the hood secretly craved. If only she could combine the two of them and create the perfect man. If only Eric could have Caleb's paper, and Caleb's job, and Caleb's perfect pedigree. Or if Caleb could have Eric's smile, or sense of adventure, or have that dangerous hood streak in him. She wanted to be able to rock some Timbs, or some Polo boots, and throw on a hoodie and hit the subway and get lost. She could do that with Eric. She could hit up a Jay Z concert or a Drake concert with Eric. She could bust out singing the lyrics to some Eric B and Rakim, and Eric would join in and sing along.

Caleb couldn't do that. She and Caleb had little in common, while she and Eric had everything in common. It's just that one filled in the pieces of her past, while the other filled in the missing pieces of her future. And so for the time being, she kept both of them in pocket. And she was cool with that. She would keep Eric until she was ready to get rid of him and build her Cosby like family with Caleb.

"I like!" Rosalynn told her, stepping into the bedroom and peering around.

"Thanks," Tameka said, turning and growing animated. She wanted to hide her thoughts, and hide her tears. Her girlfriends from college were touring her new place in order to give it their seal of approval.

"It is really pretty!" Tammy chimed in. "I should have looked in Harlem. I'm kicking myself. I'm stuck in DUMBO, with a stupid view of a big ugly bridge, while you're in the middle of all the action!"

"Girl, DUMBO is not exactly a bad piece of real estate," Tameka told her. "Being down under the Manhattan Bridge overpass means you're still in Manhattan."

Rosalynn peered around Tameka's room, taking in her bedroom furnishings. "Wow, I need another job."

"Right," Tammy said nodding. "Tameka is straight balling."

Tameka smiled and waved them off. "Girl, please!"

Inside she wanted to turn a flip. She had known Tammy and Rosalynn since college, and respected their opinions. Tammy was a good girl, from a good home. Her father was a doctor, and she actually did live the 'Cosby' lifestyle. She was a free spirit, kinda like Denise was on the show. She was the hippie, the one who wore the colorful outfits, and rocked her hair in a natural fro. She majored in Film and minored in Drama while at NYU. They were typical rich kid majors. She was now working at Random House as an editorial assistant. It was always Tammy's approval that she sought the most. No matter how BOHO Tammy tried to be, she was still a Black American Princess. She had class that was bred into her, and so if she approved, it meant that she was on the right track.

"Girl, if I would have known a marketing major makes this kinda bread, I would have changed my major!" Rosalynn declared. Rosalynn was the product of a middle class background. Both of her parents were teachers, and Rosalynn was a journalism and mass communications major at NYU. She was now working for the local NBC affiliate station in the programming department.

"Girl, I got lucky!" Tameka told them. "Very lucky!"

Tameka turned and peered out of the window and thought about her job. She was an executive assistant at Omnicom Group, the largest marketing firm in the country. She worked in one of the busiest ad departments in the world, and she was already catching the eye of some of the company's big wigs. Her knowledge of the streets had already benefited Omnicom in some of its efforts to market several of the company's client's products to an urban audience. She had been beneficial in more than just a few of the campaigns. And so she had been given a raise and more responsibility. It was this raise that put her over the top and allowed her to purchase the home of her dream—her beautiful Harlem brownstone.

"Girl, we are on our way up!" Rosalynn told her.

Tameka turned back to her friends and smiled. "We are!" She and Rosalynn shared a hug.

"I can't wait to get my own place!" Rosalynn told her.

"You know I have four bedrooms?" Tameka said, lifting an eyebrow.

Rosalynn shook her head vigorously. "No. I couldn't."

"Are you kidding me?" Tammy said, jumping in. "Rosalynn, you'll be living on 127th street! Between 5th and Lennox! You'll be right in the middle of all the action! You can get to your job in ten minutes!"

"Roz, I'm at four thousand square feet, and that's just from what I've renovated so far," Tameka added. "Once I get around to doing the rest of the unit, this place is going to be way too big! I would love for you to come and stay with me!"

Rosalynn covered the lower half of her face and wiped away her tears. "I can't believe this!" She hugged Tameka tightly. She had been staying with her sister and her husband and kids, and space was getting tight, and the situation was getting awkward. She was now grown, but sometimes her older sister seemed to forget that fact. She was dying to be able to get her own place, but prices were way too high for her to make that jump alone.

"Roz, you know you're my girl!" Tameka told her.

"How much?" Rosalynn asked.

"We can do a thousand a month, all bills paid," Tameka told her.

"Oh my god!" Rosalynn said. She was nervous with excitement. She fidgeted, trying to pull out her i Phone and dial up her sister.

"Let's hit the streets and celebrate!" Tammy told them.

Rosalynn shouted into her cell phone. "I'm moving in with Tameka! I can't believe it! I'll call you back later!" She turned, clasped Tameka's arms, and started bouncing up and down.

Rosalynn was cool, Tameka thought. The two of them had a lot in common. Neither of them was raised with a silver spoon in their mouth. Although in college she made some decisions that were less than upstanding, Rosalynn had kept her shit together and just worked more hours at her job at the Wal-Mart in Jersey. She wished that she would have had the conviction to do the same.

"C'mon, let's go out and celebrate!" Tammy said again.

The three of them walked into Tameka's living room, where

10

Tameka began to turn off lights.

"We'll get the car, while you lock up," Rosalynn told Tameka. She and Tammy headed out the door, leaving Tameka alone.

Inside of her apartment, Tameka peered around, taking it all in once again. She was proud of what she had—even if she had to sell her soul, and every now and then, her ass, to make it happen. Her apartment was laid. Her Feng Shui, Japanese theme continued into the living room and dining room. She had a low slung, Japanese style coffee table, a low slung creme colored sectional, and beautiful Japanese artwork, and spectacular Japanese vases spread throughout her home. She even had a real Japanese Banzai tree sitting in the corner near her fireplace.

"I did this," Tameka said softly, as she turned off the living room lights. She did it. And she had just cemented the last piece of her living expense puzzle by inviting Rosalynn to move in with her. She was damn sure glad that Rosalynn had accepted her proposal without much convincing or even begging on her part. That way, she would never have to reveal to anyone that she desperately needed Rosalynn's thousand dollars a month to help pay her bills. She had drastically overspent on the place, and had cleaned out her savings on the renovation. And so, once again, she had to use another person to get what she wanted. It was getting easier to do each time, Tameka thought. She was going to use Rosalynn's money until she was ready to get rid of her, and get her Cliff Huxtable to move in with her. Pawns, Tameka thought. They were all just pawns. She would use them, move them around, and sacrifice them when she needed to.

"Stupid, bitches." She smiled, closed her apartment door and locked it.

# Boyfriend # 2

# Chapter Two

Tameka sat in her lavishly furnished living room sipping on white wine from a long stemmed glass that she found at a quaint little shop on her last trip to New Orleans. She sipped and nodded and vibed to Sade's "No Ordinary love" that was wafting from the high end stereo system that she had picked up on sale at Best Buy. The stereo's Bose speakers enriched her place with a theater like experience that had her Brownstone sounding like a concert hall. The beautiful British singer's voice made Tameka close her eyes and sway gently with the melodic sounds pouring out of the speakers.

The ambiance of the room was enhanced by the scented candles burning in colorful flames, and the drawn shades in her living room provided her with a view of the streets from her Harlem brownstone. For the first time in a long time, she felt like a queen. Cleopatra didn't have shit on her, Tameka thought. She sat back and nodded to the smooth sounds that resonated throughout her apartment. The silky sounds had propelled her into a sultry mood.

Tameka took a few more sips from her chilled wine and exhaled. She peered around her apartment taking in her trappings, satisfied with the direction in which her life was going. She was checking off more and more things on her list as time went by. Sade's voice in her ear was the perfect finish to a great day. Almost, the perfect finish, she corrected. The only thing left was for her evening to end with a bang. And by bang, she meant

13

a good hard stroking from her Gangsta Boo. She smiled, as she thought of Eric.

*I gave you all the love I got*
*I gave you more than I could give*
*I gave you love*
*I gave you all that I have inside*
*And you took my love*
*You took my love*

Tameka was enjoying her nice quiet evening at home, relishing her solitude after a hard day at the office. She was waiting for Eric to arrive. He was her fix, her relaxation, her high. He was everything she needed when it came to relaxation and then some. She enjoyed having him around on evenings like this. She always had a good time with him, as he was her escape from everything. He was a Brooklyn thug with a bad boy swag that drove her absolutely crazy. He reminded her so much of the niggas from the hood that she grew up around. There was never a boring moment with him.

She laughed as she thought about Eric's deep, raspy voice that made him sound like Method Man. She reflected on his sexy athletic build that was like delicious eye candy to her. Her gangster boo stood at six-one and rocked his hair braided in forever neat cornrows that hung all the way down to his shoulders. He had a thick, but nicely trimmed beard, and wore it well on his face. His full lips and tatted up body reminded her so much of 50 Cent's. She couldn't wait to feel his lips against hers, and to have her body entwined with his. Tameka loved the way his strapping build pressed against her smooth, brown skin, and how he would wrap his rock hard arms around her like a nice warm blanket. He made her feel safe. And lying in bed with those massive muscular arms wrapped around her always made her quiver and tingle. It was a deep, stirring tingle, one that stirred from between her legs and slowly made it's way upward through the rest of her body. She was starting to feel that tingle just thinking about him.

Tameka glanced at the clock on the wall.

"Hurry up, Eric," she purred softly. She was ready to get some.

Tameka took a few more sips from the wine and continued to nod to the next Sade track, "The Sweetest Taboo." It perfectly described her relationship with Eric—taboo. She knew deep in her soul that Eric was wrong for her. He was like cigarettes to a cancer patient, or cake to a diabetic. But still, she yearned for that enjoyment; she needed it. She loved that instant gratification that came with him being around, despite the risks and time that it took to manage two separate relationships. Eric made her happy in two ways; sex and weed. She loved these evening hours when he rolled through to supply both. The wine she was drinking was a temporary pleasure, a mere appetizer to appease her until the main course arrived. And that main course was due to arrive soon.

At nine-thirty, the doorbell rang, and Tameka perked up instantly. Her rendezvous was two hours late, and it upset her a little. Of course she would let him know how she felt about his tardiness, but if he came correct, then all would be forgiven by the end of the night. But for now, her mind was on the fact that she had downed three glasses of wine, replayed the Best of Sade CD twice, and had even lost a tiny bit of her sexual appetite. She was certainly ready to curse his ass out now that he had finally arrived. Who the fuck did this nigga think he was, she wondered? No man in his right mind would have the audacity to make her wait so long, or to stand her up. She was that bad of a bitch, she thought. When she called, men came rushing to see her. What made Eric think that he was so different?

# Boyfriend # 2

Tameka thought briefly about opening the door and canceling the perfect evening she had set up for them. As a matter of fact, she had been only a few seconds away from blowing out the candles, shutting off Sade and pouring the rest of the wine down the sink. But then the doorbell rang, and her sour mood slowly began to transform into a smile.

Tameka debated whether or not to curse Eric out, but she was unsure how the conversation would turn out after she said what she had to say. She wanted to let him know what was on her mind, but she didn't want him to turn around and leave. The cravings deep down within her body were desperate to be satisfied. So getting rid of the only dick she had set up for the evening was not an option. So, she would have to be more tactful in her expression of displeasure.

Tameka sighed, placed her wine glass on the table, and rose from her couch. She strutted to the door still clad in her sexy sapphire colored, floral print and lace robe that stopped mid-thigh. She also still had on her six inch Baby Phat stilettos. Her oiled down legs gleamed like they were in the sunlight, and her long, dark brown hair fell against her shoulders like a soft cloud. She knew that she was oozing straight sex appeal. The fact that she was completely naked beneath her robe revealed her intentions for the evening. She wanting to throw open her front door, greet Eric, and get down to business. At least, that had been the plan. Still, she was pretty sure that the evening would fade away with moans and groans and cries of pleasure bouncing off her bedroom walls.

Tameka threw open her front door. Eric stood on her front stoop cheesing. He was all smiles at first, and then upon seeing her attire, realized what this evening was really going to be about. His twinkling eyes went from warm to wanting in an instant.

"Hey beautiful," he greeted in his raspy tone.

# Boyfriend # 2

Tameka smiled and walked her eyes down his attire. Tonight he was rocking a pair of Mek jeans, and some fresh construction Timberlands that looked like he just took them out of the box. He sported a fitted shirt beneath his butter soft leather jacket, and he wore his Yankee fitted cap tilted and low over his cornrows. He also had a long, gleaming chain drooped from around his neck that fell against his abs. At the end of his low hanging chain he was rocking was an enormous diamond studded cross. He was the epitome of a Brooklyn thug. A balling Brooklyn thug mind you, but a straight up hood cat nonetheless. It was a look that drove her crazy. Tameka wanted to thrust herself into his arms and melt. The irritation she felt earlier had dissipated once she saw Eric's smile and how good he looked. She wanted to lick him like a lollipop, and at the same time, she wanted to be his dessert.

"You gonna let me into your new place?" he asked.

"Yeah, come in." Tameka said dryly. She stepped to the side and allowed Eric to cross the threshold into her new home.

Eric walked in and looked around. He was impressed.

"Nice, baby," he uttered.

"So, you like it?" Tameka asked.

"You got taste. I can get used to a place like this," he said. "So, where's the bedroom?"

Tameka smiled. She was still a little pissed. But he had a way of disarming her even when she was extremely heated with him.

"That can wait. I want to show you the place first."

Eric removed his leather jacket and tossed it onto the nearest chair. Tameka took him by the hand and led him through her brownstone. Her first stop was the kitchen. She pointed toward her stainless steel 48" refrigerator/freezer, and her 48" duel fuel stove.

"The fridge is Sub Zero, and the stove is Wolff," Tameka

told him. "The saleswoman said that this was the best."

Eric twisted the red knobs on the stove, causing the front burner to come alive with flames. "Whoa. You can do some real cooking on this thing, ma. You gonna hook a brother up with some nice steaks?"

Tameka smiled and nodded. "My plan was to hook you up, but I thought you would be the one supplying the meat."

Eric threw his head back in laughter. "I like that, yo. I definitely like that."

Tameka took him by his hand, and led him into one of the guest bedrooms. Eric spun, taking in the room.

"This is nice, ma," he told her. "This ain't the main joint though, is it?"

Tameka shook her head. "No. This is one of the guest bedrooms."

"This joint here is bigger than most master bedrooms," Eric said nodding. "You did a good job on the renovation. A real good job."

"Thanks."

"So, you know what spot I can't wait to see," he said, smiling seductively.

"I can't tell," Tameka said, craning her neck. "The way you took your sweet time getting here."

"My bad," he said, smiling. "I had some business to handle."

"Oh yeah?" Tameka asked, lifting an eyebrow. "What was her name?"

Again, Eric threw his head back in laughter. "See, there you go. You know you my one and only."

Tameka rolled her eyes and nodded. "Un-huh."

She clasped his hand, and led him through the house and into her master bedroom. Eric peered around nodding.

"Yeah, this is really nice....I forgot you were into that Asian theme. Yeah, I can see us gettin' it poppin on that bed," he said, taking in the Feng Shui decor and the low slung platform bed.

"You like it, baby?" Tameka asked.

"I love it. It ain't gonna break though, right?" Eric asked with a sly smile. He pressed down on the bed, checking it's sturdiness. "Cuz you know how I get down, right?"

"No, it's not going to break," Tameka said rolling her eyes again. "Everything's stable, superman."

"A'ight, we'll see. But you know I ain't paying for no new furniture if it do."

Tameka laughed and nudged him playfully.

Eric pulled Tameka into his arms and stared into her eyes "You're so fuckin' beautiful, girl. You know that right? How did I become so blessed to be with a woman like you?"

Tameka damn near melted in his arms. Men didn't say that to women like her. Men didn't say that to her. That was the thing about Eric; he saw past her faults and he made her feel special. Hood chicks like her were never made to feel special. Hood cats only rolled through to make booty calls. Sure, they did the movie thing, and the club thing, and maybe even took a sister out to eat every now and then, but it was all about getting some pussy. E made her feel special with his words. And she clung to those words like Muslims to a Malcolm X speech.

Tameka peered into Eric's dark, onyx eyes and found many of her life's answers. She and Eric were the perfect pair. They were both hood, they were both scarred by the ups and downs of life, and he was the perfect hood cat for many a hood chick. If only she could be content with just being that hood chick, and not being a bourgeois Black wife, her life could be so simple. He was really the hood cat of any woman's dreams. Deep down in her heart she knew that he was meant for her. In all of his bad boy swagger, he was hers. His words had her completely open, and she was ready to take him there.

"You gonna speak Japanese to me while I fuck the shit outta

you," he asked laughingly.

"Are you gonna make me?" Tameka asked.

"I have made you speak in tongues before," Eric said with a smile. He pulled her close. "What you got for me?"

"What you got for me?" Tameka replied with a sassy tone.

Eric smirked. He knew exactly what she was talking about. He reached into his front pocket and pulled out a fleshy dime bag of weed. Tameka's eyes lit up.

"This is what I got for you," Eric told her. He grabbed his cock. "And this."

"Why you so bad?"

"Why you so fuckin' sexy?" he countered. He was ready to pull her into his arms again and strip off her robe.

Tameka snatched the dime bag from his hand and strutted away. Eric followed her into the living room. Tameka seated herself on the couch. On the coffee table in front of her was a White Owl cigar ready to be split open and rolled into a blunt. Tameka was so ready to smoke haze. She wanted the cannabis streaming through her system like the blood that was coursing through her veins. Weed always made her relax, and it made sex with Eric much more exhilarating. Puffing on a blunt was definitely not something she could ever do with Caleb. That was another difference between the two. With Eric, she could relax and be the hood chick that she was deep down inside.

Tameka split the White Owl cigar open down the middle with a razor and slid the guts out onto the table. She was a professional when it came to rolling blunts. Like a master, she removed the haze from its cellophane package and plucked out the unwanted seeds. She then licked the edges to seal up any tears, and then took the wrap and folded it in the center. Tameka spread the weed evenly down the length of the blunt, and then peered around for her lighter, ready to spark it up. The hood chick in her definitely came out when Eric was around.

Eric took a seat next to Tameka as she lit the cannabis. She placed the blunt between her lips and inhaled deeply, savoring the moment. She missed the smell of the sweet chronic smoke from her younger days. She missed blowing big time kill with her brothers and friends back in high school. The sweet smell reminded her of the good old days back in the hood.

Tameka took a few more pulls from the burning blunt and passed it to Eric. She then leaned back and crossed her smooth glimmering legs. She was in relax mode. She wanted the savor the idyllic mood and to allow Scotty to beam her up like she was on an episode of Star Trek. Eric took a few pulls and returned it to Tameka. They smoked for a few moments, while Sade's voice continued to serenade them.

*No place for beginners or sensitive hearts*
*When sentiment is left to chance.*
*No place to be ending but somewhere to start.*
*No need to ask.*
*He's a smooth operator,*
*smooth operator.*

The song described Eric perfectly, Tameka thought. He was a smooth operator. She walked her eyes up and down Eric taking him in. He was built, that was for sure. She loved his clothes, his cologne, his looks, and his swag. She loved her hood cat. He made her heart full whenever he came around.

The weed smoke also made her start with all the "What if's…" What if she and Eric could really make it? What if she did decide to chill with him permanently? Was she the only woman in his life? Was he even the settling down and getting married type? Most hood cats weren't. Was Eric? Could she ever trade in her long term dreams of Cosby type lifestyle? Could she substitute Cliff Huxtable for Treach or 50 Cent? What if, she thought? What if?

# Boyfriend # 2

Tameka examined Eric carefully, as he puffed on the blunt. Was he was too trapped in his ways, she wondered? Was he too caught up in his thuggish persona, and that gangsta lifestyle? Brooklyn was his first love, that was for sure. The streets came next, and hustling followed, which put her in fourth place. He did, however, continuously make time for her. And the time they spent together was always out of this world. Shit, she thought. The weed smoke had her mind buzzing way too much for such deep thoughts. For the moment, he was her escape, and that was that. The other shit; she would have to decide later. Right now, she was just going to live in the here and now with him. As far as Eric was concerned, it was all about right now.

Eric leaned back against the couch. He and Tameka's eyes were glazed. She loved the way he looked in his Mek jeans. She loved the way he wore them low slung, showing off his six pack whenever his shirt rode up. It was all making her hot. She was ready to untie her robe, and straddle him right then and there. She could feel her pussy beginning to throb.

"You good, babe?" he asked, leaning into her.

"Yeah, but I can be even better," she hinted.

He smiled. "Oh word?"

Tameka nodded. She was giving him an open invitation to handle his business. She was ready to feel his hard dick inside of her. She wanted to feel his lips against her nipples, and she was ready to feel his soothing touch. Tameka's body needed pleasing. She wanted to break in her new place with the right man and a vigorous fuck. She wanted to bless each room in the brownstone with an orgasm.

"I miss you," Tameka uttered.

"You do, huh…how much do you miss me?" Eric asked.

Tameka gently rubbed his crotch. She smiled at the bulge that quickly developed inside his denim jeans. Her soft touch began to stir the beast within him. She couldn't wait for that beast to be released and pound her pussy savagely. She felt like it was long overdue for a punishing.

Eric leaned over and kissed Tameka passionately. Their warm wet tongues intertwined like two vines. Their eyes connected, and Tameka took his hard dick into her soft palm. She stroked him gently, causing him to close his eyes and moan slightly. His breathing became heavier as the excitement built. Tameka relished these moments of pre-sex, almost as much as she loved the sex itself. She loved the build up, the racing hearts, the anticipation. Her mind became awash with waves of lust as she stared at her thug lover.

Tameka peeled the robe away from her shoulders and Eric's eyes lit up at the sight of her naked body. He loved to see her body. He could just sit back and stare at her naked body for hours at a time, because she was just that fine. But this was not one of those times. Tonight was not about sitting back and watching. Tonight was a night for action. He devoured her breast and sucked on her nipples like they were pieces of candy. Slowly, and gently, his hand worked it's way down her thigh until it found her sweet spot. She was more than just moist, she was ready. His finger slid inside of her pussy, causing her to arch her back and stir.

"Ooooh, baby…" Tameka cooed.

Tameka pushed Eric's finger deeper inside of her. She wanted to feel him inside of her. Her body yearned for the sexual execution that was promised by the throbbing dick in her hand. Her eyes flared with hungry lust, and she nibbled at Eric's ear while continuing to stroke his dick like a toy. Eric pulled his fingers from inside of her and sucked on them. It drove her crazy whenever he did that. A man who loved the taste of pussy was every woman's dream, and she was no exception. And Eric ate her pussy like he was eating at his favorite buffet.

"Damn, you taste so good," he said.

"You a freak," said Tameka, with a naughty smile.

"But you love this freak."

"You know I do." She told him. "C'mere baby."

Tameka pulled Eric closer to her. Their tongues wrestled with each other again for a brief moment, before Eric stripped away his clothing and dropped between Tameka's legs. She parted her long silky legs like the Red Sea, allowing Eric full access to her luscious pink flesh. Eric dove face first for her pussy, like a submarine diving deep into the ocean. She cried out once he began to suck on her walls and clit.

"Oh shit, Ooooh, baby….Ooooh, don't stop, Ummm," she moaned, as she gripped the back of Eric's head and guided him to her ultra-sensitive G-spot. His tongue twirled inside of her and boxed against her clit. Tameka closed her eyes, clasped the sofa cushion, and held on for dear life. Eric's head game was the absolute best.

"You like this?" Eric asked, twirling his long, moist, warm tongue inside of her. "Say you like this?"

"I like it, baby!" Tameka moaned. "I like it!"

Eric wiggled his tongue around inside of her, and then engulfed her labia. He sucked at her pearl tongue with a steady pressure, like he was trying to suck some venom out of snake bite. The steady sucking pressure was driving her crazy. And then, he slid two of his finger inside of her. The sucking on her pearl tongue and the fingers sliding gently in and out rubbing her g-spot, was too much for Tameka.

"That's it!" she cried out. "I'm cumming! I'm cumming!"

They were the two words that Eric loved to hear. He continued to suck and finger her, until she let out a steady, watery cry, and squeeze the back of his head.

"OOOOOHHHH, Eric!" Tameka cried.

Eric placed his mouth on her pussy, and sucked as hard as he could. He could feel her juices flowing into his mouth. She could feel the cum streaming through her vagina and into his mouth. It brought tears to her eyes. Tameka stiffened. She couldn't move for several moments, as her body's pleasure juices were sucked out of her. She even tried to speak, but couldn't. The only thing that came to mind was to call Eric a black mother fucker! He had her ass hooked. She knew that if she ever caught him sucking another woman's pussy like this, there was going to be a homicide. Those juicy, sexy, tangerine like lips were hers, and hers only. This was the only pussy they would ever be allowed to suck again. She could never voluntarily let him go. Niggas that ate pussy like he did, only came along once in a lifetime. She was ready for the second part.

"I wanna fuck. I want you inside of me now," she purred.

Eric situated himself on the couch, and Tameka slowly mounted his ten inch erection. She moaned as the beast impaled her insides. She wrapped her arms around her lover and rode his dick slowly at first, but steadily increasing her gyrations in speed and intensity.

"Ooooh, you feel so good, baby. Your pussy is so good," he told her. He could feel her juices still running down his dick.

The gentle but sharp caresses of Eric's cock inside her and the rough kisses on her nipples made Tameka's body light up with pleasure. Eric was devouring her body as if he needed it to live. He thrust upwards into Tameka as she rode him relentlessly. The deep penetration inside of her caused her to clench her hands into a pair of tight fists.

"Got, damn!" Tameka cried out. Her entire body went stiff as Eric's big dick piston slid in and out of her.

"Oh my god....oh shit, you feel so good, daddy...I'm gonna cum again!" she exclaimed.

Tameka could feel her juices running out of her. Her eyes continued to water with enjoyment. The way Eric twisted her body like a pretzel on the couch should have been a crime. She quickly went from riding his dick, to being face down in the cushion with her ass and body arched, while he rammed his massive cock into her from behind. He fucked her like he had supreme authority over her pussy.

"That's it!" Tameka cried out. "That's it! Get that pussy, Daddy! It's yours! It's all your! You killing it, Daddy! You killing it!"

Sweat poured down Eric's face. Tameka liked it rough. She had a pussy that fit his dick just right, so he didn't know how she was able to take it. Most of the girls that he got raw with, couldn't take it. But Tameka was a soldier. And that was one of the things that he loved about fucking her. He could go all out with her.

Eric smacked Tameka's ass and then pulled her hair. Doing so was like turning on a light switch. It just made her go harder. She didn't have time for love making, and tender kisses. She didn't have time to give instructions or to wait for a nigga to catch his breath after a quick nut. She needed a professional; a damn maintenance man. Tameka needed a nigga that was able to lay pipe, and fix her plumbing on a regular. And if the plumber brought a snake with him, so much the better. She loved nothing more that to have something long, and hard being shoved into her hole.

"Shit, your pussy is so tight," Eric moaned as he went deep inside her.

Tameka cried out as Eric hit deep. Her soft voice crying out, combined with her tight pussy, made Eric cum like crazy. He shot his wad so forcefully into the condom that he almost blew the tip off.

Tameka arched her back and came once again. The feeling of Eric deep inside of her throbbing as he came, made her cum too. Together, their bodies shook and jerked with a spastic rhythm that made it seem as if they were both being electrocuted.

Eric and Tameka huffed and puffed, with both of their

bodies going as limp as wet noodles. Eric laid down fully on top of her, and for several moments, neither could speak.

"Your pussy is so good, baby," Eric said, once he was able to formulate words again.

"Is it?"

"Hells yeah, my dick is still jumping," he said with a smile.

"I know," she said, lifting a sly eyebrow. "I can still feel you jumping inside of me."

Eric rose from the couch. He extended his hand, helping her rise as well. Tameka faced Eric, wrapped her arms him and peered around her apartment. She had just blessed one room with her thug love. Eventually, the rest of the rooms would hear her cries of pleasure as well.

"You straight?" Eric asked.

Tameka nodded. "Very straight." She peered over at her clock. She had handled her business in enough time to catch the newest episode of Atlanta Housewives. And now that she had gotten her fix, it was time for her to get rid of her Brooklyn Pipe Layer. What the fuck would be the purpose of him sticking around, she thought? Her night was complete.

Tameka stretched and faked a yawn.

"You okay, baby?" asked Eric. "I ain't put you to sleep, did I?"

Tameka pursed her lips. "Boy, please." The last thing she wanted was to massage his ego. He had put in work. He had put in really good work. And that's why she was done with him for tonight.

"I am sleepy," Tameka told him. "I gotta go in to the office extra early tomorrow."

"Word?" Eric asked her.

Tameka nodded, lying her ass off.

"What about our round two?" Eric smiled. "You know one time is not enough for a cat like me. I'm just getting started."

Eric rubbed on Tameka ass, and she gently knocked his hand away and stepped back.

"I think I came too much," she told him. "I'm starting to get a headache."

"I got something to relax you and take your mind off that headache," Eric told her.

Tameka held out her hand. "Advil liquid gels?"

Eric shook his head. "Fresh out. Only thing I got left is hard dick."

Tameka grabbed Eric's cock. "Hard dick? I don't think so. You ain't ready for a round two."

Eric folded his arms and stared at her. She could feel the blood flowing back into his dick, causing it to stand up again. She had a choice. Another fuck session, or Housewives?

"Damn, baby, I got to get up early tomorrow," Tameka told him. She chose Housewives. She had came three times already, so she was straight. It wasn't her fault that he didn't get his like she got hers. Sex was an individual sport, she thought. You better get yours, before I get mines, she would always say.

"You gonna leave a brother hanging?" Eric asked. "I thought that I was going to spend the night here and bless the crib with you?"

Tameka lifted his clothing from the ground and stuffed it in his arms. "I know. But I didn't anticipate this headache, and I didn't think that you would come over so late."

"What difference does it make what time I came over, if I'm spending the night?" Eric asked, while getting dressed. "I'm here now."

Tameka walked Eric to the door. "I'm sorry, babe. I'll make it up to you. Call me tomorrow?"

Eric opened the door, and walked out onto the stoop. Tameka grabbed his jacket and placed it into his arms. What part of "I'll holler," did this nigga not understand, she wondered?

28

"You still pissed because I showed up late?" Eric asked.

Tameka nodded. "Yeah, that's it. I'm still pissed."

"I told you that I had some business to handle,"

"Eric, I have to get up really early and go to work. Plus, I got a headache now. Please understand."

"You aren't one of them bi-polar chics are you?" Eric asked. He pulled out his key fob, and aimed it at his Black Escalade, disabling the alarm. A loud chirp sounded through the air.

Tameka leaned forward and kissed him. "I'll talk to you tomorrow, babe."

"Alright," Eric said, relenting. "I'll call you tomorrow. You go and get some rest, and get rid of that headache."

"Thanks for understanding, Boo,"

Eric turned and headed down the steps, while Tameka closed the door. Inside, she leaned against her front door and shook her head. She had almost fallen weak tonight. She was about to break one of her biggest rules, just because she had been thinking with her cunt. She was about to let Eric spend the night.

Her brownstone was not for her thug love, it was for her future Cliff Huxtable. And no matter how bananas Eric's head game was, she couldn't lose sight of her goals. Yeah, she loved him, but love had little to do with money. And her number one rule was C.R.E.A.M. Cash Rules Everything Around Me. And although Eric was her sweet black coffee, she wasn't about to let him fuck up her cream. Besides, she got what she wanted out of him anyway; she got a good fuck down. He had served his purpose, and it was time for him to hit the bricks. It wasn't just the bitches who were pawns. Her niggas were chess pieces too.

# Boyfriend # 2

# Chapter Three

The Touraine was Manhattan's newest luxury boutique apartment building. It was nestled on the island's swanky Upper East Side. The sixteen story building offered it's residents not only 24 hour a day concierge service, but a private library, a private wine cellar with private individual wine lockers, as well as a rooftop terrace and lounge with outdoor fireplaces, al fresco dining, and starlit gathering areas. The Touraine was the newest apartment building in Manhattan's penultimate luxury real estate scene. It was a level of luxury that Tameka was certainly not used to.

Tameka stood inside of the five bedroom, five and a half bath, forty-four hundred square foot penthouse on the top floor of the luxury apartment building, taking in the sights and sounds of the party around her, as well as the furnishings throughout. Although she had been inside of the apartment numerous times over the last six months, the furnishings never ceased to amaze her. The apartment was Versace downed to the tee.

French Empire furnishings clothed in Versace fabrics were spaced throughout. Exotic woods had been hand carved into beautiful pieces of furniture, and embellished with gold leaf trim. While her style had been modern and Asian, this apartment's style was pure old school and old money. Lot's of old money!

The crowd that was gathered was distinctly Wall Street—big money Wall Street as a matter of fact. And while the apartment was old school, the moneyed people inside were not. They were the hot, young, new money Wall Street set. They were the hipsters, the mutual fund set, the derivative millionaires, and hot young currency manipulators. In their world, it didn't matter how you made it, only how much of it you made. Old money mattered only when it came time to choose their spouses. They all wanted to get a crack at Daddy's trust fund, and they all wanted the connections that old money brought along with it. Other than that, this was their time. The Kanye, Jay Z, Nicky Minaj, Lady Gaga, Katy Perry, Drake and Bruno Mars that was booming through the high dollar Bang and Olufsen sound system, reminded everyone that this was a new generation of Wall Street hot shots. And although they were her age, Tameka still felt uncomfortable around the predominantly white and super rich crowd.

"Hey, baby!" Caleb called out to her.

Tameka turned and spied her lover heading toward her.

"Why do you keep disappearing?" Caleb asked.

Tameka shrugged. She didn't want to tell him that she felt uncomfortable around his Wall Street friends. After all, one day these would be her friends too. Once she got him to put a ring on it, that is. They were spoiled, rich, white yuppies, and she had little in common with them at this point. Sure, she knew how to act around them, that was her job. She was in marketing after all, so she knew what they liked. She knew how to speak their language, and she knew how to market things to them, including marketing herself. But still, she found relating to this particular crowd a little bit difficult. White people spoke one language, rich White people spoke a different language, and young, rich, Wall Street White people spoke a completely different language. She didn't understand a lot of what they were saying, and almost none of their jokes. She didn't know when she was supposed to laugh, or smile, or look serious, while conversing with them. So she decided that she would keep drifting away to her own little corners of the room, away from any potential conversation.

"Just stepped out for a little air," Tameka lied.

Caleb peered around the room. He took in the crowd, and then stared at Tameka. "Sorry, babe."

"What?"

"We're boring you to death, aren't we? All of this stupid Wall Street chatter about the markets, and about bailouts, and financial meltdowns, and derivatives markets."

Tameka smiled. She wanted to scream yes, but knew that she couldn't. If she couldn't fit in with his crowd, then perhaps he would believe that she couldn't fit in with his lifestyle. And she was determined to have this man as her future husband. Who wouldn't want this lifestyle?

Tameka peered around the room. Moet and Chandon, Krug, and Dom Perignon had been flowing all night. They even had a champagne fountain made up of Swarovski crystal champagne glasses set up next to a massive ice sculpture in the dining room. And by them, she meant Caleb. This was his party, and his penthouse, and a celebration in his honor for being selected Broker Of The Year for Goldman Sachs. And she would be Mrs. Broker-of-the-Year if she played her cards right. Who in their right mind didn't want that? Who in there right mind couldn't live like this? And the icing on the cake was an intelligent, beautiful, caring, fine ass chocolate man.

Tameka took in her Wall Street lover. He oozed sexiness. He had rich chocolate skin, a clean shaven bald head, dimples deeper than the Grand Canyon, a smile that could light Manhattan, and all of it was rolled up into a fitted Hugo Boss tux that looked like he had been born to wear it. He was suave, debonair, sophisticated, charming, worldly, and well bred. He was a man's man. Cool, calm, calculating, rich, and extremely handsome. He was the kind of guy who always got picked as class president, or head of the football team. He was a natural born leader, and a people magnet. Everyone wanted to be around him, or near him. He could speak intelligently on every subject known to man, and had traveled the world extensively. He could tell you about visiting the Taj Mahal in India, The Great Pyramids in Egypt, or the Great Wall in China. He could tell you about his trips to the Amazon Rain Forest in Brazil, or Table Mountain in Cape Town, South Africa, or the Casinos in Singapore. He had hiked the jungles of Vietnam, and traveled across the desert by camel in North Africa. Europe, he knew like the back of his hand.

Tameka took Caleb in with her eyes, and she knew one thing and one thing for sure. She wanted this man. She wanted him in her life. While Eric was a great lay, and a good outlet for relaxing and chilling and just being herself, Caleb was the man she would be proud of to call her husband. He was her showpiece, someone who made her better. She could take him to the office and impress the bosses, or out to eat with clients and land the big contracts. He could help her get her paper up; even though she wouldn't need to because of all the paper he would bring to the union. She took Caleb in with her eyes, and she knew that she loved him. She loved everything that he was, and everything that he represented.

In a world where niggas slept on couches, played video games, and blamed the White man for not being able to get a job, Caleb was a man who dominated the world with his mind. He didn't just have a job, he had a career. And not only that, he was the best broker, in the best investment house in the country. He was her Cliff Huxtable.

"Talk to me, babe?" Caleb continued.

"I'm not bored," Tameka reassured him. "Just doing some thinking."

"At this noisy party?" Caleb said smiling, and lifting his arms into the air. "How can you think with Avril Lavigne blaring out of the speakers?"

Tameka smiled. "Is that who that is?"

Caleb nodded.

Tameka leaned in and whispered into his ear. "You're such a White boy."

"Oh really?" Caleb asked, lifting an eyebrow. "These White boys can't do this."

Caleb did the wave with his arm. Tameka howled laughing. She grabbed his arms, stopping him from embarrassing her.

"Oh, so now you embarrassed of me, huh?" Caleb smiled.

"Boy!" Tameka peered around the room to see if anyone had been watching. Where had this Caleb come from, she wondered? He was fun, but not this spontaneous. Could he actually have a secret fun and crazy side to him that she hadn't known about? Could she also have fun with this man?

"Go, Caleb!" Jake shouted from across the room. "Bust those funky fresh moves, bro!"

"Jake, don't encourage him!" Tameka shouted over the music.

Jake was Caleb's ace at the job. He was a derivatives trader—White, young, rich, handsome, and privileged. He grew up in Connecticut, was a product of Andover Prep, Harvard, and Wharton business schools. He was old money, with a massive old money trust fund. He and Caleb had been roommates at Harvard, and had been best friends since.

"It's too late!" Caleb shouted. He broke loose from Tameka's grasp and began to break dance. The crowd of white brokers and their Swedish model chics quickly surrounded him and begun clapping. It was all in good fun, and the hip party, really livened up. Soon, Jake joined Caleb in the break dancing.

The sight of Caleb letting loose and having fun had taken Tameka by surprise. She had never seen him like that, and had never expected that it was inside of him to do something like that. Sure, it could be the Moet, or the Riesling, or the Krug, or the Dom P, but nevertheless, it showed her a different side of the man. He was a man that could not only provide her with the lifestyle of a princess, and then rock her world in bed at night, but also provide her with laughter and good times. Not just stuffy old Wall Street dinners or pseudo hip parties full of stock brokers and their model chic girlfriends, but genuine good times. Could he really make her smile like Eric could? Could he do the Jay Z concerts like Eric could? Could he do Coney Island, the Ferris wheel, the Roller Coaster, and the Boardwalk? Could he be fun? And if so, where did that leave her relationship with Eric?

"Hey, Babe!" Caleb told her, breathing heavily.

"Some break dancing!" Tameka smiled. "Where did you learn that?"

"You want to steal my techniques, don't you?"

Tameka lifted an eyebrow and shook her head. "I don't think so."

Caleb wiped away the little beads of perspiration that was beginning to form on the top of his brow. "Wow, I haven't done that in a while. I better go freshen up."

"You two need to go on tour!" Svetlanna said, rubbing Caleb's ass as she walked by.

Tameka frowned and rolled her eyes at her. Svetlanna was one of the dozens of skinny, Nordic model chics at the party.

"Wench!" Tameka said.

Svetlanna smiled and winked at her. Tameka started after her, but Caleb grabbed her.

"Calm down, tiger!"

"I hate these skinny, model bitches!" Tameka told him. Normally she hid any traces of the hood when she was around Caleb. But competition brought it out of her, especially when a chic was pushing up on her gravy train. "They think they own the world, and can do anything they want to."

"Hey, don't worry about them," Caleb told her.

"No, she and her little poofy mouth friends have been all over you all night," Tameka told him. "They think I haven't been checking them out. They've been all up in your face, hanging on your every word, laughing at all of your corny ass jokes! I can just grab a hand full of that blonde ass hair, wrap it around my fist and yank as hard as possible."

Caleb laughed and wrapped his arms around Tameka. "Girl, you got a little bit of hood up in you, don't you?"

If you only knew, Tameka thought.

"I'm not worried about them," Caleb said, waving his hand and dismissing the apartment full of models. "I only have eyes for you. You got that?"

Tameka folded her arms and nodded.

"My momma told me I better bring her home somebody who can help cook New Years dinner!"

Tameka laughed.

"Somebody who knows what to do with some hot water cornbread," Caleb said holding her tight and rocking gently from side to side. "Remember, I'm from the South. I like 'em thick."

"You better like it."

"I love it!" Caleb laughed. He lowered his hand to Tameka's thick, firm ass and squeezed. She jumped slightly. "Were' my jokes really that corny?"

"Very," Tameka said trying to pout. But she couldn't. He had brought a smile to her face.

Where the hell did this man come from, Tameka wondered? It had to be the alcohol. He had never squeezed her ass like that before. Not just out of the blue. Whatever it was, she needed to keep plenty of it on tap, because she was feeling this guy tonight.

Caleb leaned forward and kissed Tameka passionately. He slid his tongue into her mouth, and the two of them kissed like they were the only people in the apartment.

"It's going down tonight," Caleb told her.

"You bet your ass it is," Tameka replied.

He had her open. The Dom Perignon, his sexy scent, the kiss, and the bulge that she felt in his pants when they kissed, had her wide open. She was going to ride her Texas cowboy like she was Annie Oakley and he was her favorite horse. Hi Ho muthafuckin Silver, she thought.

Caleb nodded, and she followed him into his master suite. She was about to tell him to wait until all the guest were gone, but then realized that she didn't have to. He continued through the master suite, and into the master bath, where he lifted a face towel and took care of the perspiration that had formed on his face and head after his dance routine. Jake walked into the bedroom.

"Yo, C, I need to get that from you!" Jake shouted.

Caleb walked from the bathroom and into his bedroom, where he slid a massive painting to the side, revealing a giant, steel, in-wall safe. He hit a couple of digits on the touch screen pad on the safe, and the safe popped open. Tameka felt her knees go weak. She had to grip the bed post to steady herself.

The inside of the safe was filled to the brim with banded stacks of bills. Caleb pulled out two stacks and tossed them to Jake.

"That's twenty thousand."

"Thanks," Jake said, lifting the stacks into the air. "I'll get them back to you tomorrow."

Caleb shrugged. "No sweat."

Jake left the room, and Caleb closed the safe. He turned back to Tameka.

"Now, where were we?" he asked.

The sight of a safe filled to the brim with ten thousand dollar stacks had blown her mind completely. She was speechless. She had never seen so much money in one place, in all her life. The safe had to have millions in it. The thought of a man who wanted her, who had a bedroom safe filled with millions, made her cream in her panties. Her pussy was dripping wet. She wanted to fuck him. She wanted to get pregnant by him. She wanted to fuck him on top of the money and then give birth to his child on top of that same pile of money. Tameka no longer gave a fuck about the crowd of people on the other side of the bedroom door. If this man wanted to fuck her in the middle of Times Square on New Years, at 11:55, so be it. Her cowboy wanted some pussy, and she had only one thing to say about it.

"Yippie Ki-yay, muthafucka!" Tameka pulled off her dress, dropped it to the floor, and jumped on her man.

# Boyfriend # 2

# Chapter Four

Eric sat inside of his gleaming black Escalade, staring at Tameka's apartment. His thoughts were on her and the evening that they were about to have. He had stopped off in the hood and bought a nice fat forty sack of Bubblegum weed mixed with Big Bud. They were his favorite types, and now his supplier had mixed the two variants and came up with a bomb ass combination. If only Tameka would hurry up and bring her ass on, Eric thought. He lit up a cigarette, pulled the smoke into his lungs, and then blew rings into the air. He was ready to inhale some sweet Bubblegum and get higher than a kite.

It was a balmy night and Eric had made big plans for he and Tameka . He couldn't wait to take his boo to the renowned Tavern on the Green in Central Park. He wanted to impress Tameka, and show her a different side of him. He knew she would love his choice for tonight's outing. Tameka had showed him that she had a taste for the finer things in life. She craved luxuries like exquisite dining, 5th Avenue shopping sprees and living the lavish life. Where she got such big money taste from was beyond him. She was a hood chick, with a college degree under her belt, and now she wanted to live like Ivanna Trump. Wasn't that some shit, he thought, laughing. She wanted him to thug fuck her, and then turn around and act like she was Ms. America. Women, Eric thought. You just couldn't figure them out. One minute they want you all up inside of them, and the next minute they pushing you out the door like you came through the window trying to sneak up and do a pussy robbery or something.

41

It was some straight up bullshit.

Eric's thoughts were on the other night when Tameka rushed him out of her apartment. He had really wanted to stay and chill with her that evening. So much so, that he sat parked outside of her brownstone and watched her place for over an hour. His ego was bruised by the fact that he had been dismissed so summarily after their intense fuck.

Who the fuck did she think she was? Eric wondered. No woman had ever treated him like that after sex. They usually wanted him to spend the night with them and hold onto them like he cared. They loved his presence. They loved the cuddling, nesting, and pillow talking after sex. But Tameka had proven to be different; she didn't care for any of that stuff. Somehow their roles had gotten reversed, Eric thought. He had arrived late that night. They fucked; she came, got her way, and then dismissed him like a broken toy.

He picked up his cell phone and dialed Tameka.

"What?" Tameka answered, after seeing his number.

"I've been sitting out here for ten minutes, how long you gonna be?" he asked.

"Babe, give me a few more minutes, you know I gotta step out looking right."

Eric sighed. "Hurry up! You gonna make us late!"

"Okay."

A little frustrated, Eric pressed the end call button on his cell phone, and then checked the time. He didn't want to be late. He reclined in his seat, inhaled deeply, and again blew cigarette smoke into the air.

Eric peered over at the brownstone. Tameka had definitely piqued his curiosity, and there was something about her that he couldn't shake from his mind. His ego had definitely been bruised.

"This bitch kicked me out the house to watch T.V.?" Eric

thought. "Is she fuckin' serious?"

A smile spread across his face, even though it wasn't funny to him. He knew that the dick he served, as well as his head game, felt good to Tameka. The way she pressed herself close to him, panted in his ear as he thrust his big dick into her, and dug her manicured nails into his muscular back when he was going in deep, was all proof of that.

So, what was up with Tameka, he wondered? What was it about her that he couldn't put his finger on? He wasn't sure, but he did know that he kept his strap beneath the driver's seat in his Escalade. So he was definitely ready for any type of bullshit. But the vibes that he got weren't dangerous vibes, they were just suspicious ones. He would definitely have to keep his guard up around her.

Tameka finally stepped out of her brownstone, and she was looking spectacular. Eric perked up and watched as Tameka strutted down the stairs holding onto the railing. He took her in with hungry eyes. She was dressed uber sexy this evening. Tameka had chosen a black sequin shoulder tie around top along with a pair of tight fitting Seven Jeans that accentuated her luscious curves. She was a plus 10 model with the curvaceous figure of a video vixen all wrapped into one. Eric nodded slowly as he took her in. She was definitely one fine ass woman.

Tameka strutted toward Eric's SUV rocking a pair of red Michael Kors stilettos, with a matching red evening jacket draped over her forearm. Her smile was so bright she could land a 747 jumbo jet. Eric was stunned.

Eric dowsed the remnants of his cigarette into the ashtray and took in a deep breath. He wanted to forget about the last time they were together and just concentrate on tonight. Jealously wasn't a good look for him, he thought.

As Tameka made her way toward him, his mind began to drift back to when they first met. He began to reminisce about that faithful trip to Mardi Gras in New Orleans, where he and Tameka met. It was a trip he had taken with some partners from his Brooklyn hood—Sean and Echo.

Echo was a wild boy with a murderous temper and a rap sheet longer than his leg. Eric and Echo had been boys since way back in the day. They were homies from the playground era. When Echo got into a situation over a drug debt, he resolved the situation the only way he knew how; with his gun. He killed a rival dealer, shooting the boy four times in the chest and head. As a result, Brooklyn became too hot of a town for Echo to lay his head. The beef was escalating between his boys and the dead cat's crew, and to top it off, the cops had a warrant out for his arrest. So, Echo turned to Eric for help. Eric volunteered to drive his friend down to New Orleans where he would be able to stay with family.

It took several days to drive to New Orleans, putting several hundred miles on Eric's Escalade. But at the end of the day, Eric didn't mind, because it was for a friend. Plus, word was out on the streets, that New Orleans was definitely a target rich environment when it came to scoping out the ladies.

The men were new to the city of New Orleans, and while down there, they wanted to experience Mardi Gras. They had heard the stories about the wild parties, the topless women, the public drinking, and the reckless behavior that went on for blocks. Eric wanted to get drunk with his boys and meet the finest women that New Orleans had to offer. He had often heard about New Orleans and their famous Quadroon, and Octoroons, and all of those fly ass sisters with their long hair and green eyes. He was definitely up for experiencing some of New Orleans finest offerings.

The three of them arrived in New Orleans early Thursday morning and checked into the infamous Andrew Jackson Hotel, which was located in the heart of the French Quarter. The historic hotel was within walking distance to Jackson Square and Bourbon Street, and put the entire French Quarter at their disposal.

The French Quarter was an entirely different world from the one Eric came from. The architecture was like nothing he had ever seen. Sure New York had historic architecture, but nothing like what they had put up in New Orleans. His rooms had a view of the picturesque 18th century Creole courtyard and boasted a wrought-iron balcony that overlooked the legendary Royal Street. It had been pricey, but well worth the money.

Echo might have been on the run for murder, but Eric and Sean wanted to take advantage of the situation. New Orleans, Louisiana was too good of a party town to just sit around and take in the architecture though. They all had stacks to spend, and came ready for all that it offered, including some trouble. Eric made sure to pack a few pistols which he concealed in stash boxes in his Escalade.

Eric, Sean, and Echo wanted to take in the world-renowned French Quarter, Mardi Gras, and Bourbon Street's notorious nightlife. The minute they checked into their suite, they changed their wardrobe, and rushed out to party non-stop. Brooklyn and its troubles were far away, and the three of them were fresh faces in the southern city. Somehow the ladies seemed to sense this, even before picking up on their Brooklyn accents, and as a result were all over them.

That night, the three of them hit up clubs and bars like it was the end of the world. The Apple Barrel on Frenchmen St. in the Faubourg Marigny/Bywater section was first. The cozy Apple Barrel, dubbed as Frenchmen Street's best-kept secret, offered live jazz and blues every night. The scene was hip, but a little too collegiate in its atmosphere for their taste. So they moved on the the next spot, which was the Blue Nile, also on Frenchmen St. It was a groovy little music club that offered live performances from famous, as well as, up and coming acts. Jazz, funk, and rock were all present. From there, the trio moved on to The Circle Bar, and then the Club 300 Jazz restaurant in the French Quarter.

Eric and his peoples took in everything New Orleans had to offer, including the food. They feasted on King's cake, French doughnuts, Gulf Oysters and fried Oysters, boiled craw fish, Italian Muffuletta sandwiches and Chinese inspired Beef Yaka Mein. It was what the locals had recommended, and so they tried it all.

New Orleans quickly became Eric's second favorite city. Second only to New York, of course.

The three of them spent two feral nights in the city experiencing Mardi Gras and painting the town red. They consumed every type of alcohol and flirted with various ladies, bringing women back to their suites and fucking their brains out till dawn. For a minute they even forgot that Echo was a wanted man in Brooklyn. In fact, they had completely forgotten about home period. At least until they ran into a fellow New Yorker.

It was at the Cat's Meow where Eric first laid eyes on Tameka. The historic place with its 1820's architecture and two massive exterior balconies overlooking Bourbon Street, was packed with revelers jamming to the live band playing on stage in the courtyard below. Karaoke was in full swing, and the stage was open to those daring enough, or intoxicated enough, to display their talents.

The drinks were on Eric that night. They were all leaving New Orleans the next day and taking the hour long drive to Lafayette, where Echo's elderly grandmother lived. Eric peered on stage and spotted a beautiful woman clad in a sexy and sleek, yellow club dress, dancing it up. Tameka had the mic in her hand and was singing to Mary J Blige's *Real Love*. She was on stage with two friends, yet it was *her* presence that was magnetizing. Eric couldn't help but smile and focus his full attention on

46

Tameka. She commanded not only his attention, but the entire club's, and had the place completely rocking with her performance.

"I see you lookin' nigga," Sean said, bumping Eric gently with his shoulder.

"Shorti lookin' nice in that yellow dress," Eric declared. He walked his eyes up and down her long, gleaming, toned legs that seemed to stretch forever before ending in a pair of stilettos.

Tameka was the lead singer, with Rosalynn and Tammy backing her up. When Tameka danced toward Eric's way on the stage, he made it his business to lock eyes with her and smile. She smiled back. He knew then, that she was interested in him. When Tameka and her girls finished their karaoke performance and started to exit the stage, Eric didn't hesitate to move her way through the tight crowd.

The men were like wolves at Tameka and her friends. They bid for the ladies attention and tried desperately to get some conversation. But Tameka and her friends weren't having it. They found the New Orleans men to be to drunken, out of control, and immature. Their suitors relaxed vacation attire also told them little about the men's pockets, and Tameka wasn't trying to waste conversation on anything with shallow pockets.

"Where y'at?" one local had asked Tameka, causing her to twist her face in confusion and disgust.

She had dismissed him like he was a buzzing fly. Eric approached Tameka with his winning smile and a drink.

"Hey beautiful," he said in his deep Brooklyn accent. "You gonna reject me, too."

Tameka had turned around and immediately gave Eric the once over. She liked what she saw. He was tall, dressed well, and his accent was like music to her ears. The sparkling jewelry that decorated his wrist, neck, and fingers was an extra plus for her.

"Why you had the nerve to come out lookin' like a banana

that a nigga about ready to peel," Eric said smiling.

"Oh, you got jokes." Tameka said smiling back. He had taken her back with his comment on her attire. Most of the dudes in the room were all over her like wolves, while the one with the Brooklyn swag was throwing punches.

"Always...so what part of Brooklyn you from?" Eric asked.

"How you know I'm from Brooklyn?"

"How can I not...ya whole swag screams out Brooklyn, luv," Eric said.

"It does, huh?"

"Yeah." Eric eyed her sexy figure and smiled.

"So I guess you like what you see?"

"You know I do. Let me buy you a drink."

"Why not," Tameka said.

She followed Eric to the bar and ordered a Grand Mariner and pineapple. Eric ordered the same. It didn't take long for the two to engage in a conversation about Brooklyn. He was from Brownsville and she was from Bed-Stuy.

"We right next door to each other," Eric said.

Tameka had smiled. She was definitely feeling his swag. Eric couldn't help but to compliment Tameka on her beauty and she ate it up like a starving pup. What sealed the deal for Tameka was when Eric pulled out a wad of hundreds to pay for their drinks. She was impressed. He was fine as hell and wasn't a broke nigga. Two of the most important qualities she looked for in a man. That temperate night in New Orleans produced a love connection. Tameka knew Eric was a bad boy, and she was definitely feeling him.

Echo catching a body in Brooklyn and Eric having to drive him to New Orleans had worked out better than he expected. He had gotten to know Tameka very well while in the city, and they had a lot in common. From their bumptious street attitude, to their love for smoking weed, they were like two peas in a pod.

# Boyfriend # 2

They promised each other that once back in New York, they were gonna to link up, and it was a promise that they had kept. And now, he was outside of her crib, watching her stroll up to his ride.

*****

Tameka was shocked that Eric had made reservations at Tavern on the Green, one of the most exclusive, and expensive, high-end restaurants in New York City. When she stepped into the posh restaurant, arm-in-arm with Eric, she felt like royalty. Peering around the restaurant, she took in the grand decor. They were quickly escorted to the Crystal Room, one of the restaurant's better dining rooms. It featured windows overlooking the restaurants' adjacent garden in Central Park, as well as the multitude of trees that had been wrapped with tiny white lights that created a "Fairyland" effect.

They were seated at their tables and Tameka couldn't stop smiling. Eric had definitely pulled out all of the stops with this one. And he had definitely surprised her. This was something that she would expect from Caleb, not Eric. Both of her men had thrown her for a loop in the last couple of days.

"You love it?" Eric asked.

"Yes, I do, baby. Oh my god, this is what I'm talking about," she said excitedly.

Eric smiled. "Nothing but the best for my boo."

Tameka was amazed. Eric was always full of surprises, but not like this. He had stepped up and got his grown and sexy on, and it had her creaming in her panties. Her thug love had taken it upscale a notch or two, and it had really thrown her for a loop. Now, it remained to be seen what he ordered, and how he behaved in such a setting.

The couple dined on boiled lobster with tarragon butter and sipped on chilled wine. It was a meal fit for the elite. They talked and flirted with each other during the duration of their evening together, and took in the lovely decor that surrounded them. The thing on Eric's mind was dessert. He stared at Tameka thinking about the sexy outfit she was wearing. Her ass had looked unreal while she was walking to his vehicle. He wanted to hurry up and have her for dessert.

She smiled. "I know what you're thinking about?"

"You do, huh?"

She nodded.

"What's on my mind?"

"Me, for dessert later on," she said.

"You must be a psychic," he joked.

"The eyes never lie," said Tameka.

"I bet they don't."

Eric was ready to leave. He called the waitress over for the bill, pulled out his wad of cash and placed two crisp hundred dollar bills on the table to pay the check. He and Tameka exited the restaurant to continue their pleasant evening someplace more intimate.

*****

Eric came to a stop in front of Tameka's brownstone. Tameka had him so hard, that a large bulge was protruding through his slacks. The foreplay went on from the time they'd left the restaurant up until their arrival at her Harlem brownstone. Eric was ready to fuck. He kissed Tameka fervently, cupping her breast, ready to finish where he'd left off the other night.

50

# Boyfriend # 2

"You know what I want to do for you?" Eric asked in a soft voice in Tameka's ear.

"What's that, babe?" she asked, smiling heavily.

"I wanna fuck the shit outta you until my dick don't work, which will be never, and then get up in the morning and make you breakfast. You'll be the first woman I've ever cook breakfast for."

Tameka didn't seem too excited about his proposal. It meant that he would have to spend the night, which is something she wanted to avoid. She didn't want Eric getting too comfortable up in her crib. First it would be one night, then another. The he'd be spending the weekend. Then weeks at a time. And then he'd never leave. The next thing she knew, he'd be cooking dope up in her place, maybe even getting her home raided. That was definitely not part of her plan. No, this place was her dream place. It was for her dream mate. And while Eric had definitely showed her a different side tonight, he still wasn't that man. He was still rough and rugged, and nothing would ever change him from being that. And nothing ever should, she thought. She loved Eric, because he *was* Eric. She loved her thug, in all his glorious swagger. But it was what it was. She loved him, but she still had a dream that she wanted to pursue. And she wasn't going to let anything, not even love, or good times, get in the way of that dream life. Eric sensed her hesitation.

"What's wrong wit' you?" Eric asked.

"Nothing."

"You don't want me to spend the night?"

Tameka remained silent.

"Who you fuckin'?" he asked softly.

"No one," she lied.

"So, I ain't good enough to spend the night at your swanky, tricked out crib?" Eric asked, offended.

"I just have a really busy morning tomorrow and have to be

up at the crack of dawn."

"You a fuckin' trip, Tameka."

"I'm a busy woman, babe," Tameka told him. "You need to understand that."

"Yeah, whatever!"

"I'll make it up to you, babe, promise," said Tameka. She tried to kiss Eric, but he turned away from her. "So it's gotta be like that? Why are you ruining our nice night together?"

"You're the one fuckin' it up," he told her.

Tameka sighed. "You know what...goodnight, babe. Call me tomorrow."

Eric didn't reply. He sat slouched in the driver's seat and didn't bother to look at Tameka. He was clearly upset. Tameka shook her head and slowly stepped out of his truck. She slammed his door and walked to her brownstone. Eric sat back and watched her leave.

"Fuck him," Tameka said to herself, as she climbed the steps to her brownstone. "No, you aren't fucking good enough to lay up in here. Does that answer your question?"

Tameka pulled out her key, unlocked her apartment door, then turned back to Eric and blew him a kiss and waved. She pushed open her door and stepped inside.

She loved Eric, but she wasn't about to become just another baby momma, dope dealer 'wifey' bitch from the hood. No, this pussy was doctor, lawyer, stock broker pussy. And she wasn't going to be making the trip up state to take no little hollering babies to visit their locked up daddy. That was not going to be her lifestyle. She had seen too many of her friends back in the hood fall into that, and she refused to become that bitch. No, she had put a minimum price tag for laying up in this pussy, and it was stock broker money. You want to lay up and cum all weekend, then you'd better be cashing at least a million dollars in checks over a year's time period. She was sorry, but that was just the way things were going to be. Niggas who want million dollar pussy, needed to be million dollar niggas, and that was that.

Tameka locked her front door, walked to her window and peered out of her blinds. Eric was still sitting outside in his Escalade.

"God damn!" Tameka exclaimed. "Drive off, muthafucka!"

She turned, walked to her sofa and lifted her remote. She had recorded Basketball Wives, Hip Hop Wives, and The Real Housewives of Beverly Hills. She leaned back on her sofa and selected Beverly Hills.

"Now these bitches, they know how to put a price on some pussy," Tameka said, smiling. She knew that one day she would get there. She was going to be one of the Real Housewives of Westchester County, New York, or Alpine, New Jersey.

# Boyfriend # 2

# Chapter Five

Caleb strolled to his apartment window and peered out over Central Park. He had just finished working out, and his shirtless torso was glistening with sweat. He peered out over the city, taking in the sights and thinking to himself how fortunate he was. He was the prince of the city, the toast of Manhattan, and Goldman Sachs newest golden boy. He could do no wrong in their eyes, and everything was finally paying off for him. All of his personal investments were soaring through the roof, and his bank account was growing larger and larger with each passing month. Plus, he had that other thing that he did. That other thing that he did to get his investment money, and to keep swelling his bank account up every so often. He didn't know how many more times he would do it, or if he would do it again after this time. He damn sure didn't want to get caught and throw everything away just by being greedy. But then again, greed was what it was all about, wasn't it? That's what surrounded him everyday at work, that's what he had been brought up to believe, and that's what this entire country had been built upon. *Greed!* Greed was good, *right*?

Caleb turned and walked back to his master suite, where Tameka was laid out on the bed. She was asleep. He had laid it down pretty good just an hour earlier. So good, that he had put her ass to sleep. Sound asleep. He loved it when he laid pipe that good. Sure he thought of himself as a master pipe layer, but today he felt like really patting himself on the back. He had made

Tameka speak in tongues. Caleb rubbed her ass and smiled. It was time for him to hit the shower.

Caleb came out of his Under Armour shorts, and strolled into his master bathroom. He stood in front of his full length vanity mirror and took in his muscular physique. He was pleased with what he saw. His arms and chest were bulging, and his abs were ripped and tight. In fact, he was *very* pleased with what he saw.

Caleb turned and stepped into his walk-in shower and turned on the water. The hot water from the numerous nozzles struck his body forcefully, massaging his back and soothing his aching muscles. The water shooting down from the rain head shower nozzle above, poured down on top of him, like he had been caught in a downpour in a tropical rain forest. The water felt soothing, and utterly relaxing. He lifted his soap and face towel, and commenced to bathing. He lifted his in-shower remote, and turned on his in-shower internet radio system. Pandora came alive.

Faith Evan's *You Used To Love Me* came alive.

Caleb smiled. It was the song that was playing when he met Tameka at the airport. He closed his eyes and thought back to that day.

***** 

"I'm sorry!" Tameka said, peering up at him from the floor of the airport. She quickly gathered her belongings. "I am *so* sorry!"

"That's okay," Caleb smiled. "I love it when strangers slam into me at the airport."

Caleb extended his hand. Tameka clasped it, and he pulled

her up from the floor.

"I am so sorry!" Tameka apologized again. "It's just that I'm late, and I'm about to miss my flight!"

Tameka ran toward the loading gate, only to be waved off by an airline worker. Curious, Caleb followed just behind her.

"I'm sorry, ma'am, but that flight has already boarded," the airline worker told her.

"*I need to get on that plane!*" Tameka insisted.

The worker shrugged. "I'm sorry, I can't help you."

"Bullshit!" Tameka shouted. "That's my damn flight! I don't want to be stuck here in Atlanta!"

"Ma'am, the plane has already pulled away from the gate!"

Tameka stomped the ground hard. "This is bullshit!"

The worker pointed toward a kiosk of telephones. "You can call reservations and see when the next flight is leaving. Where are you headed?"

Tameka looked at her like she was stupid. "The same place that plane just left for."

"New York?" the worker asked, ignoring Tameka's flippant remarks.

"Yes," Tameka said, exhaling.

"Two hours."

"Two hours!" Tameka shouted. "What the hell am I supposed to do in the airport for two fucking hours?"

Caleb stepped in and smiled at the airline worker. "That's okay, ma'am. I'll handle this."

"What?" Tameka asked angrily. "How are you going to handle this? You work for the airline or something?"

"Well, you can be angry, and shout and pout, which is going to get you nowhere, or you can make the best of a bad situation," Caleb told Tameka.

"And how do I do that?" Tameka huffed.

"By having lunch with me."

"No thanks, I just ate," Tameka said with a frown. "That's what made me late for this damn flight. No one ever tells you that Hartsfield is the size of a small city, and that your flight is going to be at the complete opposite side of the airport! You don't even have time to grab something to eat!"

Caleb laughed. "First time at Hartsfield?"

Tameka frowned. "Yeah."

"Figures."

"What's so damn funny?" Tameka asked.

"You have to take the train," Caleb explained. "If your flight landed in A Terminal, and you're trying to make it to D Terminal, the only way you're going to make it is to take the airport's subway train."

"The airport's subway train?"

Caleb nodded.

"The airport has its own subway train?"

Caleb smiled and nodded. "This is one of the biggest airports in the world."

"I wish someone would have told me that!" Tameka said. She let out a half smile.

Caleb lifted her luggage. "Is this all you have, or is the rest on its way to New York without you?"

Tameka nodded and again smiled. "That's it. Thank God!"

"So, how about that lunch?"

Tameka walked her eyes up and down Caleb. He was sexy. He wore a tailored business suit, along with some high dollar wing tips that screamed money. *Lot's of money!* Her first thought, was that he owned his own business, but she quickly dismissed that thought. If he owned his own business, and he was at the airport, then he would have chosen something more comfortable to travel in. No, this was a man with clients, and bosses that he had to answer too. But judging by the expense of his suit, he was definitely an executive. He was too well dressed for a lawyer, she surmised. Unless of course he was some type of high dollar corporate attorney. That would explain the suit and his need to travel in it. He was heading straight to a meeting once his flight landed or either leaving town after just having a meeting. One or the other. Either way, he was pretty high up on the income scale.

"Lunch?" Tameka peered down at her watch. "I don't know. I can't miss my plane again."

"Oh, my apologies," Caleb smiled. "I meant lunch on my plane."

Tameka recoiled. "Lunch on your plane?"

Caleb blushed. "Well, not my plane. The company's plane. It's a Net Jet."

The look on Tameka's face told him that she didn't understand.

"A fractional ownership?" Caleb tried to explain.

Still Tameka didn't understand.

"The company I work for owns a percentage of several jets, and we use those jets to fly around the country on business."

"Oh," Tameka said, finally understanding. "Why didn't they just buy one whole jet?"

Caleb threw his head back in laughter. "Actually, they own several. But that's for the guys' way up on the totem pole. Guys like me have to use one of the smaller biz jets."

"So, you're asking me to have lunch with you on your jet?" Tameka asked. His jet, company jet, fractional ownership, *whatever*! She was impressed.

"Well, you seem like you could use a lift?" Caleb smiled.

"A lift?" Tameka asked, lifting an eyebrow. "You give someone a lift in your car, not your jet."

"I'm heading to New York; you're heading to New York, why not?"

"You're heading to New York?" Tameka asked surprised.

Caleb nodded.

# Boyfriend # 2

"Wow, my luck, huh?"

Caleb extended his arm. "Will you join me for lunch, Mademoiselle?"

Tameka placed her arm through his, and Caleb led off.

"My knight in shining armor," Tameka told him. "What's your name?"

"You always get on airplanes with strangers?" Caleb smiled.

"You seemed like an okay guy," Tameka told him.

"So does Dexter, but he's still a serial killer."

Tameka laughed heartily. "You got me. You definitely got me on that one. So, Caleb, are you a serial killer?"

"No."

"So, what are you?"

"I'm a Junior Executive at Goldman Sachs."

"An executive?" Tameka nodded. "I'm impressed."

Caleb opened the door for her, and then led her down the steps onto the tarmac. A Dassualt Falcon Business Jet was waiting for them. A gentleman rushed up to them, and took the luggage from Caleb's hand.

"And your name is?" Caleb asked.

"Tameka."

A stewardess helped Tameka up the steps onto the business jet, and she and Caleb seated themselves in a pair of cream colored overstuffed leather chairs. Tameka walked her eyes through the cabin. Everything was swathed in cream colored leather or gorgeous Birch wood that had been polished to a high gloss. The cabin smelled like new car leather from a luxury car.

"Will you be dining, sir?" the stewardess asked.

"Yes." Caleb told her.

"Very good, sir," she told him. "I take your order and prepare your meal after takeoff."

"Thank you," Caleb said nodding.

The pilot stuck his head out. "We're about ready for

takeoff."

Caleb nodded. And the pilot disappeared back into the cockpit.

It was all too much for Tameka. She felt as if she were dreaming.

The plane begin to roll toward the runway.

"I can't believe this plane!" Tameka gushed. "This thing is beautiful! Now, this is like, what first class should *really* be like."

Caleb lifted a remote, and pressed a button. A large screen against the wall came alive. He pressed a second button, and a motorized Birch wood table folded out from the wall, giving them a surface to eat on.

"Holy shit!" Tameka exclaimed. He was blowing her mind.

"What do you want to watch?" Caleb asked, while pointing the remote at the large flat television screen.

Tameka shrugged. "It doesn't matter."

Tameka could hear the engines come alive, and then feel the pull of the plane racing down the runway and then lifting off. They were airborne, heading home. And she was doing it on a luxurious private jet.

"Comfy?" Caleb asked.

Tameka nodded. Caleb pressed a couple of buttons on the remote, dimming the lights, and changing the channels. She didn't care what he put on the monitor. She wasn't planning on watching much television anyway. She wanted to stare at the beautiful, rich, chocolate executive sitting next to her, who had the use of a corporate jet. She could feel moisture forming between her legs.

Caleb flipped the channels until he found some music videos. Fantasia was playing. Tameka leaned back in her seat.

"I could get used to this," she purred.

"I'll bet you could," Caleb smiled. "So, what brought you to Atlanta?"

"I'm actually coming from New Orleans," Tameka told him. "Mardi Gras. I was on vacation."

"Ah," Caleb nodded. "New Orleans, a beautiful and very romantic city."

"I didn't see the romantic part of it," Tameka said. "But I definitely saw the partying side of it."

"Oh, Mademoiselle. New Orleans is much more than that. You just need a proper gentleman to show it to you."

"And who would that proper gentleman be?" Tameka asked with a smile.

"When do you have to be back in New York?" Caleb asked, lifting an eyebrow.

"I'm on vacation until next Monday. But I wanted to get back and get some things straightened out. I'm trying to purchase some property."

Caleb waved his hand, dismissing her worry. "Ahhh, the thing about property, is that it'll be there. It's not like it's going to get up and walk away, now is it?"

"I supposed not."

"Good," Caleb said, winking at her. "So, that means you really don't have to be back right away."

Tameka shrugged.

"So, why were you so worried about missing your flight?"

"Who wants to be stuck in the airport for hours and hours?" Tameka asked.

Caleb nodded. "You're right. Daphne."

The flight attendant rose. "Yes, sir?"

Caleb peered at Tameka. "Tell the pilot to turn the plane around, and take us to New Orleans for dinner."

"Yes, sir," the flight attendant said. She disappeared into the cockpit.

Tameka could feel the plane turning. She found a man who was taking her to dinner in New Orleans on a private jet. She creamed in her panties.

*****

Caleb finished showering, turned off the radio and stepped out of the shower. He wrapped a thick towel around his wet body and peered into the bedroom, hoping that his shower and the radio hadn't awakened Tameka. To his surprise, she was gone.

Caleb strolled into the bedroom, and peered down at the spot where she had been laying. He found a small post it note. He lifted it and read it aloud.

"Didn't want to disturb you. Had to get going. Smooches, Tameka."

Caleb shook his head, crumpled the note, and threw it in the direction of his fireplace. The note hit the mantel and fell onto the floor. He would pick it up later. Right now, his thoughts were elsewhere. He just couldn't get a firm grasp on Tameka, and what she truly was about.

# Boyfriend # 2

# Chapter Six

Tameka slowly removed herself from Eric's gentle grasp around her. She had been entangled in his arms throughout the night. She pulled back the covers and placed both feet on the parquet flooring. She peered around the room, taking in her surroundings. She was in his Brooklyn apartment in Canarsie.

Eric was sleep. His snoring made it evident that he would be comatose to the world for a few hours. It had been another intense fuck for them, she thought. Her pussy was still throbbing. The way Eric put it down on her, had made her head spin like she was on a merry-go-round and had her body stretched into convulsions. Tameka smiled as she reminisced about the way Eric snaked his tongue into her pussy, and then sipped on her juices like he was drinking from a fountain. She loved the way he fucked her from the back while having her face down in the pillow with a firm grip around her neck. She liked it rough like that. She felt she needed that passionate sexual experience. She needed to escape. And Eric always did it for her.

Rosalynn was trying her last nerves back at the brownstone. She was coming up with her share of the rent on time, but the other issues with Rosalynn had been giving Tameka a headache of late. When her roommate wasn't working, she was in her room blaring music, or having her boyfriend spend the night, which was a no no. And to top it off, Rosalynn was a bit of a slob. She constantly found herself cleaning up behind her roommate and complaining to her about keeping the place tidy. Rosalynn constantly left piles of dishes in the sink, or would leave her underwear and clothes all over the house as if they were a department store display. And the worst of it, was that she borrowed things without asking and never put stuff back where she found it. It all went against her meticulous personality. For her, everything had to be in its place, and everything had a place. But Rosalynn, she was like Oscar from the odd couple.

Tameka exhaled and thought about her relationship with her friend. She was definitely beginning to regret that she had asked her friend to move in. There were times when she wanted to shout to Rosalynn, "Why don't you move back in with your sister and her fuckin' family!" But she held her tongue for the moment and hoped that the situation between them would work itself out. They had arguments here and there, but things hadn't escalated into a full blown fight. If it ever came to that, she would have to whip Rosalynn's ass, and send the bitch packing, she thought.

Tameka's thoughts turned to her college years. She didn't remember Roz being so messy or disorganized back then. Hell, in college, Rosalynn was the more independent and upstanding one, while she had been known to be the rebel. Somehow, somewhere along the line, their roles had switched. And now, she found herself wanting to be Harriet the homemaker, while Rosalynn simply wanted to lay up on her back and screw her boyfriend all fucking night. She had become the prude, not wanting to have dudes coming and going in and out of her place, while Rosalynn had become the more free spirited one. What the fuck had happened, Tameka wondered? Was she getting older, more mature, more responsible? Where had the time gone, she wondered? Time?

Tameka looked at the time; it was twenty minutes after 2am.

"Dammit," she mumbled. She peered around for some clothing. She refused to don a robe, so it was a good thing that

# Boyfriend # 2

Eric's place was warm enough for her to walk around naked. She rose from the bed, walked over to the dresser, removed a cigarette from the pack, and then moved toward the window. Tameka lit her cigarette and peered outside. She inhaled the cancer stick and took a deep breath.

Letting the smoke slowly work itself out of he lungs, she glanced around her lover's room taking in some of Eric's decor. His apartment was the epitome of a bachelor's pad. It was nothing like her brownstone back in Harlem. It was definitely absent a woman's touch.

Eric had a 72" flat screen perched on top of a black dresser, with several cords and cables running down and across his parquet floors and into the back of an X box 360. Dozens upon dozens of video games and movies cluttered the dresser, and also shared space on the floor with numerous empty beer and liquor bottles. Remnants of old blunts, old cigarettes, weed residue and ashes were scattered everywhere. The walls were clad with rappers and big booty women in compromising positions. Everything in the room was for a man. *She* was the only womanly thing in Eric's bedroom.

Eric's bed was the softest thing in the entire place. He had told her that it cost him four grand, and that it was imported from France. It looked pretty expensive, she thought at the time. It was carved from solid ebony and white oak. Eric had even taken the time to cover the bed in sheets of pure silk. That had impressed her the most about the whole set-up. The fact that her gangster boo had been able to pick and choose some sheets that were on point. She loved to wrap herself in the sheets and she loved how the texture felt against her skin while lying in bed.

Tameka took a few more pulls from the cigarette, each time allowing the smoke to leisurely make it's way out of her mouth. She relished these moments. A good smoke, after a good lay. She never allowed herself to smoke in front of Caleb, for fear that he may think less of her. Caleb didn't smoke, and the only time he drank was at dinner or at a party. And it sure wasn't beer that he was drinking. It was always some high dollar bullshit that she could barely pronounce. But here with Eric, here standing in the dark, in the shadows of his room, she could relax and smoke, and just be her.

Tameka stared out the window taking in the lights. Brooklyn at night was always a place to be and hang out. She remembered the good times and bad times while growing up in Bed-Stuy. Being in Brooklyn with Eric made her reminisce about those times. It wasn't easy growing up in the Stuy, but it made her the bitch that she was today. In a way, she had become a Harlemnite. She had fallen in love with Harlem and everything about it. She loved the history of Harlem, the people, the sights, the sounds, the culture. And although she would always be a Brooklyn girl at heart, she now felt that Harlem and Manhattan were the places to be They were the places where she shopped, ate and lived. In a way, she now thought of Brooklyn as her past and Harlem as her future. These days, she rarely visited her old home. But she did love it whenever Eric brought her back to her old stomping grounds.

Tameka turned and gazed at Eric as he slept. He was lying on his back and out cold. The silky bedroom sheets barely covered his nakedness and his six-pack rippled across his stomach like a wave. His tattoos showed like an art display across his dark skin. He was handsome and rugged, and Tameka loved every bit of his rough exterior. He was like a black diamond in her mind.

Tameka stared at Eric as he slept like a baby. Taking in his chiseled frame, made her pussy start to throb and drip like a leaky faucet. He was a wonderful spectacle of a man—a Brooklyn thug that excited and revved up every bone in her body. She couldn't get enough of him. She had flashbacks of what he'd done to her body only a few short hours ago. She closed her eyes and reminisced on the way Eric twisted her petite frame into a pretzel as he penetrated the depths of her core with his machinery. It almost made Tameka feel violated because of how deep his dick went inside of her.

Tameka walked her eyes up and down Eric's naked body. Only moments ago, she had been ready to leave his place and go home. But after examining his body once again, she found her bare feet virtually cemented to the floor. Why the fuck I'm so horny? She asked herself. She had came numerous times during their intense fuck. In fact, immediately afterward, her body felt spent, and fatigued. So, why was she tempted to finger herself while standing by the window, she wondered? Her eyes devouring Eric's physique was one reason, she knew. And the fact that it was all so accessible to her was another. He was her play thing, and they played hard. Again, she felt her pussy throbbing.

Tameka took a few more pulls from her cigarette and then dowsed it. She walked to Eric's bed and sat on the edge, where she continued to gaze at his physique. A naughty smile crept across her face, giving visualization to the naughty thoughts dancing across her mind. Slowly, Tameka peeled away the covers that barely covered Eric's nakedness and moved her hand up his thigh. She eyed his flaccid penis which sat softly like a sleeping snake. Although it lay limp and dormant, she still thought it impressive. Tameka leaned closer to it and gently took his sleeping tool into her mouth. She devoured the head of his penis, and began spanking the mushroom tip with her tongue. She wrapped her lips around his shaft like a warm blanket.

Soon, Tameka's head was bobbing up and down in Eric's lap, and the more she sucked on his rod, the harder it became. She was a bona fide freak, and she loved how his erection developed more and more in her oral cavity, and how it went from feeling like a wet noodle, to a long steel pipe being jammed down her throat.

Tameka moaned as she sucked his dick, causing Eric to rouse from his sleep. Despite his stirring, she never lost focus on pleasing him. Soon, Eric began to moan. His manhood had grown to full staff. Tameka loved the feeling of it throbbing in her mouth as she slid her lips up and down on it. The feeling of his long shaft gliding in and out of her mouth, made her pussy spring to life. She could feel her juices flowing.

"Damn, baby. Ooooh, what's this about?" Eric asked. He raised himself slightly and peered down at Tameka going to work on him.

"Ssssshhh, let me finish," Tameka replied, pausing only for a split moment to answer him.

Eric had no arguments. Tameka had her sweet lips wrapped around his cock and was deep throating it.

Eric squirmed and cried out to her. "Oh shit! Ooooh, damn baby…shit feels so good."

Tameka hummed and toyed with his balls, working every lower inch of him with precision. His hand began to caress the back of her head, while her hand held his penis tightly.

"I wanna fuck you again, baby," Eric told her.

Tameka was ready to make his wish come true. Her appetite for sex had grown exponentially. She wanted to wrap herself in their growing lust and intertwine with him. She continued her deep-throat, with her tongue descending down to the base of his dick, causing her boo to shiver ever so slightly. Then, she gently raked her teeth across the tip of his penis, causing him to quickly clasp her head and pull away.

"Oh shit…you gonna make me cum like that," he uttered. He felt his fluids beginning to build up for an eruption, and it was too soon for him to cum.

Tameka let out a naughty, yet seductive smile.

"Damn, what got into you tonight?" Eric asked. "I see you can't get enough of it,"

"Just fuck me," Tameka said, slowly mounting him.

She wanted her walls to crumble around him. She wanted her boo thang to ravage her body and do to it whatever he wanted it. Her mouth raped his tongue and it felt as though she was going to suck his soul out of his body. The two of them kissed passionately. The warmth of their bodies became entangled and a warmth spread between them that felt like the summer's heat. Eric was ready to pierce her with his erection, and Tameka's body was wet with anticipation.

She wrapped her thighs around Eric's body and lowered her dripping wet punany onto his erection. Eric felt her pussy lips touch the head of his cock, and grunted. The penetration into Tameka was delicate for a short moment. As soon as the head of his dick was between her sweet lips, he felt the suction from her body. Her pussy pulled him deeper and deeper inside of her. Once Tameka reached his base, she began riding his dick like a cowgirl riding a thoroughbred. She leaned into him, planting her manicured nails against his strapping chest, and rhythmically began stirring.

"Damn baby, your pussy is so damn good. Umm, shit... Ooooh, you feel so good," he moaned, cupping Tameka's succulent ass and pulling her closer to him.

His brain began shutting down as his body reacted to his woman bouncing and grinding atop of him. Eric tried as hard as he could to make the pleasure last, but the way Tameka was working her pussy, made it only a matter of time before he had to release.

Tameka's soft sensual tunnel massaged and pulled at his dick. It took only a few more glides up and down his shaft with her tight tunnel before he lost control and exploded.

"I'm fuckin' comin!" he shouted.

# Boyfriend # 2

His cum shot deep into her body as his hips thrust upward and into her several more times. After a few moments his balls felt empty, and he lay spent beneath her. But it wasn't only Eric that experienced a pleasurable release, Tameka got hers too. She orgasm continuously, before resting her head against his masculine frame. Completely exhausted, they both breathed out heavily.

"What was that about?" Eric asked.

"Just be quiet…"

It was rare that they didn't use condoms, but it was a spur-of-the-moment action, and Tameka had her IUD as a back up to prevent pregnancy.

"You better not get pregnant on me," Eric told her.

"And, if I was?"

"You tryin' to trap me?"

Tameka chuckled. "Nigga, I ain't tryin' to have any kids, so what the fuck you talkin' about?"

"A'ight…as long as we got that understanding…but you still on your pills, right?"

"You ain't gotta worry."

Tameka closed her eyes and felt the rhythm of his heart beat against her ear as she rested against him. It was strong. He was strong. With her eyes still closed and the sound of his heart beating in her ear, she asked, "You love me?"

Eric chuckled. "What?"

"I asked do you love me?" she repeated.

"And why you asking after this?"

"Just answer my question," she told him.

"Yeah, I got love for you."

"No, I don't wanna know if you got love for me, I want to know, do you love me? It's a yes or no question."

Eric sighed.

Tameka snuggled tightly alongside him and waited for an

answer. She elevated her head and peered into his eyes. She wanted to see his reaction. Eric gave a deadpan look in return. She assumed his silence was his answer.

She let out an annoyed sigh. "Fuck it. Never mind!"

Tameka was disgusted. She went all out to please this nigga in the bedroom and she couldn't even get an answer from him. She was ready to pull herself from his warm embrace and leave. But before she made a move, Eric unexpectedly gave her an answer.

"Yeah, I love you," he told her. "More than anything on this fuckin' earth. You're the only woman I can spend the night with, and the one woman I love waking up next to. And you know it fuckin' bothers me that I let you spend the night at my place anytime you want, but you won't let me stay the night at your place."

Tameka smiled. "It does?"

"Yeah, it do. You fuckin' some next nigga?" he growled. "That's why I can't stay the night at your damn place?"

She chuckled. "No, only you, baby. You're the only man in my life. The only man that I ever truly cared about."

"I better be."

Tameka kissed his chest gently. Her thug-a-boo was so sweet. She loved the fact that he was jealous. It showed that he really cared.

"I ain't gonna lie, Tameka…being wit' you be havin' a nigga ready to slow his roll, and right now, I ain't tryin' to hear about you fuckin' wit' some next nigga," Eric told her.

"And you better not be fuckin' wit' no next bitch either," Tameka shot back.

"Shit, wit' pussy this good, damn, you ain't gotta worry about that. Your shit got a nigga on lock, fo' real," he said jokingly.

Tameka laughed. "You silly."

"I know, right. But fuck it, I do love you, cuz there ain't no other shorti out here as real as you."

Tameka beamed. She had Eric where she wanted him; he was in check.

Eric hugged her lovingly. He didn't want to let her go. It was a side of him that few people rarely saw. But Tameka was able to peel back some of his thick thuggish layers and expose his gentle and loving side. She'd heard stories and rumors about him on the streets, and she knew how dangerous he could be. But tonight, the only danger she faced, and went toe-to-toe with, was the snake between his legs.

Tameka remained wrapped into his arms like he was a blanket around her. She smiled, and for a brief moment thought about Eric becoming her Cosby.

# Chapter Seven

Caleb took Tameka's hand into his as they strolled through Bergdorf's. Tameka peered around like a kid in a candy store. The shoes and the handbags throughout the store fully had her attention.

"You've never been in Bergdorf's?" Caleb asked incredulously.

Tameka shook her head. She was a hood chick through and through, and she had never ventured inside of a Berdorf, a Saks, or a Neiman Marcus, for that matter. Sure, she had been inside of Macy's, but Dillard's had been her top of the line store while she was growing up in the hood. That, and Foley's. Stores like Neimans, Saks, and Berdorf's had been way out of her financial reach. And now that she found herself inside of one, she was like a fish out of water.

"I took you for a clothes horse," Caleb said with a smile.

"I am," Tameka told him. "But I know how to shop *wisely*. I hit up the outlets in Jersey and Philly, and I am a complete internet whore."

Caleb and Tameka shared a laugh.

"Oh, so that's where you get all of those fly clothes that make your booty look so fat," Caleb said with a sly smile.

"My ass looks fat, because it is," Tameka smiled. "I'm one hundred percent sista girl beneath this skirt."

Caleb bit down on his bottom lip and shook his head, while thinking about her shapely figure. "I know you are."

75

"Boy, go on!" Tameka playfully slapped him across his shoulder. Her playful banter with Caleb quickly came to an end, once she saw the handbag she had been salivating over for months on the internet. "That's it! I can't believe it! It looks even better in person!"

Tameka lifted a three thousand dollar Nancy Gonzales leather purse made from crocodile and boa constrictor. It was a purse that had been her hearts desire since she first laid eyes on it. But then, something on the next display pulled in her eye. It was a lime green Hermes Kelly Bag. And *that* was a purse that she had desired since she first started watching movies. Like millions of other women around the world, she was smitten when she saw Grace Kelly rocking one on screen. Tameka felt like she could faint. She had virtually died and gone to handbag heaven.

"Oh my God!" Tameka said, clasping the Kelly bag. "I can't believe it. A Kelly Bag. And it's in lime green!"

Tameka placed the bag on her shoulder and peered into a nearby mirror, checking herself and modeling the bag. She turned toward Caleb. "What do you think?"

"Nice," Caleb said hesitantly. "Not sure about the color."

"The color! This color is a classic! They rarely make this color. This is a special edition! A modern day remake of a classic! Are you kidding me? Don't make me hit you!"

Caleb laughed and held up his hands. "Okay, okay, calm down. Dang, girl, you about to get violent up in here."

"I don't play about my purses or my shoes," Tameka said, continuing to peer at herself in the mirror. "This is my dream bag. I want this bag so bad."

"Buy it."

Tameka lifted the price tag. "Six thousand dollars!"

She immediately pulled the bag off of her shoulders and placed it back on the rack. She then lifted the three thousand dollar Nancy Gonzales purse. Caleb peered at the price tag on the

Nancy Gonzales bag.

"See the difference?" Tameka told him. She placed the Nancy Gonzales bag on her shoulder and peered at herself in the full length mirror. "I guess I'll be rocking the Nancy Gonzales bag."

Caleb shook his head. "Where are you going to carry *that* thing?"

"I can wear this everywhere," Tameka told him. "It depends on what I'm wearing. I can dress it down, and rock it with some jeans and some heels and wear it casually. Or, I can throw on a dress and carry it to church. It's flexible."

"And the lime green bag?"

"Oh, that one. That one is to make all the haters sick. You rock that one when you going to a fancy party or a fancy restaurant, or somewhere where you want to make bitches sick."

Caleb laughed. "Tameka, you're crazy."

"Just keeping it real."

"All right, I got you."

"You ready?" Tameka asked.

Caleb grabbed the Hermes Kelly bag and followed her to a nearby register. Tameka placed the Nancy Gonzales bag on the counter. She was shocked when Caleb walked up behind her and placed the Kelly bag on the counter next to the croc and boa purse.

"What are you doing?" Tameka frowned. "I'm not getting that one!"

Caleb pulled out his wallet, and then pulled out a black American Express card, and handed it to the sales clerk.

"Caleb! I can't let you do that!"

"Don't worry about it."

"No, that purse is too much!" Tameka protested.

"I said I got you," Caleb told her.

Tameka shook her head. "No."

Caleb nodded to the sales clerk, telling her to go ahead and ring up the purchase. She swiped Caleb's card and handed it back to him.

"I can't believe you just did that," Tameka told him. "And used the *Black* !"

Caleb laughed.

"Let me see that thing," Tameka told him.

Caleb handed her his Black Centurion card, and Tameka clasped it like it was fine china. She had only heard about the card, but never actually seen one, or even knew anyone who had one. And now, she was actually holding one in her hand. She had definitely come a long way since the days of eating fried bologna sandwiches in the projects. She was moving in circles that she never imagined she would, and playing in a whole different league. Major niggas with major figures, her girlfriends used to say.

The saleswoman bagged up Tameka's purses and handed the shopping bag to her. Tameka snapped out of her thoughts, handed Caleb his Black Card, and grabbed the shopping bags. She leaned over and kissed Caleb on his cheek.

"Thank you."

"Don't mention it," Caleb smiled. "Just think of me the next time you are out there making those bitches sick."

Tameka laughed heartily.

The two of them headed out of the mall to the exit. Caleb handed the valet his ticket, and the kid raced off to retrieve the car.

"Nobody has ever done anything like this for me before," Tameka said. "Especially no guy."

"Well, you need to date better guys."

"Perhaps I do," she said with a smile. "Anybody in particular in mind?"

"Maybe."

# Boyfriend # 2

Caleb's playful banter and the fact that he had a Black Card in his wallet was turning her on. She had a man standing next to her that was a self-made man, a power broker, a guy who was climbing the ladder of success at break neck speeds. And for now, she was along for the ride. It was a ride she didn't want to get off of. She just needed to play her cards right, and perhaps, eventually, she could become the lovely wife. *Mrs. Stockbroker. Mrs. Daddy War Bucks. Mrs. Billionaire Bitch* rolling in a Rolls Royce, jetting to Paris, vacationing on her private island, hanging out with Oprah, and sipping on champagne and eating caviar all day. It was a life she wanted more than anything. And she would do anything to get it.

The valet pulled up and lifted the scissor doors to Caleb's brand new, half a million dollar, pearl white, Lamborghini Aventador. Tameka peered down at the exotic car, still not believing that it was her man's whip. She could see the rear mounted engine through the glass engine cover, and it turned her on even more. What other chicks from the hood had actually ridden in a five hundred thousand dollar Lamborghini? What other chicks could say that they had felt buttery soft, fine Italian hand-stitched leather beneath their cornbread fed ass?

Caleb helped Tameka into the car, walked around to the driver's side and climbed in. They closed their scissor doors simultaneously, and Caleb revved the motor. Tameka peered out of the vehicle and noticed just how many people were staring at them, and at the car, with their mouths gaped open. She smiled, pulled out her Chanel sunglasses and put them on. She was the luckiest chick in the world, she thought. People were staring at them, wondering who they were, and what they did for a living. She felt like they were Jay and Bey sitting inside of that Lamborghini.

Caleb pulled away. "So, where you wanna grab something to eat from?"

"How about Ruth Chris?" Tameka asked.

"Sounds good. You know I love steak."

"I feel like some Maine lobster and some garlic butter shrimp," Tameka told him. She peered around the cabin of his new Lambo. "So, how fast have you taken this thing?"

Caleb shrugged. "I've gotten it up to about a hundred and fifty."

"One hundred and fifty miles per hour?"

"Yeah."

"Chicken shit,"

"What?"

"This car does over two hundred miles per hour, and you've only gotten it up to a buck fifty. What's up with that?"

"I'm still breaking it in."

"I think you're scared."

"I ain't never scared, baby girl. Believe that."

Caleb raced the engine. The feeling of power vibrated throughout the cabin. The rumbling V-12 engine mounted just behind her seat caused a constant vibration that only served to moisten her even further. It was as if someone had her vibrator on extremely low power; like it was in tease mode. The Lambo, the Black Card, and the sexy, handsome man sitting just to her left, had all conspired to make her super horny. She wanted him to fuck her on top of the hood of his Lamborghini. She wanted to cum all over the top of it. She wondered how many times that had been done before. Especially by hood chicks. How many of them had actually had their juices run down their legs and onto the hood of a half a million dollar exotic car?

Tameka lifted her skirt, showing off her firm thigh. "You want some of this?"

Caleb peered down at her caramel leg. "I *always* want some of that."

"Take me back to your place in Jersey, and fuck me on the

hood."

"What?"

"I need you to fuck me on the hood of the Lamborghini."

Caleb smiled. "Say the magic words."

"You gonna make me beg?"

"Say it."

"Please?"

"Please what?"

"Please fuck me on the hood?"

"Make me."

"What?"

"I said, make me want to do that."

Tameka peered around at the streets outside. There was certainly no shame in her game, and she was desperate for him to fuck the shit out of her on top of his new Lamborghini. She could feel her pussy aching. She needed him inside of her.

Tameka took her hand, unzipped Caleb's pants, and leaned over and begin to kiss his dick as he drove. She could feel the car turning, and she knew that Ruth Chris had just been put off until later. They were headed for his mansion in Jersey, where she was going to get her wish. He was going to bend her over the top of his car, and fuck her like there was no tomorrow. She wrapped her lips around his dick and sucked like she was trying to remove venom from a snake bit. She sucked his dick like someone's life depended on it. She sucked his dick like her life depended on it. She sucked his dick as if her living the good life, depended on it.

# Boyfriend # 2

# Chapter Eight

Eric slowly cruised toward the Onyx night club on Atlantic Avenue. He navigated his ride through the police barricades carefully, so as not to get single speck of dirt on his prized possession. His Escalade was gleaming from the fresh three hour wax job that he had the detail shop put on it, and from the massive 26" chromed rims that shined like mirrors. It was after midnight and he was rolling deep with his Brooklyn crew, and had Tameka riding shotgun. The stereo system was booming Jay-Z's *'Where I'm From'* and weed smoke was pouring out of the cracked windows like a fine mist. The purple haze they were smoking had them all high as a kite, and they were ready for a party filled night. To them, life didn't get any better than this, and all was right in the BK.

The crowd and long line outside of the club entrance was chaotic; hordes of people were cluttered on the block from one corner to the next. The women were clad in their sexiest outfits, with more flesh showing than the bunnies between the pages of a Playboy magazine. The ladies looked phenomenal in their high heels and stilettos, short skirts and tight jeans. The men were in their hip-hop attire, sporting platinum jewels, and filled with bad boy Brooklyn swagger. The traffic was at a snail's pace, and judging by the number of high end cars that lined the one-way street, it was evident that the ballers were heavy in attendance at the infamous club Onyx. The beautiful autos coasted to the curb like supermodels down a runway; Bentley's and H2s, Lambos,

Benzes and Porsches. The streetlights bounced off the million-dollar motorcade blinding all within sight of them.

Plies and Young Jeezy were listed to perform tonight. The fact that their names had been advertised on the promotional fliers, along with word of mouth spreading throughout the New York streets, coupled with continuous radio announcements, a heavy crowd had showed up. People of all ages and ethnics came to party and see a lively show. It brought out the goons too.

NYPD had to show a strong presence to deter any crime or violence outside of club Onyx. They had to shut down the block with their barriers to direct the heavy traffic, as well as post officers on guard to quell any disturbances that might crop up. The club was infamous for hosting premiere hip-hop events, as well as for bringing in the cream-of-the-crop rappers and R&B artists to perform on any giving night. But along with the well-known acts and scantily clad ladies, came trouble and fights. The club owner and the police felt it was better to be safe than sorry. It was Brooklyn, and there had been already one shooting and fatality at the club only a year ago.

Eric parked his truck at the end of the block, and he and his peoples stepped out like they were superstars, with their ice gleaming, and jeans sagging, Yankee fitteds wore at an angle adorned their heads, while costly name brand attire screaming jazzy adorned their bodies. With the police everywhere, guns were left concealed in stash boxes and the weed was quickly extinguished. The last thing they needed was trouble from the cops or an arrest; nobody wanted to see lock up and spend all night in central bookings, especially with such an important event happening tonight.

Tameka felt like the first lady in Eric's crew. She played her boo closely, walking arm-in-arm with him toward the madness at the front entrance. Eric's boys, Sean, Easton and Chucky, followed closely behind the two of them. Tameka knew she looked amazing in her sexy outfit. She was turning heads as she strutted toward the club in her low-cut, red, mini-dress with cinched ties on the sides, and a pair of stilettos that elongated her already statuesque legs. She was Eric's trophy tonight, and was a tantalizing piece of eye-candy for all of the men who would be in attendance.

Tameka and Eric proceeded toward the door, ignoring the massive crowd of people lined up to see the performance with Piles and Jeezy. It was a madhouse outside, with everyone trying to push their way past security. Eric moved toward the entrance and stepped toward the beefy bouncers that stood behind the velvet ropes and barricades. He locked eyes with one of the men that held the crowd back from behind the ropes.

"Yo, we up in there," Eric said. He was flanked by his woman and his peoples.

"It's bottle service only, E," the bouncer told him.

"So, unhook the ropes then, my nigga, and let my people slide through. I'm buying three bottles," Eric said.

"It's three hundred minimum for a bottle," the bouncer said, lifting an eyebrow.

Eric looked at the bouncer like he had been offended. He reached into his pockets and pulled out a wad of hundreds and fifties, lifting the cash for the bouncer to catch witness to.

"Yo Breez, why you insulting a nigga like that?" Eric asked with a sly smile. "You should already know."

The bouncer nodded. "Just doing my job, E."

"Then do it wit' somebody else," Eric told him.

The bouncer unhooked the velvet rope and allowed Eric and his peoples to slide inside the club. The rest of the crowd looked on with envy and hate. It was getting ugly at the entrance, with the have-nots being reminded what they didn't have, while the ballers filtered into the venue with their crews. Tameka glanced back at the unruly crowd, and a small number of ladies that were still standing outside on the line gave her some venomous looks. Their look made Tameka smirk. She loved it when bitches hated on her and wished that they could be her. But it wasn't her fault, she thought with a smile. She didn't do long lines or fuck with average niggas, and her advice to them would be to do the same. Upgrade their game like her. She was VIP status wherever she went, no matter who she went with. Whether it was VIP executive status with Caleb, or Brooklyn bad boy swag status with Eric, she was always going to be with the creme of the crop. Raise ya game, bitches, Tameka thought, as she winked at the chicks still standing on line waiting to get in.

Tameka and Eric strolled into the club still arm-in-arm. Her boo was looking good, she thought, taking him in. He was clad in a pair of Mek jeans, and sported a pair of fresh Timberlands that were right out of the box. He wore a crisp collared shirt with a long, glimmering, diamond linked chain that had a diamond encrusted cross peeking out from the collar. And of course his braids were freshly done. They were spiraling down the back of his head like artwork and falling against his shoulders.

As Tameka and Eric maneuvered their way through the lively club, the DJ began spinning Piles and Jeezy's popular track, *Loose My Mind*. Tameka was ready to dance. The tune hit her and the rest of the club goers like a shock through the heart. Everyone instantly became animated, and the still swelling crowd that was packed inside of the 10,000-square foot space really became hyped.

"This shit crazy, way to bad. Rozay, baby, waste 2 stacks. Hottest thing in the lot, that there mine. Can't spell sober, lost my mind..." Tameka shouted at the top of her lungs, singing along with the track.

Eric and the members of his crew laughed out loud. But Tameka didn't care. Young Jeezy was one of her favorite rappers. She was a fan of his for life, and couldn't wait to see his performance.

The music was booming throughout the club's monster stereo system, and the sweet smell of purple haze had begun to waft throughout the building. The rap and R&B tunes had all of the revelers hyped, and the lavish bar that spread around the room was making sure that everyone was feeling good. The Onyx Club had proved to be the perfect venué for the night's festivities. The owners had spent a grip making sure that the club was just right. It boasted a sound system that was second to none, and it had a state of the art lighting system that changed the clubs lights according the beat of the music. The club also had no less than twenty 46" LCD flat screens mounted all throughout. The flat screens were poised above the patron's heads, and tonight, they were playing nothing but Piles and Young Jeezy videos. Club Onyx was definitely the premiere club for the city's elite, and tonight, those elites had turned out in numbers. A swarm of rappers, professional athletes, major hustlers and hot women had gathered beneath the sea of crystalline rods that hung from the ceiling, to dance, drink, party, and stunt. The atmosphere was electric.

Eric wanted nothing but bottle service all night. He had reserved a private booth that was nestled in the back of the club, that was elevated above everything else. His elevated booth gave him a three hundred and sixty degree view of the entire club. Even Tameka had been impressed by this move. Eric's entourage piled into the expensive booth and was ready to have a great time. The beautiful hostesses in their short shorts and glittering tight tops approached the table with several bottles of Moet and Crystal. Drinking glasses were quickly filled and Eric snatched his own personal bottle out of the ice-bucket and took it to the head, downing the liquor like it was water.

Tameka nestled against her man and was ready to show off with him on the dance floor. The music still had her hyped and ready to get her dance on. She lifted a stemmed glass that was nearly overflowing with Moet and sipped at the bubbly. She peered around the table, taking in the faces of her Brooklyn crew, and a smile crept across her face. She couldn't help it. She was happier than she had been in a long while. She was surrounded by real niggas doing real things, and parties like this reminded her of the good times back in the day.

Tameka gazed at Eric and smiled. Silently, she mouthed three little words to him under her breath. "I love you baby."

"I love you too," Eric replied without any hesitation in front of his goons. He wasn't afraid to admit it, even amongst the crowd he was around.

Piles and Young Jeezy arrived at the club after two in the morning and the place went bananas. Fanatical fans and groupies rushed toward the small stage to be closer to the rappers, while security and personal bodyguards played the men close, keeping a watch out for any potential danger or an overzealous fan. The rappers jewelry sparkled like wet ice, and their raucous performance had the club's energy through the roof. The two performed their hit song, and a few more hot tracks and had the club going absolutely insane.

Tameka remained by the booth next to her boo and had a perfect view from where she stood. She watched Jeezy and Piles perform, and marveled at how the women went crazy each time the rappers screamed and rhymed into the microphones. Admittedly, their performance even had her losing control a little bit.

Soon, Tameka found herself not being able to control her enthusiasm any longer, and she began dancing. She winded and gyrated her thick hips to their songs and soon, the folks around her started to focus more on her than the show on stage. And Tameka loved the attention. She knew what she had been blessed with, and she knew that she was able to grab any man's interest easily. Between her sexy wardrobe, and her exotic and damn near erotic dance moves, she knew how to make men stop and drool. Her curves made her a natural born man magnet.

Eric remained lounging in the VIP booth, with his eyes focused on his woman. He loved that Tameka had every man in the club's eye's on her. It swelled his pride to know that he was hitting what other men wanted. He tapped his boys and smiled.

"That's my fuckin' bitch right there...she do her thang," he exclaimed.

"She damn sure do," Sean replied.

The two men shared a quick laugh and surveyed the scene. Women were posted everywhere, all clad in their best. The club looked like a 2 Live Crew rap video, combined with a Big Poppa video shoot. Scantily clad woman looking like video models were everywhere. While ballers with bottles of bubbly, plenty of ice, and giant entourages threw money away like it was free. It was if they were throwing blood in the water and stirring up a shark feeding frenzy. The model chics couldn't decide which tables to be at, so most of them just started to table hop and collect as many numbers as possible.

With the night progressing toward dawn, things were moving smoothly. Piles and Young Jeezy did their thing, packed the club, performed, and then made their exit. And even though the concert part of the evening was over, Club Onyx was far from winding down.

Tameka moved her little dance and show onto the main dance floor with the other lively club goers. Her low cut mini dress kept riding up her thick thighs each time she dropped to get her eagle on, exposing more of her seductive flesh. She had niggas in the club hypnotized. The big money men kept sending their boys at her, requesting her presence at their tables. They were dying for just one night with her.

Eric sat in the comforts of VIP, with his Moet bottle

clutched in his hand, while his goons kept an eye on things around him. He was continuously sipping, and getting more and more tipsy with each passing moment. His boy, Sean, was in his ear about business, and about an escalating beef with a Brooklyn hustler named Skinny.

"That nigga got ya name constantly comin' out of his mouth, E," said Sean.

"Fuck Skinny," Eric spat.

"We owe his cousin a lot of money," Sean reminded him. "We gonna have to do sumthin' before this shit gets ugly on the streets.

"It already has," Eric told him.

Eric sighed and tried to focus his thoughts elsewhere. He wanted to forget about his debt and about his problems with Skinny and the streets. Skinny was a middle man to his cousin Peon. Skinny was six foot three, and a hundred and twenty pounds soaking wet. But his status was large. He was a major player, and a dangerous man. But Eric was also a dangerous man. The two men were bumping heads in the Ville. Eric was allegedly in debt to the organization for a hundred thousand. It was cocaine money, something Tameka didn't know about. She thought he only dealt with weed, but Eric was ready to come up and become a major figure, and that meant making major moves. The hundred thousand he owed was to Peon. Peon was the Nino Brown of Brooklyn. His status was larger than life, and his reputation for violence preceded him. He was many dealers or drug crews' suppliers. 80% of the drugs shipped into Brooklyn came from Peon, and Peon been around for a long time and had connections everywhere. His little cousin, Skinny, was his eyes and ears in Brooklyn. Eric didn't like Skinny, he felt the man was a snake, a liar, a cheat, a thief, and that he couldn't be trusted.

Eric argued that Skinny was embezzling money from his own cousin's organization and blaming other low level dealers and drug crews for the lost income. He was also using the names of dead gang members to hide his illicit activities. The result was much lost of life and violence in Brooklyn. Other crews and dealers were scared of Skinny, and would rather pay up money that they didn't owe, rather than square of with him and his murderers.

Eric on the other hand, refused to be bullied and intimidated by Skinny. He had guns and killers on his team too. And he did owe money to Peon, but it was nowhere near the hundred grand that Skinny had written in the books. Skinny was a greedy and conniving bastard. He was a man that Eric despised. And if they had to go to war, then so be it. Eric was ready. He had a reputation to protect, and he would die protecting it.

"E, I'm telling you, this shit is gonna get way outta hand," Sean said, still in Eric's ear about the troubles. Unlike Eric, Sean was nervous. He was ready to resolve the beef.

"Fuck Skinny!" Eric declared. He wasn't to be moved.

"We gonna war then, yo."

"I looked scared?"

Sean sighed. He saw their team heading for serious trouble and fading. With Echo hiding out in Louisiana with his grandmother because of a murder warrant, and his cousin Tyme doing a bid on Riker's Island, their two main shooters were out of the game.

Eric continued to drink and relax. He eyed Tameka and smiled. Sean gave up trying to reason with him and walked away. Moments later, a blood gang member, a tough-looking young male with gold teeth, walked by Eric's booth and glared at him.

"What the fuck you lookin' at nigga?" Eric shouted.

"Bitch ass muthafucka!" the man shouted back.

Eric quickly rose up and clenched the Moet bottle tightly in his hand. "What you say, nigga?"

"Fuck you!"

# Boyfriend # 2

There were no more words to be said. With the speed of lightening, the champagne bottle was abruptly smashed over the gang members head, and a brawl ensued. Men came rushing in from all directions to aid both individuals, and Eric was caught in the middle of the chaos . Through it all, he continued to throw punches and kicks.

From the dance floor below, Tameka peered up at the chaos happening in the VIP section and raced to find Eric. She knew he was in the middle of the fight. It was in his character. She no longer cared about anything else, but the safety of her man. The music had stopped and club patrons found themselves running away from the brawl, fearing gunshots might follow next.

It was shear pandemonium. Bottle and chairs were being thrown across the room and the fight started to spill out into the streets. Tameka spotted Eric and Chucky beating on a lone individual. It was a bloody mess. Eric's clothes were torn and he had suffered a cut across his forehead. Tameka grabbed Eric from behind.

"Baby, let's go!" Tameka shouted. She had to forcefully pull Eric off the man they were beating down.

They ran out the back exit and rushed toward the truck. Sean was the last one behind. Police came storming into the club, detaining anyone they deemed to be a suspect or participant in the fight. Outside, everyone piled into the Escalade. Chucky got behind the wheel and Eric and his crew sped off. Tameka was pissed, while a drunken Eric was nonchalant about the entire thing.

"What is wrong with you?" Tameka asked. She was still breathing heavily, and her heart was pounding from the excitement. "What the hell was all that about?"

"Some clown ass nigga tried to punk me," Eric answered.

Tameka sighed and shook her head. "You gotta chill baby. I don't want to see you get hurt."

92

"I won't Tameka. I just lost it. But I'm good."

She sighed again. Eric pulled her closer into his arms and said, "You know I gotta reputation to uphold, baby."

"You need to hold me down, that's what you need to hold down," she quipped back.

"I plan, too."

Chucky came to a stop at a red-light which was a few blocks from the club. Eric sat in the backseat with Tameka in his arms. He seemed aloof for a moment, and Tameka noticed his distanced.

"You okay?" she asked.

"We need to talk though. I'll let you know what's goin' on wit' me."

"What baby…everything okay?" Tameka asked.

"Look…"

But the sudden sounds of gunshots and shattering glass sent the couple ducking in their seats, along with everyone else in the Escalade.

*Bak! Bak! Bak! Bak! Bak! Bak! Bak! Bak!*

Tameka screamed. Eric threw his arms around her and tried to shield his woman from the danger outside. Everything happened fast. The shots were rapid. And then, the danger was over as quickly as it started.

Sean and Easton jumped out from the truck with their guns in their hands and quickly returned fire at the red Dodge Charger speeding away from the crime scene. But they missed.

"Oh shit!" Eric exclaimed.

He looked over at Chucky, who was slumped behind the wheel and shot. Easton and Sean ran back to the truck. They knew they needed to get to a hospital fast. Sean got behind the wheel and sped off, while they tried to keep Chucky alive in the backseat. He had been shot twice in his side.

"Aaaaaagh!" Tameka screamed. Blood was pouring out of

Chucky's side, and a lot of it had gotten onto her hands.

They reached Brookdale Hospital quickly. The Escalade came to a full stop near the emergency room entrance, and Sean jumped out to get their friend some medical help. A short moment later, no less than a dozen medical staff came running out with a gurney, placed Chucky onto it, and then hurriedly wheeled him inside the emergency room. Eric and Tameka watched from a short distance. They didn't know if Chucky would live or die. Tameka was shocked, but she wasn't traumatized. She was from the hood, and she had seen plenty of niggas shot before. It used to be the world she lived in a long time ago. But she thought she was done with the ignorance and the gun play. The fact that she wasn't, had her pissed off more than anything.

Tameka turned to Eric. "What the fuck is going on? Who you got beef with?"

Eric looked at her for a moment. His clothing and hands stained with his friend's blood. He had a deadpan gaze. Tameka wanted an answer. Eric took her by the arm and led her away out of ear distance from everyone else.

Away from everyone else, Eric sighed deeply, and then peered into her eyes. "I fucked up, a'ight."

"Fucked up what?"

"I owe money, a great deal of money, and I gotta pay it back. But I'm into this beef wit' this muthafucka named Skinny. He a rat ass nigga, and got me pulled into some serious shit wit' his cousin."

"How much do you owe?" Tameka asked.

Eric hesitated, not wanting to answer, but he knew she needed to know the truth.

"I got into trafficking cocaine a few months ago," he finally said softly. "I'm tryin' to come up and make things right for us, baby. But on books, they sayin' I owe a hundred stacks. But

# Boyfriend # 2

Skinny tryin' to get into my pockets and inflate that shit to make his own pockets rich, and that's why I'm warring wit' this nigga. I ain't no fuckin' fool."

Tameka sighed. Niggas and egos, she thought. It was always about that, more than anything else. She had seen too many of the cats she grew up with be buried, simply because of an ego.

"You a'ight?" Eric asked.

Tameka nodded.

"We gonna be good, baby," Eric told her. "We gonna be okay, cuz I'm gonna handle this shit, a'ight."

But Tameka wasn't so sure. Being with Eric was fun and adventurous, and she loved being the first lady of his crew, and the sex was phenomenal. But now? Things were beginning to get really crazy. She was a ride or die chick, but her life had been put in danger. Danger was where she stopped being a ride or die chick, and started being Tameka. Self preservation came before anything else. This definitely was not the life she was trying to live. She knew that she had some thinking to do, and she knew that she wanted to get the fuck away from Eric right now. She also knew that she had to play it cool, and keep her cards close.

Tameka heaved a sigh. "No more secrets, Eric."

"I promise you, ain't gonna be anymore secrets."

She hugged him tightly and rolled her eyes behind his back. She knew that she had feelings for Eric. Deep ones, in fact. But nothing, and no one, was going to put her life in danger. She didn't go through four years of college to get shot at like a ghetto hoe from the hood. Being a dope dealer wifey had it's perks. The champagne, the VIP treatment at the clubs, the look of envy on all those other bitches faces. But still, being a dead dope dealers wifey held no perks. She knew that she had some serious thinking to do. She needed to get away with Caleb for a while.

# Boyfriend # 2

# Chapter Nine

Caleb's ski out chalet was nestled in the midst of Pennsylvania's famed Poconos Mountains. The Poconos were one of the preeminent destinations for North-easterners wanting a quick getaway from the hustle and bustle of work. Resorts dotted the two thousand-four hundred square mile mountain range, giving way to the occasional rustic mega-mansion every now and then. The Poconos were where the Wall Street and Madison Avenue CEO's maintained their vacation homes. It was also where the Hartford based insurance CEO's, New York's fashion and publishing execs, as well as the East Coast's pro-athlete set kept their rustic mini-mansions, lodges, and massive log homes. At thirty seven thousand square feet, Caleb had one of the largest log home mansions in the mountains.

"This place is beautiful!" Tameka exclaimed. She carefully climbed down the gentle slope, and made her way beneath one of the mountains numerous breathtaking waterfalls. "I never knew this place was here!"

"Not many people do," Caleb told her. He pulled off his shirt, tossed it onto the ground, and then made his way into the winding river. "Most people think of Pennsylvania as only being Philly, or Pitt, and those that do vacation in the Poconos, only think of it as a winter destination. They are missing the beautiful rivers, and waterfalls, and all of the other things that this place offers."

"I've never been skiing before," Tameka told him. She

peered around, taking in her surroundings. She wanted to take in every rock, every tree, every blade of grass. She was like a kid in a candy store. Her outing with Caleb was proving to be just the decompression she needed, after her wild outing with Eric. The contrast between the two couldn't have been more different.

"Then we'll have to come back during ski season," Caleb said with a smile.

"Can you ski?" Tameka asked. She raked her hand through her hair and tossed it back over her shoulders. Thank God for infusion weaves, she said to herself. She could be free to swim and get her hair wet, and have a little fun. And fun was what she needed. It would help to take her mind off the fact that she had damn near became target practice on the streets of Brooklyn.

"I can ski," Caleb said with a nod.

"Liar!" Tameka said, smiling. She waded through the water to where Caleb was standing. "You can't ski."

"I can!" Caleb lifted his arms in the air and spun. "What? I don't look like the athletic type of something? What are you trying to say, Tameka?"

Tameka giggled. "I'm just saying, you don't look like the adventurous type." She rubbed her fingers across his six pack. "You know you got it going on."

"Naw, it's too late," Caleb smiled. "You've already bruised my ego."

"Awww," Tameka wrapped her arms around his waist and laid her head on his shoulders. "I'm sorry, babe."

"You're gonna have to pay for that."

"Hmmm, sounds freaky."

"I was thinking more like this!" Caleb lifted Tameka into the air, and tossed her back in the water.

"Caleb!"

"Not only can I ski, but I won the amateur snowboarding competition three years in a row!"

"Damn, fool! I was just playing! Now, you're going to pay for that!" Tameka raked her arms across the river, sending an enormous waver of water washing over Caleb. Her laughter was genuine. Water fights were more up her alley than gunfights.

"Oh, you wanna have a water fight?" Caleb asked, wiping the water off of his face. He raked his hands across the water, sending an enormous wave back in Tameka's direction.

"Ahhh!" Tameka screamed, as the wave washed over her. "Caleb! I'm going to kill you!"

She splashed water in his direction, and he began to splash water back toward her. The two of them playfully engaged in a water fight, slowly moving closer toward one another, until Caleb was able to grab her arms. She was beautiful to him. Not just her shapely figure, but her wet hair, her pearly whites and crooked smile, her big dark brown doe like eyes. He stared at her, and she stared back at him. And he was beautiful to her. Once again, she found her perceptions flying out the window. The guy she thought was just a boring broker; she was now having a water fight with. He had shown her that he could in fact cut loose and have fun. Good fun. Good, wholesome, clean, and above all, *safe* fun. And then, he kissed her.

"Where'd that come from?" she asked.

Caleb shrugged, and released her arms.

"You brought me here to take advantage of me, Mr.?"

"I didn't have to bring you up here to do that."

Tameka smiled. "I know, but the beauty of this place makes it a lot easier. The waterfalls, the flowers, the chirping birds, the beautiful scenery. This shit is damn near erotic. You bring all your little girlfriends up here?"

"Can't tell you that."

"Why not?"

"Cause I want you to think you're special."

Tameka tossed her head back and laughed. "Well, ain't that a bitch?"

Caleb laughed heartily. He turned, and waded through the water to the waterfall, where he stood just in front of it. It framed his beautiful physique. He looked as though he were a statue of a Greek god, standing inside of a gorgeous water garden. Tameka followed. She wanted him to kiss her again. Perhaps even get a little freaky beneath the waterfall. That would definitely be something to tell her girls about. Making love in a beautiful forest beneath a waterfall? That was the type of fairytale that she previously was able to only dream about. And now, the opportunity, like so many other recent opportunities, had presented itself. She was truly living a dream now that she had Caleb in her life. *This* was the life that she wanted, Tameka thought. *This was the life.* Not dodging bullets in the back of an Escalade. But still...

Caleb stepped beneath the flowing waters, and rinsed the river off of him. The waters flowing down on him from the waterfall were fresh, crisp, and cleansing. They were sourced from the melting snow caps of the nearby mountains, which also made them cool. He felt like he was in an Irish Spring commercial.

Tameka stared at him as he stood beneath the cool waters. He was so calm, so poised, deep in thought and concentration while the waters flowed down over him. He was her brown Adonis, with the mind of Aristotle, and money and class of a privileged Aristocrat. He was her dream man. Why she had ever doubted that, she did not know. And why she even continued to fuck with Eric and his boys, was something she didn't understand either. What kind of hold did Eric have on her, she wondered. And how had he managed to get it? She had never allowed herself to get caught slipping, or to get caught up by a niggas dick, head game, or swagger. *Never.* So why she couldn't cut Eric loose was a mystery to her. Especially when she had a better, safer, richer alternative waiting in the wings. What the fuck was going on, she wondered? What was wrong with her mind? Was it the danger? The excitement? The thrill of being able to sneak around, have her cake, and eat it too? What?

Tameka peered up at Caleb. She wanted to join him beneath the water falls, but she didn't want to take many more chances with her hair. Sure, her stylist was on point, and her infusion was top notch, but chancing the force of the waters rushing down on her head once again was something she wasn't game for. The worst thing she could do would be to ruin the moment clasping for strands of weave because her bonding glue didn't hold under the force of the water. Besides, she was rocking Indio Remy, and at $300 dollars a bag, she wasn't about to keep getting it wet.

Caleb stepped from beneath the waterfall and wiped the water from his face. He peered at her. "You ready to start heading back?"

Tameka nodded.

Caleb waded through the water to the banks of the river, where he lifted a towel and dried himself off. Tameka followed closely behind. She lifted her own towel, dried her body, and then wrapped the wet towel around her narrow waist, fashioning it into a skirt. The two of them gathered their belongings, and then made their way up the banks of the river back to their waiting steed. Tameka made the mistake of walking behind the beautiful black Arabian.

"Never, do that!" Caleb told her.

"What?"

"Never walk behind a horse like that," Caleb told her. "You do that, and he gets surprised or scared, it's a trip to the hospital."

"Why?" Tameka asked, genuinely confused. She was from the hood, and the only horses she had ever been around, were the Ford Mustangs that the bad boys threw rims and ground effects kits on back in the day.

"Because he'll kick the shit out of you," Caleb explained. "This is how you do it."

Caleb placed his hand on the horse and gently stroked it, and pet it. He then kept his hand on the horse, while walking around it.

"You want me to run my hand over his ass?" Tameka asked.

"If you don't want to get your teeth kicked out, or end up with a concussion, a fractured skull, or a broken neck, then you'll keep your hand on him while you walk behind it."

"I'll just walk in front of it from now on." Tameka said, giving an exaggerated smile.

"And always mount a horse from his left side," Caleb told her, while peering over the horse at her. "You're on the wrong side."

Tameka exhaled. "I am *not* Yosemite Jane!"

She started to walk around the horse, but Caleb held up his hand and stopped her. Again, she exhaled, changed directions, and walked around the front of the horse. Caleb placed his left foot in the stirrups and mounted the horse. He then reached down, and helped Tameka mount the horse.

Tameka wrapped her arms around Caleb waist, and he tugged at the reins, giving the black Arabian the signal to get moving.

"Where did you learn about horses?" Tameka asked.

"Texas."

"Texas! Are you serious?"

"Yeah. What's wrong with Texas?"

"Nothing. I mean, you just don't seem like anybody that would be in Texas."

"What's that supposed to mean?" Caleb asked with a smile.

"I don't know. I just can't see you being in Texas. You know, when you think of Texas, you think of cows, and oil rigs, and cowboy hats, and..."

"You're kidding, right?"

"What?"

"You've never heard of Dallas, or Houston? Texas has cities, you know."

"I know."

"I don't look like the macho cowboy type to you? Is that what you're saying?"

"Stock brokers with Harvard degrees aren't from Texas."

"I can't believe what I'm hearing! You are really trying to stereotype people. I guess I should have a pocket protector and a pair of glasses?"

Tameka squeezed his waist. "Aw, did I bruise your itty bitty ego?"

"Fuck you."

Tameka laughed. "Awww, I hurt him little feelings. You are my big strong macho man. You're my rough and tough cowboy."

"You know what, when we get back to the crib, I'm going to show you what a buckaroo I am."

"What?"

"I'm going to mount that ass, and I ain't gonna stop until you start screaming yeee-haw, and singing the Yellow Rose of Texas."

Tameka laughed. "Damn! And I don't even know that song."

"Don't worry, I'm gonna put it on you until you make something up."

"What? Hey, wait a minute. I think I left my boyfriend back at the river. Where did you come from?"

"Tameka, prepare to get fucked down."

Tameka could feel herself getting wet between her legs. She didn't know where this new Caleb came from, but she loved it. Now, if he backed up all of his smack talking once they got back to his cabin, then she would really be head over heals in love. Maybe even enough to get rid of Eric. If Caleb was going to cut loose and be her million dollar man during the day and her freak daddy in the bed at night, and at the same time be able to cut loose and have fun with her, then there would be no need to keep Eric around. She could drop his dangerous ass like a hot rock.

# Chapter Ten

The Jet Blue flight touched down at McCarran International airport in Las Vegas early Thursday evening. Eric had sprung the surprise trip on her after she hadn't returned several of his phone calls. He must have known that he was on thin ice, Tameka thought. And so, he had conjured up some tickets to the one place she wanted to go more than any place else in the world, Las Vegas —Sin City. It was her first time in the city, and she couldn't wait until she stepped off the plane and set foot into her paradise.

Eric knew that they needed to get away. After the incident in Brooklyn with Chucky getting shot, Tameka had grown more than just cold and distant, she had virtually disappeared. And he definitely didn't want that to happen, especially because of some bullshit beef that would be over soon. He couldn't stand the rift that had developed between the two of them.

Eric knew that Tameka had escaped from that kind of street life a while ago, and that she didn't want to be caught up in any drama. She had a good thing going for her; a promising career and a great new place. She had too much to lose. The shooting had created some serious doubt about their relationship. He knew that she was second guessing the entire thing. She was wondering if he was worth the trouble. And so now, he was determined to show her that he was. If only he could get her to look at the shooting as an isolated event, and get past everything that had happened.

Eric knew he had to soothe over Tameka. He had to make things up to her, and come big with something special. He wanted her to forget about all of the craziness, and so a trip to Las Vegas was the biggest thing he could think of. It was far away from New York and all of his troubles, and it was a city that Tameka really wanted to see. So he surprised her with two plane tickets and accommodations for three days in one of the most luxurious suites on the Vegas Strip. It was costly, but it was worth it. He knew he had to bowl her over with romance, sex and the best time of her life. He wanted to keep Tameka in his life.

Tameka stepped into the busy terminal clad in a sexy sarong that was tied around her curvy waistline. She was also wearing a sexy top that showcased her full, taunt breasts, and a pair of four inch heels that accentuated her long toned legs. Again, her looks caused the men in the airport to shoot side glances her way. And again, Eric was proud to have her under his arm as they strutted through the terminal. To him, it felt like he was walking with Ms. America in the airport terminal.

They waited in the minor crowd with other arriving passengers, until they were able to grab their bags off the airport conveyor. It was a speedy process. Tameka had her Gucci rolling luggage and Eric had his Nautica duffel bag in tow in a matter of moments. They quickly moved toward the exit. Tameka carried an excited smile as she stepped out of the airport and peered around. They were definitely in Vegas. There were signs everywhere of performances happening at the MGM Grand, and every cab had advertising of shows and acts on the roof and side of their vehicles as they picked up passengers outside the terminal. People were everywhere, many hoping to take advantage of the many casinos that swamped the city. Like most others, they all had dreams of winning it big and leaving Sin City as millionaires.

The couple waited in the Taxicab loading area, and the line

stretched almost the size of a city block. The long line quickly caused a bit of frustration amongst them. Tameka sighed. She was eager to get into a Taxi and race off to her dream destination. She was dying to experience Vegas in it's fullest.

The cab driver loaded their bags into the truck. Eric jumped into the cab behind Tameka and they were off into the city. Tameka nestled against her boo and took in the picturesque view of the Vegas strip. There were numerous outdoor lighting displays on Fremont Street, as well as elsewhere in the city.

"Oh my god, it's so beautiful here," Tameka said.

She was ready to take in everything the city had to offer her. She had money to spend and was ready to hit the hotel and then the casinos, and take in a few Vegas shows with her man.

The cab slowly pulled up to the entrance of the MGM Grand hotel & casino—the mega resort on the Las Vegas strip. Tameka and Eric gazed up at the towering 30-floor building. The resort was legendary. It boasted five outdoor pools, several lazy rivers and numerous waterfalls, all spread over six and a half luxurious and decadent acres. The mega resort also housed numerous shops and night clubs, along with exclusive restaurants, two food courts, a major convention center, and the largest casino in Las Vegas. And then there was the legendary statue of Leo, the MGM lion, that was a sight to see onto itself.

Tameka was ready to leap out the cab and indulged herself in the finest and best that the resort had to offer. She was ready to dine in the restaurants and be pampered at the spas. She was ready to take in some of the concerts, and most of all, hit the casino floor.

The couple entered the resort all smiles. There were hordes of people in the grand atrium, all of them marveling at the gold leaf, decadent furnishings, and dramatic ceiling that seemed as though it extended into the heavens. A larger-than-life gold lion stood proudly in the center of the round lobby. It sat majestically on a raised pedestal of flowers and other decoration, and appeared to act as a doorman, guarding the luxurious lobby.

Tameka was in awe at the glass-sided lion habitat inside the casino, in which six lions could be seen dwelling. The ferocious man-eaters prowling and lounging within the confines of the enclosure was damn near erotic. The resort even had a see-through tunnel that ran through the habitat for close-up viewing.

The use of gold was prominent throughout the casino, gold stars, gold lighting fixtures and tons of gold lions. It was a display of wealth and grandeur straight out of the gilded ages. The billion dollar structure had those seeing it for the first time, in total awe. The MGM Grand was a labyrinth of golden age magnificence. It screamed to the inhabitants and gamblers, welcome to OZ, and everyone was ready to follow the yellow brick road to find their wizard.

Eric and Tameka headed toward their luxurious suite on the 30th floor. They strutted hand-in-hand en route to the double doors that would open up to their seventh heaven. They followed behind the bellhop who wheeled their luggage toward their suite.

"Here we are," the bellhop said.

Eric placed the hotel room key into the door and pushed open the entryway into his wonderland. The suite had two bedroom suites, and a massive living room, as well as it's very own kitchen. Stepping into the opulent milieu, Eric and Tameka gazed at the stunning city by way of the floor-to-ceiling windows that encircled the room. Eric walked toward the large windows and gazed at Vegas. He could see the city stretching for miles, and was even able to see the end of Sin City, where the desert began. The suite also boasted twin rotating sofas, and a king size bed in each bedroom. There was also two large master bathrooms, each with a garden Jacuzzi tub, and separate steam showers, with rainfall shower heads..

"I'm never going home," Tameka said with a smile.

Eric chuckled.

The bellhop set their bags in the middle of the floor and Eric gave the man a twenty dollar tip. When the doors closed behind the bellhop, Eric turned toward his woman.

"Welcome to paradise," Eric told her.

"Oh, yes it is." Tameka nodded. "Indeed it is."

"This is what it's about, baby...living like this. Enjoying wealth." Eric told her.

"I know people in Brooklyn that will kill to see shit like this," Tameka said.

"And some have," Eric said flatly.

Tameka laughed. "You're silly."

Tameka strutted around the place and her eyes lit up like a child. There were large plasma flat screens hanging everywhere and everything came with a remote control—even the chair for massages.

"Damn, baby...you know what would make this evening so perfect right now," Tameka asked.

`"What's that?"

"To smoke something right about now...some Kush or Haze. Oh, I would love to get high in a room like this."

Eric smiled. He went over to his duffel bag, crouched down and started to unzip it. Tameka looked at him confused.

"Babe, what you doing?" she asked.

"It's a surprise."

Eric dug through his belongings and removed a small shampoo bottle from the duffel bag. Tameka became even more confused. She stared at Eric perplexed, and then followed behind him as he walked into the kitchen. He twisted open the bottle and began pulling out a sealed baggy. Tameka eyes lit up.

"Oh my god, baby, no you didn't just smuggle weed onto a plane."

"It worked, didn't it?"

Tameka was flabbergasted. She smiled. "How?"

"Easy, I just simply emptied the container of shampoo into a jar and put the smuggled goods in a sealed baggy and place it inside the bottle and then poured the shampoo back in. And I added a few spices to fuck up any sniffing dogs who attempted to smell it. Genius, right?"

"You could have gotten caught."

"Nah, I've done this type of thing before. Just gotta know how to move and act. Your vibes can give you off," Eric explained. "But c'mon, I didn't and now we got a gram of weed to smoke on this trip."

Tameka smiled. Eric was crazy. It was one more reason why she loved fucking with him. Despite all of his crazy shit, she still couldn't cut him loose all the way, and this was why. Caleb would have never attempted to pull something like this off. Eric's nuts hung low, and it was this Brooklyn swag that had her going crazy.

"You got any white owls?"

Eric reached into his jacket pocket and removed two.

"You love me, right?" Eric asked. He held the cigars in the air.

"Damn, what haven't you thought of?"

"I don't know yet…" he laughed.

"While you're doing that, I'm gonna be in the shower," Tameka said.

She walked to the bathroom leaving Eric in the kitchen to split open the white owl cigar and roll up the weed. Eric smiled as he watched her sashay to the bathroom in her sexy sarong. Her nice round ass protruded from the smooth fabric.

"Um mmmm, love the way you walk, girl," Eric said, shaking his head..

Tameka spun her head around and let out a naughty grin "You can join me in the shower if you want."

"I might just do that."

"I'll leave the door unlocked," Tameka told him.

She disappeared into the bathroom leaving Eric with impure thoughts. He heard the shower coming alive and pictured Tameka getting undressed and stepping into the steaming warm shower.

Eric hurried rolling up the weed. He wanted to take Tameka up on her invitation. Having sex in the bathroom and throughout the suite was the perfect way to start their three day trip in Las Vegas. That pussy was calling him. He heard the shower running and Tameka purring in the bathroom. He imagined that she was playing with herself, because of her loud moans.

"Damn, fuck this."

Eric left two rolled joints on the counter and hurried into the bathroom. He stripped away his clothing, leaving a trail to the shower door. When he stepped inside, the steam from the warm shower hit him instantly. He noticed Tameka's sexy silhouette behind the glass shower door. His Jones came to attention.

"You coming in with me baby, or you're just gonna stand there and get your thrills by watching me," Tameka asked.

"I'm already naked."

Eric stepped into the angled steamed shower with Tameka and the two embraced under the cascade of warm water.

"You're so fuckin' beautiful...you know that right," Eric told her.

Tameka blushed, and the two began to kiss fervently. The softness of their wet skin moved them both into throbbing arousal. Nipples became hard and Eric's cock came to attention between Tameka's thighs.

The evening continued into pure ecstasy. The sun had set hours ago, and the night stars now decorated the sky. Tameka and Eric got high on the love seat and peered out at Sin City. The city lights appeared to go on forever. They were so numerous, and stretched until the eye could no longer separate the sky from the desert.

Tameka took a pull from the joint and remained nestled against her boo in the cushioned love seat. Both of them were clad in complimentary robes from the hotel. Earlier, the two had evoked sensations that each didn't know they had or were even capable of.

Eric's cell phone rang, but he was hesitant to answer the call.

"Go ahead an answer it baby. It might be an important call," Tameka told him.

"You sure, baby?"

Tameka nodded.

Eric stood up and grabbed his cell phone off the counter. Tameka sat back and took a few more heavy pulls from the burning joint clutched between her fingers. Her eyes were tight from the potent weed percolating into her system. She watched Eric handle his business on this cell phone.

"Yo, I'm in fuckin' Vegas right now, so y'all niggas handle that before I get back. I'm wit' my lady."

Tameka smiled.

The need for some more sexual gratification suddenly stirred up inside of her. The Kush was making her horny again. Eric had his back turned to her. He was busy on the phone berating someone in New York. Tameka stood, slowly untied her robe and let it fell to her feet. Her pussy was throbbing again. Maybe it was the weed or being in Vegas that was stimulating her, but whichever it was, it certainly had her going. Tameka wanted to fuck again.

Eric remained on the phone for five minutes. He was so busy handling his business on his cell phone, that he didn't notice his girl had gotten stark naked and was waiting for him to finish with his conversation. When Eric hung up, he turned and nearly dropped his cell phone.

"Oh shit! Damn."

Tameka smiled.

Her caramel skin shined as if recently oiled. Her curves were shapelier than the letter S. As she stood there, her nude body glistening like the sun's rays lighting up the sky in the afternoon, Eric couldn't keep his eyes from mentally devouring every inch of her. He admired her perky youthful breasts, her toned body, and her long legs.

"Damn you're beautiful. I fuckin' love you girl," Eric said, as he pulled her into his affectionate embrace.

His tongue darted in and out of her mouth like a burning spear. Eric lowered her gently to the floor and wrapped himself between Tameka's warm and inviting thighs. Her nipples became hard under his probing lips. Eric proceeded to make love to Tameka with slow deliberation, teasing Tameka with his thick manhood against her. Her eyes lit up from the fire he kindled inside of her. Eric's skillful handling had given her astronomical pleasures that made her spew out orgasm after orgasm.

As their night continued, Tameka rested her head against her king. Her body and mind was satisfied to the third degree.

"What's on your mind baby?" Tameka asked.

Eric smiled and then dropped the bomb on her. "I want you to marry me."

"What?" Tameka was taken aback.

"Yeah, let's do it…here and now, in Vegas."

The proposal came unexpected. It hit her like a bullet to the chest. Tameka wondered what the fuck Eric was doing. Where in the hell had this proposal come from? This shit was crazy, Tameka thought. She sat up instantly.

He stared at her, never diverting his attention from her astonished gaze. He was waiting for her reply. He knew that he had rolled the dice big time. But desperate moments, called for desperate measures. He had fucked up by letting things get out of hand, and now, he needed to get her back in pocket.

Tameka sat in quiet shock. Her rough thug had suddenly transformed into a care bear. She didn't know what to tell him. She wasn't ready to get married.. What part of the game was this? Her two perfect worlds were colliding. The already complicated world she had with Eric had become even more complex. Eric had his place; he was her boy toy. He was her thug boo. So why in the fuck was he trying to be her Cosby?

"Tameka..." Eric called out to her softly.

Tameka lifted her hand silencing him. She rose from the floor, and walked into the master bathroom, where she locked the door behind herself. Tameka stared at herself in the full length mirror. She didn't have any words, and she definitely had no *answers*. Especially an answer to Eric's ridiculous question. *Would she marry him? Would she marry him? What the fuck, man?* Marriage was forever. That was something for two people who wanted to be together forever. It was for two people who never wanted to be apart. Was that for them? Was Eric the dude she couldn't live without? If he decided to leave, could she live without him? Could she live *with* ? The world of the streets, the drugs, the shootouts, the late night rendezvous, rolling with his goons, was that her world? Was that the world that she wanted to live in? She needed Caleb. She needed to call. She needed to see him, to talk to him. She just wanted to hear his voice. Las Vegas, the place she wanted to see more than any other place in the world, had just become the place she wanted to get away from, more than any other place in the world. She needed Caleb. She needed her girlfriends. She needed to hit them bitches up, go shopping, and talk this shit over with them during a long, expensive lunch. It was becoming too much for her to deal with alone. She needed advice from her girls.

# Chapter Eleven

Tameka pulled up to Tammy's apartment in DUMBO and revved the engine of the Bentley Continental GT Convertible that she was driving. The rumble of the massive W-12 engine sent vibrations throughout the entire car, and caused enough of a commotion to summon her friends from inside of the apartment. Tammy was the first one out the door.

"What the hell?" Tammy asked, turning up her palms. "What are you doing? Where did you get this thing from?"

Rosalynn, Tameka's roommate was out the door next, followed by Bridgette, who was their suite-mate in college. Bridgette, like Tameka, was from the hood. She was a product of Marcy projects, and worked at The New York Times as an editor, journalist, and contributing writer covering African American issues. She was fiercely intelligent and 100 percent down for the cause. She rocked her hair natural, occasionally wearing twist and braids, but for the most part, kept it combed out in an afro.

"Girl, what bank did you hit?" Bridgette asked. "I'm listening to see if I can hear NYPD sirens coming for your ass right now."

Tameka laughed. "It belongs to my Boo!"

"Eric?" Rosalynn asked, lifting an eyebrow.

"Child please!" Tameka said, waving her hand and dismissing such a ridiculous statement. "My *real* Boo Thang!"

"Must be nice!" Bridgette said smiling. "A trip to Vegas with one, and a Bentley from the other."

"Girl, all you have to do is put it on 'em!" Tameka said. She opened the door, climbed out of the Bentley, and stated bouncing her ass. "Put that twist action on 'em!"

The girls giggled.

Rosalynn shoved Tameka lightly on her shoulder. "Uh, you nasty, Bitch."

Again they all laughed.

Tammy began to slowly walked around the metallic black Bentley, taking in the multiple coats of hand applied paint and clear coat finish. The Bentley's polish glimmered brilliantly in the bright New York sun.

"Girl, I'm telling you, all you gotta do is learn how to pop it," Tameka continued.

Bridgette laughed. She opened the door, and climbed inside of the car, caressing the white, diamond-stitched, leather seats, and the highly polished burled wood appliques on the dash.

"Girl, I ain't never sat on some leather like this!" Bridgette declared.

"This thing is beautiful!" Tammy declared. "How the hell did you get him to let you drive it?"

"Girl he ain't tripping over this Bentley," Tameka told her. "He's too focused on his brand new Lamborghini. He don't even drive this thing."

"Girl, does he have a brother?" Bridgette asked, folding her arms and craning her neck.

"Girl what if Eric sees you rolling in this thing?" Rosalynn asked. "What the hell do you think he's going to do?"

Tameka waved her hand dismissing the idea. "Girl, ain't nobody worried about Eric's ass."

"Girl, he gone put them thangs on you if he catch you," Bridgette declared.

"Girl, please!" Tameka said craning her neck. "I wish a nigga would. Beside, he ain't even like that."

"Okay, he ain't like that!" Bridgette told her. "Most niggas ain't like that, at least until they think somebody else is swimming in their pool!"

Again, they laughed.

"And then all bets are off!" Rosalynn added. "Why are they like that? They be out there doing their thing, and tripping, and acting a fool, and as soon as they think you're stepping out, they lose their damn minds!"

"That's cause lucky bitches like Tameka give us all a bad name," Bridgette said with a smile.

"And what's that supposed to mean?" Tameka asked, placing her hand on her hip.

"It means, you got a man who tosses you the keys to something like this, and you still creeping on his ass," Bridgette explained.

"Girl, I got this," Tameka told her. "You let me worry about this."

"Oh, now you got this?" Bridgette asked, folding her arms and pursing her lips.

Tameka nodded.

"You wasn't so sure when you was up in Vegas tripping about Eric's little proposal," Bridgette told her.

"Is he creeping on you?" Tammy asked.

"Who?" Tameka asked. "Eric?"

"Caleb," Tammy clarified.

Tameka thought about Tammy's question. Was Caleb stepping out on her? Her first instincts told her that he probably wasn't. He was always available whenever she called. He always answered, and there was none of that bullshit that guys do when someone else was in the room that they didn't want to talk in front of. So, no. Caleb wasn't stepping out on her. Now, ask her that same question about Eric, and she wasn't so sure. Eric was the player type. He was a hood cat, rolling in an Escalade sitting fat on some rims. He dressed fly, had some long hood paper, and was too smooth of a cat to not have all the little hoes in the hood trying to give him some. Besides, she knew Eric, and she knew his type. She had met dozens of them growing up in the hood, and they were all the same. They were dope boy, player types, who fucked everything that came their way. She was sure he had bitches, and plenty of them. She was just one of his many stops throughout the week. So, why did she put up with that, she wondered? Because he was fun, because he was hood, and because he kept it real. He did remind her of the fellas in the hood she grew up with. He brought over the killer bud that she loved smoking, and he was fun to be around. So, what was the real deal, she asked herself. Why couldn't she cut him loose? She kept saying that she would, but saying it and actually doing it were two different things. Cutting him loose had proved difficult. Even after the shooting and the stupid ass club fight. She was a hood chick at heart, no matter how she tried to act around Caleb, and no matter how much she wanted that upper middle class life, the projects were a part of her. There was just something about rolling in that black Escalade with the twenty-six inch chrome rims, with the system bumping, and the weed smoke pouring out of the tinted windows. There was something about being first lady with a Brooklyn crew. It was a position that all the girls in the hood coveted back in the day. But this wasn't back in the day though, was it? She was grown now. So, why couldn't she cut him loose?

"So, what's up?" Tammy asked. "Is he stepping out on you or what?"

Tameka's thoughts shifting back to her present company and the question she was being posed.

"No," Tameka said shaking her head. "Naw, girl, he know better."

Tammy and Rosalynn exchanged looks.

"Bitches, don't judge me!" Tameka told them.

"Ain't nobody judging you!" Bridgette told her. "That's just your guilty conscience eating at your paranoid ass!"

"I know you bitches, and I know that look," Tameka told them. "Look, don't be sitting here trying to judge my actions, cause ain't none of you hoes on the up and up, remember that! All of us got dirt. I went to college with your asses, and I know where y'all bones are buried."

Rosalynn wrapped her arms around Tameka. "Just be careful, okay?"

"Careful like what?" Tameka asked and then exhaled. She was growing tired of the conversation.

"Be careful playing with people's emotions and feelings," Tammy told her. "You don't want to get caught up."

"Yeah, and Eric don't seem like the type to be too cool if he caught you," Rosalynn told her. "Especially now that that fool done asked you to marry him. Meka, his feelings are involved. And niggas with huge egos and broken hearts are nothing to be played with."

"Girl, Eric is not like that," Tameka told them.

"What I'm saying is, don't lose a Bentley, trying to hop up in a Cadillac!" Bridgette told her.

"And don't forget about the incident at the club, and after the club," Rosalynn told her. "Eric and his crew are dangerous. Really dangerous."

"True that!" Tameka said nodding.

"Girl, do not lose the big bucks messing around with the hood," Tammy said, running her finger over the Bentley's paint.

"Do you think I'm crazy?" Tameka asked. She reached into her pocket, and pulled out Caleb's Black American Express Card and held it up. "Do you think for one minute that I would fuck this off?"

"What is that?" Rosalynn asked.

"Ooooh, bitch!" Bridgette declared. "Is that what I think it is?"

Bridgette snatched the credit card from Tameka's hand.

Tammy and Rosalynn gathered around Bridgette and examined the card.

"His Centurion Card?" Tammy asked, wide eyed. "He gave you his Black Amex?"

"His *unlimited*, Black Amex," Tameka said with a crooked smile.

"Are you fucking kidding me?" Bridgette exclaimed. "What the fuck are we still doing here?"

Tammy hopped in the back seat of the convertible Bentley. "Why aren't we shopping?"

"For real!" Rosalynn asked, walking to the other side of the car and climbing into the other back seat.

"That's why I came to pick you ladies up," Tameka told them. "Shopping, dinner, and a day at the spa, all on Mr. Caleb. You know, we need to talk."

"Bitch, if I catch you fucking with Eric again, I'm going to kick your ass!" Bridgette told her. "If I catch you giving that pussy up to anybody else, I'm going to beat your ass!"

"Yeah, you want advice, and you already know the right answers," Rosalynn added.

"I agree with Bridgette," Tammy added. "You fuck up, an ass whipping is in order."

Tameka laughed.

She was right though, Tameka thought. She had been taking a chance. A stupid chance. Why was she risking running off her Daddy Warbucks just for a little fun and some weed every now and then? Hell, she could send her maid to the hood for some weed, once she locked Caleb down and had that ring on her finger. That was the marriage proposal that she wanted. The *only* marriage proposal that she wanted. What the fuck was Eric thinking?

Bridgette walked around the Bentley and climbed into the passenger seat, while Tameka climbed behind the wheel into the driver's seat.

"Where to first?" Tameka asked.

"Chin Chins," Bridgette said, rubbing her stomach. "Your girl is hungry."

"To the Spa," Tammy offered. "We can snake while we get pampered."

"I could use some pasta from Romano's," Rosalynn suggested.

"Okay, so what I'm hearing is that you hoes are hungry?" Tameka asked.

"Yes!" Bridgette said emphatically.

"Okay, off to grab something to eat then," Tameka announced.

"And then to the spa," Tammy told her.

"And then shopping," Bridgette added. "Can a sista get a new Louis Vuitton?"

"You got that," Tameka declared. "Louis for everybody!"

Cheers and whoops went up from the Bentley.

Tameka pressed the start button, bringing the motor to life. She raced the engine, and she and her crew pulled away.

"Tameka, I'm telling you girl, you better not fuck this up!" Bridgette said, running her finger over the triple stitching on the leather dash. "You want to marry a muthafucka, you marry a nigga who has you rolling in a Bentley. I'm telling you, girl. Do not fuck this up."

"Don't worry," Tameka smiled. "I won't."

# Boyfriend # 2

# Chapter Twelve

Tameka wrapped her arms around Eric and pressed her soft tits into his muscular back. She hugged and comforted him, while standing beneath the steaming hot waters from the shower. Eric felt as though he was washing away his sins, by having the ugliness he endured earlier wash off his body and down the bathroom drain. Both his hands were flat against the wall like he was holding himself up for support, and his head was lowered in an almost reverent way while his eyes remained closed. He tried to relax as Tameka's hands worked their magic, trying to massage away the tension in his shoulders and neck. The shower had become their cocoon for the moment.

Eric had already washed the blood from his hands, and yet he felt as if he were still not clean. He could still feel the stench on him.

"It's okay, baby, I'm here," she whispered into his ear. Tameka caressed him gently, giving soft pecks on his back and neck.

Eric had rushed to her crib with blood on his hands, and upon seeing him at her door, Tameka stood shocked and wordless for several moments. Finally, after gathering her wits, she rushed him into her home. Inside, she saw the blood and grief on his face.

Eric went on to tell her how some mysterious cats had tried to kill him. He had been ambushed while walking to his truck. It had all been done under the cover of night. Three young hooded thugs had rushed him. All he remembered at first, were the shots that they had fired. The bullets had ripped through his truck, shattering his windshield, causing him to leap into action. He had to snatch the Ruger from his waistband as quickly as he could and return fire. The silhouettes of the men in the darken street moved closer. That was when he had to leap from his vehicle, take cover, and continue shooting. He hit one in the leg, and then the face, the second one caught one of his bullets in the chest. And the third one, well, that one had been the problem. He had snuck up behind Eric and jumped him with a giant Bowie knife. He had planned on plunging the sharp blade into Eric's flesh, but Eric pivoted quickly, shooting the young kid in the chest causing him to fall back against the cold pavement. The threat was over, but the danger still loomed.

Eric had climbed into his truck and drove in a hurry to Tameka's brownstone. It was the first place he thought about, once he realized that he had to get away from his own place. He tossed the gun down a sewer drain on the way to her spot, but he knew that he still needed to clean himself up. The three men that tried to kill him could have either came from Skinny or other foes that wanted to see him dead. The streets were becoming a cesspool of jealousy, with a dangerous breed of young killers, each wanting to take a little piece of pie for them self. The game was changing, and changing fast which each passing minute. Eric still owed a great deal of money to Peon. And it was money he needed to obtain fast. Skinny was turning out to be a bigger problem than he had anticipated. And it was a problem that he did not need at this stage of the game. He needed to clean that shit up.

Tameka had stripped Eric of his dirty and bloody clothing, and started the warm shower for him. He was quiet as Tameka lathered his skin with the scented soap she kept in her bathroom. Eric stood silent, and contemplated his actions, and thought back to the evening's events. What were the consequences he would have to face? There was the cops, and if those cats had been sent by Skinny, then he had definitely escalated the situation. But then again, if Skinny had sent henchmen after him to put him in the grave, then it was Skinny that had escalated the situation. Things were definitely out of hand. He had too much going on, too many dollars on the line, to get involved in stupid ass beef with Skinny right now. Shit was spiraling out of control.

Tameka wrapped her arms around Eric. She felt his troubles. She wanted to make things better for him. Despite the fact that he was bringing nothing but drama her way, she still couldn't just flat out cut him loose. He reminded her so much of her homies from the hood. And just as she couldn't abandon them, she could no sooner cut Eric loose. At least not now, at least not in his hour of need. Perhaps some of his frustration lied with her, she thought.

She had turned down his marriage proposal in Vegas. Her excuse to him, was that the time wasn't right. Deep down, she knew that it would never be right. He was still heavily involved in the streets and it's drug culture. And despite her project roots, Tameka didn't want to be a part of that violent drug sub culture. She had a promising career, and much to risk if she kept Eric in her life, let alone married him.

Tameka thought about her life and her situation. She didn't go through four years of college to become a hustler's wife. She had seen the result of women caught up in that world. Visitation through glass, or at a federal facility on weekends, was not how she envisioned her future. In fact, she had resolved to slowly getting past Eric, and slowly moving away from the lifestyle that he offered. She had even thought about slowly cutting out smoking weed. She had come to the conclusion that it was time to leave the hood behind. But somehow, Eric had her caught up in the middle of everything again.

# Boyfriend # 2

Eric stood in the hot shower allowing the water to strike the top of his head and run down his body. He was a little salty about Tameka turning down his marriage proposal. Tameka gave him her reasons, and he had even promised he would leave the game. He just had to pay off his debt first, and take care of some unfinished business. He needed some serious money to retire. And it was only serious money that would make him leave the dope game. But he needed to handled this business with Skinny first.

Tameka's soft kisses against Eric's hardened flesh caused him to moan. Her pecks against his neck and back felt good to him. He wanted to forget about the shootings. He didn't know if the men he shot were dead or alive, and really, he didn't care. It had been a matter of survival, and he was just fortunate that he came out the victor.

Eric turned to face his woman. Tameka rubbed his strapping, bare chest, teasing his nipples and caressing his waves of abs that ripped into his skin endlessly. Her dark, chocolate nipples were hard and ripe like fruit ready to be picked from a tree. Tameka reached her hand around to the back of his head and pulled her lover closer. She kissed him passionately. Their tongues danced like choreographed ballerinas while their full lips moved in harmony. Eric's hands roamed down the sides of Tameka's tender body, finding their resting place on the curves of her full, round ass. He loved the smoothness of her skin. He filled his hands with her succulent ass, pulling her body closer to his.

"You like that, don't you, baby," Tameka whispered into his ear.

"You know I do," Eric said softly.

Her touch, her kisses, her stokes against his rising, thick flesh, made Eric momentarily forget about the violence in his life. The shower cascaded down on them like a tropical waterfall, soaking their two beautiful ebony, brown skinned bodies. The two of them found themselves wrapped together in a harmonious tryst—naked and wet, with hormones raging like a sexual machine.. Tameka was ready for Eric to fill her horny cunt with his hot sperm..

"Ooooh, fuck me, baby," she cooed in her lover's ear.

She humped her pussy against his thigh, and sucked and licked every inch of his beautiful brown skin. Slowly, they twisted into position so that Eric could penetrate his woman from behind. Tameka now found herself the hunted. Eric curved her over under the steaming shower head, and she placed her hands against the shower walls, as he pierced her wet slit with his thick flesh.

"Ooooh, fuck me, baby," Tameka cried out.

He gripped her curvy sides and pounded his frustration into Tameka like a savage. Her tits flapped underneath her as she took the strong dick inside of her doggy-style. Reaching around, Eric fingered her clit and worked up a steady rhythm. Again and again he pumped his stiff dick into her, and Tameka took it all. Their breathing intensified. Sex in the bathroom was something that drove her into a frenzy. She came first, shaking wildly, and feeling her womanly liquids squirt from her pink folds. And then it was Eric's turn. He pumped his hot semen into her, bringing much needed relief and relaxation from an otherwise tense evening.

Tameka and Eric climbed out of the shower, and made their way to her bedroom. Eric collapsed onto the bed, and Tameka laid down on top of him. She rested her head on his shoulder, and rubbed her hand on his muscular chest. Eric lifted the remote on her nightstand, aimed it toward her stereo and pressed play. Jodeci came alive.

*Forever, forever, forever*
*So you're having my baby, and it means so much to me*

# Boyfriend # 2

*There's nothing more precious, than to raise a family*

Tameka meant to close her eyes only for a few minutes to get some much needed rest. It had been a long week for her, between her career, her friends and juggling her dual relationships with Caleb and Eric, she was tired. Eric's drama was taken a mental and physical toll on her. She was worried about him, and she was worried about herself. She wanted to cut him loose, but she loved kicking it with him. The emotional ups and downs had fatigued her to the bone.

Tameka woke a few hours later to find that Eric had departed. He had managed to creep away silently and swiftly, without disturbing her. Not that waking her would have been an easy task, as tired as she was. Tameka stretched and yawned, and then climbed out of bed and made her way to her window. She peered out of her blinds to find that his truck was gone. And the crazy thing about it, was that she didn't know how she felt about his disappearance. Her rule had been to never let him spend the night. But that was under normal circumstances. Tonight had not been normal circumstances. She was worried about him. Tameka hoped and prayed that Eric wasn't out there trying to retaliate. But even more so, she hoped and prayed that he was safe. And that feeling took her by surprise.

"Fuck!" Tameka declared. The realization finally hit home to her. She actually cared about Eric. Somehow, someway, somewhere along the line, her plaything, had now genuinely become her Boo thing. She had allowed herself to slip. She had allowed herself to start giving a fuck. Tameka shook her head, as she peered out the window into the distance. She could hear Deborah Cox's song playing in her head. *How did you get here? Nobody's supposed to be here.*

"How the fuck did you get here?" she asked herself. "How did you get into my head?"

# Boyfriend # 2

*****

Eric sat in the passenger seat of Sean's pearl colored Escalade. Both sat and waited patiently. The night was cool, and the streets quiet. Eric took a pull from the Newport burning between his lips and gazed at the front entrance of the three-story structure. The building was rundown, but still operable enough for it's poor and hapless residents to live in. The place was nicknamed The Shooting Gallery, because of its use. Not shooting as in bullets and gun fire, but shooting as in shooting up. It was the place where meth heads, crack heads, and heroine addicts all came to smoke and shoot up their drug of choice. It was also the place where Skinny was known to get high with his girlfriend.

Sean was aware of the shooting, as were the rest of the streets. He had called Eric up while Tameka was asleep, and both had agreed that it was time to retaliate. Skinny had to go, and he had to go ASAP. Sean was fuming. Eric assumed Skinny was behind the attempt on his life—twice. In the first incident, Chunky got shot. In the second it was Skinny's boys that ended up taking a trip to the hospital and to the morgue. Sean initially wanted Eric to keep a low profile, while he and the rest of the crew handle things, but Eric wasn't having it. He refused to look like a punk. Skinny wasn't going to have him go running underground. So they decided to take care of the problem upfront.; they would kill Skinny now and worry about the consequences with Peon later. Peon was a business man, but his cousin, Skinny, was a piece of shit. Everyone knew that.

Sean had two nine-millimeters resting on the truck's floorboard. They were fully loaded and ready to be used. It was

129

after midnight, and Sean and Eric was ready handle their business and get the shit over with. Eric peered at his watch, and then passed Sean the burning cigarette, while continuing to watch the front entrance of the building.

"Damn, I wish Echo was here. He love shit like this." Sean said, as he took a pull from the cancer stick.

"Yeah, you and me both," Eric replied. "Nigga knew how to hunt a muthafucka down and light they ass up. That's why his ass is on the run now for two bodies."

Sean and Eric both laughed. The levity was much needed, as the atmosphere within the truck had grown thick with anticipation.

"Can't believe Skinny had the audacity to try and get at you twice," Sean said.

"I tell you what, after tonight, he ain't gonna have a third time."

"I told you, E, watch out for that muthafucka," said Sean.

"Yeah, well...we gonna show this muthafucka how you get up close and really kill a nigga," Eric said through clenched teeth.

Sean took a few more pulls from the cigarette, then looked at Eric. "Your shorti, she know you a killer?"

Eric looked at his friend. He hesitated to answer him. The cold, black eyes that stared back at Sean were the complete opposite of the kind and gentle eyes he showed Tameka. He had his secret; secrets and demons that she didn't need to know about. His hands were stained with men's blood.. He had his world, and she had hers. The crazy thing was, their worlds weren't all that far apart.

"She knows some things, but not everything. You know that," Eric replied with a sly smile. .

"I know that, but this here...this is what we do. This is different. What if the truth comes out before that other thing pans out, you think she'll be able to stick around?"

"This truth, it ain't gonna come out," Eric replied deadpan.

Sean let out a short laugh. "You're delusional man."

"I'm about my business, and if we have to drop a few niggas occasionally to keep this business, then so be it. I got Tameka in pocket, and she knows all that she needs to know. She doesn't need to go peeking in any closets."

"I feel you. Just be careful," replied Sean.

The two men sat quietly for a short moment, and then Eric let out a short laugh. "You know I proposed to her in Vegas."

Sean looked flabbergasted. "Get the fuck outta here."

"Yeah. But she turned down my proposal. She said it wasn't right. She ain't wit' the business, and felt the time wit' us ain't right."

"She wants you to give this shit up?"

Eric nodded.

"And what you thinking?" Sean asked. "Is this a keeper or something?"

"I don't know…she goin' down one road, and me another. We so much alike, but can be so different at times. She doesn't wanna become a hustler's wife. She talkin' about she left that type of life behind her years ago, and for us to be together like that, I gotta do the same too. I just might get this serious bread up and step away," Eric told him.

"You serious?" Sean lifted an eyebrow. "And what about your boy? What he gonna say 'bout this?"

Eric shrugged. "What can he say. I decide who I wanna roll with, and who I wanna roll over."

"He ain't gonna like that."

"We been at this for a long time, Sean. Too long."

"I know," Sean replied. "But what else you gonna do? Nigga, we grew up doin' this shit. We ain't no nine to five niggas, E. We gangsters. We take what we want."

Eric took another drag from the cancer stick and looked in deep thought. He then dowsed the cigarette out in the ashtray and glanced at the time.

"Fuck it, let's go send this nigga's momma shopping for a black dress."

Sean nodded. Both men retrieved the 9mm's from off the floor and exited the truck. They coolly walked to the dilapidated building and immediately headed for the top floor. They'd gotten word that Skinny liked to get high with his bitch at her place. It was valuable information, and it was information that Eric aimed to take advantage of. It wasn't a secret that Skinny liked to get high, but where he liked to smoke his drugs was a well kept secret. Eric had to pay high dollar to get a hold of such valuable information.

Sean and Eric reached the top floor and walked toward the apartment. They could hear rap music playing inside. It was loud. Eric glanced at Sean and nodded. Both held their guns at the ready. The hallway was dark, and the smell of urine and trash saturated the area.

"Fuck it, let's do this," Eric said.

Sean kicked in the feeble front door, knocking it off the hinges, and the two rushed inside. Both men made a bee line for the bedroom. They caught Skinny and his whorish and cracked out girlfriend butt-naked on the bed, with cigarettes burning in an ashtray, and a crack pipe being ready to be shared between them.

"What the fuck!" Skinny shouted.

"You fuckin' crack head!" Eric shouted. "You tried to have me kill."

He rushed to where Skinny was sitting, and began pistol whipping him. The iron tool smashed into Skinny's head violently, causing blood to spew everywhere. Skinny was instantly crippled by the ferocious blow to his head. His girlfriend began to howl, but Sean promptly shut the bitch up with a blow to her head.

"Hush up, bitch!" he shouted.

Eric beat Skinny to a bloody pulp with the nine-millimeter. It was personal with him. Soon, Skinny lied stiff against the mattress, with his girlfriend whimpering next to him. He was suffering from numerous fractures—a broken cheekbone, eye socket and jaw. Surprisingly, he was still able to speak.

"My cousin is gonna fuck you up over this shit," Skinny managed to say from his blood covered mouth. "Ya dead, Eric!"

"Oh yeah…you first, trifling muthafucka!" Eric exclaimed.

He had no time for words. Eric raised the gun at Skinny and fired.

*Pop! Pop! Pop! Pop! Pop!*

Skinny lay contorted on the mattress in a pool of blood. And before his girlfriend could let out a blood curling scream, Sean gunned her down too.

They left the couple naked and warped against each other, and made their way out of the building and back to Sean's Escalade. Inside of the truck, Eric felt relieved. He had finally taken out the trash.

"Yeah, I'm out." Eric told him. "I'm gonna get this money together and I'm done with the dope game."

Sean looked at Eric. "You sure you know what you're doing?"

"Gotta start a new chapter in my life," Eric said. "I gotta get this bread another way."

"That ain't you, E," Sean chuckled. "We'll see."

Sean started the Escalade and drove off slowly. Eric sat back and thought about Tameka, and about getting his paper up. He knew what he needed to do to make things happen. Why he was hesitating, was beyond him. He was lion. And there were no pacts between lions and hyenas. It would soon be time for the lion to roar.

# Boyfriend # 2

# Chapter Thirteen

Isa was New York's latest and greatest in a long line of trendy off-beat restaurants. Located in Williamsburg, Isa was an adventure in rustic dining. The restaurant sported a log cabin motif, with an authentic,open, wood-fired, brick oven and grill. The Brooklyn based establishment resembled Caleb's ski lodge in Pennsylvania. It boasted a hand made rustic wooden bar, rustic wooden dining table, and rustic wooden chandelier to augment the candle-lit establishment. Piles of wood were stacked against the walls throughout the establishment, and the sweet smells of burning wood, and fine cuisine wafted throughout the restaurant. Caleb and Tameka were seated in the center of the restaurant, peering at two menus.

"I can't decide!" Tameka said, peering around excitedly. She had heard about this place from the ad execs at work, and had always wanted to check it out, and now she was here. Isa was super expensive, and it was virtually impossible to get reservations at the place. Especially during dinner. That Caleb was able to work his magic through his credit card's concierge service was really impressive. She definitely needed one of those Black Cards once she became wifey, she thought.

"Try the blackened Swordfish," Caleb suggested.

"I want to," Tameka countered. "It all looks so good. But look, this Smoked Salmon looks delicious! And the Bourbon seared Mackerel! And then there's the lemon seared pork loin with cracked peppered and garlic dust! I can't decide!"

Caleb smiled, closed his menu and stared Tameka in the eye. "You trust me?"

"What are you talking about?" Tameka replied, eying him suspiciously.

"Do you trust me?"

"I guess," Tameka said hesitantly.

Caleb took her menu and closed it. He turned to the waiter. "The lady will have the blackened Swordfish, seared with Bourbon, and I want the chef to add honey butter and lemon juice, and then sprinkle it with the cracked pepper and garlic dust. And for myself, I'll take a Bourbon seared steak, well done, with a Bourbon and honey glaze. We'll both have the seared potatoes, baby carrots, and a bottle of Chateau La Fete Rothschild, please."

"Very good, sir," the waiter nodded. He collected Caleb and Tameka's menus, and quickly disappeared.

"This better taste good," Tameka declared.

Caleb smiled at her. "Trust me, I know what I'm doing."

"Swordfish?"

"It is delicious. The way they prepare it, it's smooth, soft, and almost creamy on the inside. And the searing will seal in the flavors. You'll be able to taste the North Atlantic."

"I don't know if that's a good thing."

"Woman, trust me," Caleb said with a smile.

"Why?" Tameka asked, lifting an eyebrow. "You always order for your women? Is that why you claim to know what you're doing?"

"I thought women liked a man who took charge?"

"Hmmmm," Tameka leaned back and placed her finger beneath her chin. "Are you one of those regressive brothers? The type that like to keep us barefoot and pregnant and in the kitchen?"

"Oh, so chivalry is regressive?" Caleb wagged his finger

toward her. "See, that's why us brothers are checking into mental hospitals at alarming rates. You women can't make up your minds."

Tameka laughed. Being out and about with Caleb transported her to an entirely different world. No bloody clothing, no turf wars, no assassination attempts, no drug wars, no dodging bullets. Just good times, flowing wine, and expensive restaurants and shopping sprees. He took her mind off of Eric and his drama. She needed this dinner, she thought. She needed a night out with Caleb. A worry free night of romance and laughter.

"You throw a fit if we don't open the door for you, but when we do, you accuse us of being cavemen," Caleb continued. "If we tell women that she can stay at home, you accuse us of wanting a maid. If I order food for you, then I'm being regressive and I want you barefoot and pregnant. You see what you women are doing to us?"

Tameka laughed even harder. "Calm down. Calm down. I must have hit the nail on head for you to protest that hard."

The waiter returned with two wine glasses, and a bucket filled with ice and a bottle of Chateau La Fete Rothschild. He popped the cork on the wine, and poured Tameka a glass, and then poured Caleb's. He then placed the wine back inside of the bucket and retreated.

Tameka lifted her wine and tasted. "Wow!"

"What?" Caleb asked.

"This is the good stuff!" Tameka said, pointing toward her glass.

"First time?"

"For what?"

"For Chateau La Fete?"

Tameka nodded.

"Dang," Caleb said with a smile. "Then I've missed an

opportunity."

"And opportunity for what?"

"The first time you sip a bottle of Chateau La Fete, you should be in a Jacuzzi, or a hot tub, surrounded by candles, lying back on your man's chest while he feeds you strawberries dipped in white chocolate."

"Damn!"

It was Caleb's turn to laugh.

"I'm sorry I missed that," Tameka said, leaning back in her seat. "Can we just pretend that I haven't tasted it yet, and get that Jacuzzi thing going later on?"

"We'll see," Caleb smiled.

"We'll see?"

"Yeah," Caleb nodded. "I want to see if you're going to be a good girl first."

Tameka ran her tongue over her lips. "Oh, I was thinking that you wanted me to be a bad girl. You know some candles, a little wine, and a shoulder massage, that'll definitely turn me into a bad girl."

"And what will this turn you in to?" Caleb asked.

Caleb reached into his pocket, and pulled out a tiny light blue box. He sat the box on the table, and pushed it toward Tameka. She gasped.

"What is that?"

"It's a gift."

"A gift?" Tameka covered the lower half of her face. "In a Tiffany ring box?"

Caleb nodded.

"Is that what I think it is?" Tameka asked. She began to tear up. Her right hand flew to her chest, and she waved her left hand in front of her face to give her some desperately needed air. She couldn't believe that she had a tiny ring box sitting in front of her. What did it mean, she wondered? It couldn't have been that easy.

It couldn't have been. Was he asking her to marry him, she wondered? Is that what this was about? The expensive wine, the romantic dinner, the ring from Tiffany's, it all screamed proposal. The only thing missing was him getting on one knee and actually popping the question. Oh, shit!

Tameka could feel herself beginning to hyperventilate. She could also feel tears beginning to well up in her eyes. She wanted to scream *yes*. She wanted to shout at the top of her lungs that she would indeed marry Caleb. Her mind raced at the thought. Who would she call first, she wondered? Would she call her Mom, her sister, her cousin, or her boss, and tell that mother fucker that she quit, and that he can go fuck himself? Surely Caleb would want her to stay at home and be a housewife. She would sleep all morning, shop after lunch, and then rush home, prepare dinner, and then fuck his brains out every evening. It would be the ideal life. But what she would do with her brownstone, she wondered? She could just rent it out, or sell it. Would Caleb want to sell his mansion and move into her Harlem brownstone with her? Would he? That would be too perfect. They could finish the top floors and the basement, and get it ready for the family they would have. She even knew exactly where she would put the nursery.

"Tameka, this ring is just the beginning," Caleb said softly. "This ring is about tomorrow. About the promise of tomorrow. I bought it, to symbolize where we are in this relationship, or at least, where I hope we are."

Now she was confused. What he was talking about, she wondered? *A promise ring*? What the fuck? They weren't in fucking high school! *A promise ring*?

"Open it," Caleb said, pushing the box closer to her.

Tameka lifted the box from the table, tore off the Tiffany ribbon, and opened the box. Inside, sat a flawless, canary yellow marquis shaped diamond on a platinum base. Tameka gasped.

"Oh my god! Caleb, this is beautiful!"

Caleb took the ring from the box, took her hand into his, and then placed the ring on her finger. Tameka held the ring up into the light.

Outside of the restaurant, peering through the window stood Eric. He watched as Tameka held her ring up to the light, examining it. He watched, as she smiled, and glowed, and gushed.

Inside of the restaurant, Caleb took Tameka's hands into his. "This is a promise ring. I promise to be faithful to you, and I promise that one day, one magical day, we'll take that step to be together for the rest of our days."

Tameka burst into tears. It was not what she wanted, nor expected. She was hoping that she had landed the big enchilada, a full blown engagement ring. But what the hell, she thought. The fact that he called it a promise ring didn't make it any less special, or any less expensive. Beside, he had just put a ring on her finger, and pledged his dick to her and her only. So, in effect, he *was* hers. She had just eliminated all potential competition. She was going to land her big fish for sure now, because he had just put a ring on her finger, and promised her that she was the only game in town. So, he had no one else to choose from. Her dream was all but assured.

Tameka turned and wiped the tears from her eyes. This should have been one of the happiest moments in her life, but her mind was now elsewhere. Her mind was wondering about Eric. How did Caleb's factor into the situation, she wondered? It was definitely a game changer. She worried about Eric, and all of the things that he had going on. He was definitely under her skin, and she knew that she couldn't cut him loose just yet. She was in it with him for the moment, perhaps even for good. Even once she married Caleb. Would Eric accept being her secret lover? Those were the things that she would have to figure out. Could she have her hubby, and still keep her boyfriend?

"You all right?" Caleb asked.

Tameka nodded. "I'm just happy."

Tameka leaned over and kissed Caleb passionately. She was happy. Everything that she had wanted her entire life, was now within her grasp. She was going to be wifed by a dude with major figures. Now, it was only a matter of playing her cards right. It was only a matter of figuring out how she could keep *both* men in her life, *permanently*.

Eric had wanted to try out Isa's. He had heard so much about it, so he figured he would stop in, grab him and Tameka some take out, and then head over to her crib for some great head and good sex. But here she was, sitting inside of the restaurant, examining a big ass rock on her finger. To say he was surprised was an understatement.

She had turned down his ring, and turned down his proposal. But she accepted this other niggas? What the fuck was that about? Where do bitches do that at? To say that he was heated, would be to downplay his feelings. He was hot as fish grease. Tameka really thought that she was a player. She really thought that she was doing something. And that steamed him more than anything. He was a hood cat, and the one thing that rubbed him the wrong way more than anything else, was disloyalty. Eric stared at Tameka for a few moment longer, taking in her reaction. She kept holding up her big ass rock, smiling, and kissing her square ass beau.

Eric turned, walked back to his Escalade, and climbed inside, where he cranked up the system, and lit up a joint. His thoughts were on Tameka. He thought about her crooked smile, her laughter, and about how much fun they had when they were together. He had planned on blowing some blunts, and kicking back and watching a movie with her while they ate. His plans were out the window now. So many of his plans with regards to Tameka were out the window now.

# Boyfriend # 2

Eric backed his SUV up, and then pulled out of the parking lot. He was a G, and he was going to play the situation like a straight up G. He puffed on his joint, blew the smoke out of his window, and turned his thoughts to his next move. He was going to make sure he stayed at least five moves ahead of everyone else. Bitches loved to play checkers, but it would soon be made known that life was a game of chess, he thought. And in this game of life, he was the chess master.

# Chapter Fourteen

Five hundred thousand. Half a fucking million. That was what Peon was demanding for the death of his cousin, Skinny. It was either pay up, or be murdered. But the half of million Eric was in debt to Peon was just one of his problems. He was a hot head, with a Brooklyn ego that was almost as large as the borough itself. It bothered him to see Tameka sitting up in the restaurant smiling and enjoying herself. She was giving old boy a look that he thought she had reserved for just him. He knew what the plan was, and he knew what he had to do. So, he didn't know why the shit bothered him the way it did. He knew, it was all about his ego.

Peon was growling at Eric about loyalty and distrust. But Eric didn't care anymore. What Peon was saying, was mostly going in one ear and out the other. Besides, he had already made up his mind, and opted for the first choice; he would pay the money. Besides, his choices had been pretty limited, and already made for him. He had woken up to Peon standing over him in his bedroom, blowing cigar smoke down on him. There were also half dozen armed thugs scowling at him. So that was that. His choice had been made, he was going to pay.

"You owe me muthafucka!" Peon told him, while blowing smoke rings into his face. "The only reason you ain't lying in your own pool of blood with your throat cut, is 'cause you do good business in the streets. And above all else, I'm a fuckin' businessman. You're a fuckin asset for the moment, Eric, and the minute you're not…well, you're a smart man. I take it that you understand what I'm saying."

"I'll get you ya fuckin' money, Peon," Eric told him. "But Skinny, he was piece of shit! You know that, everybody knew it. Hell, I did you a favor. He was peeling you, and robbing all of us."

"I didn't ask you for no favors. I know how to handle my own shit," Peon said in his gruff, almost hoarse like voice. "You better get me my damn money, because the next time I have to come see you….you won't hear me speak one word to you. As a matter of fact, you won't even know we was here, or that you're ass is even dead. You're just going to catch a hot one in the ear. And I understood that Skinny was a piece of shit, but he was blood to me. And you didn't have my permission, nor my blessing to touch him."

Eric glared at Peon. He wasn't frightened, because he'd been around worse. He 'd seen the evil that men can do, and in fact, had done some of that same evil. And even though Peon was the boss in the streets, Eric knew that he was still a man. The two locked eyes at each other and their silence spoke volumes. Peon continued to smoke his cigar.

"You got one month to come up with my money," Peon told him. He and his goons, turned, and left Eric's apartment.

Eric climbed out of bed and rushed to his drawer. He pulled it open and removed a loaded .50 Cal Desert Eagle. It was a beautiful instrument—chrome, with a black grip. It was known for putting mountain sized holes in niggas. The Desert Eagle was instant death gripped in his hand. Eric stared at the gun with a glint of fascination. It was his favorite of all his pieces. He then lifted his hand and aimed the gun at his image in the mirror. He was shirtless, his upper torso swathed with a few tattoos. He was a hardcore individual, a gangster, a predator, the king of the muthafuckin jungle. And now, he had to do what animals did when they were cornered. He had to show his teeth.

Eric got dressed and slipped the Desert Eagle into its special leather holster. He looked sharp in his Mek jeans, Beige Timberlands and a fitted shirt that hugged his athletic build. He threw on his Yankee' fitted hat and stepped out his doorway. It was a clear and sunny afternoon. But inside Eric's mind and his heart was a storm. He could feel shit brewing on the horizon. And it was ominous. Before Eric could climb into his truck, his cell phone began to buzz, indicating he had a text from someone. Eric looked at the text and smirked. It was from Tameka. It read: *I miss you, and I wanna see you tonight and bring that good weed with you too.*

"This bitch!" he said, shaking his head. "What a fucking twisted little web we weave?"

He didn't respond right away. He would deal with Tameka later on, he told himself. Instead, he got behind the wheel of his Escalade and sped off..

Being in debt to Peon for half a million was the main thing from his mind at the moment. He had eighty grand in cash that he could get to right away, along with four bricks of raw that was street ready. He needed to make some moves and get rid of his supply, and then he would see what he had, and how much he needed to get access to. So it was time to hit the bricks.

\*\*\*\*\*

All day, Eric drove around Brooklyn and took care of business in the hood. He contacted Sean and told him about the unwanted company he had when he woke up. Sean, being the friend he was, was ready to get his gun and have Eric's back, but Eric told him to chill. He had things under control.

As the evening enclosed the fading blue sky, Tameka had hit Eric with another text message: ***Babe, where are you, why aren't you hittin' me right back? Worry about you, wanna see you tonight.***

Eric texted her back, saying: ***Takin' care of much needed business be at ya spot around 10 tonight.***

Tameka replied with a smiley face.

Eric could only shake his head. "Scandalous bitch!"

The day went by fast for Eric, and in no time, night had covered the sky and it was almost 10pm. Eric puffed on his Newport and he drove toward Tameka's place. He was in no hurry, as he had a lot on his mind and relished a long drive to help him think about his next couple of moves. He drove up the block and parked across the street from Tameka's brownstone. The living room lights could be seen from the street, indicating she was home and waiting for him to show up. He lingered behind the wheel for a moment, staring at Tameka's place like it was something like it was some alien planet. It just wasn't the same place to him anymore.

Eric's Desert Eagle pistol lay concealed beneath his seat. He could make it ugly, but decided to play his cards cool for the moment. Eric took one last pull from the cigarette and tossed it out the window. He then readied himself to confront Tameka.

He stepped out his truck and marched toward the brownstone and rang the bell. Tameka answered the door clad in purple lingerie and clear stilettos. Her long, sinuous chestnut hair fell to her shoulders and the radiant smile across her face lit the room up like a brand new light bulb. But Eric greeted her with a frown. His eyes were cold and penetrating, almost as if they were looking through her, instead of at her. Her scanty lingerie had no affect on him, and that surprised her.

"Babe, what's wrong?" Tameka asked, noticing Eric's distance.

# Boyfriend # 2

Eric walked into the place and felt the seething bubble inside him rupture. As soon as the door closed behind him, he spun toward Tameka and charged her up like a angry wildebeest. His hand shot around her neck like vice grips, and he threw her against the wall of her home so hard that a few pictures fell from the wall and shattered against the parquet floors. Tameka's eyes were wide-eye with fright.

"I loved you!" Eric screamed.

"You're hurting me," she cried out.

Eric trembled with anger. He looked down at her left hand and snatched it into his grip. He looked for the ring on her finger, but it wasn't there.

"Where is it?" he demanded.

"What are you talking about?"

"The ring? I saw you last night with him," Eric shouted.

Tameka was taken aback. Her mouth fell open.

Eric released her from his stranglehold and Tameka gasped. She rubbed her neck trying to sooth the pain. The rage in Eric's eyes told her that he was highly unstable, and that he was capable of anything at that moment. She had never been so frightened of anyone, as she was at that moment. Never in a million years had she thought Eric capable of doing what he was doing to her. Tears came to her eyes.

"You fuckin' him?" Eric asked.

"You're following me?" It was the only response that came to mind.

"Bitch, I only went to that restaurant to surprise you. You were always talking about it so much, so I wanted to pick something special up for you and make it a romantic evening. And what the fuck do I see? I see you up in that bitch smiling and kissing the next man's face! And then, I see him put a fuckin' ring on your finger! Where is it?"

"I don't have it," she said softly.

"Where the fuck is it?" Eric shouted.

"I don't have it!" she shouted back.

"You playin' games wit' me Tameka?!"

"No! I turned him down."

"Bullshit!"

Eric lifted one of her pricy lamps and tossed it across the room. It shattered into dozens of pieces. And that was just the beginning. He turned over chairs, smashed mirrors and threw objects into the walls.

"Stop it! Stop it! Stop it!" Tameka screamed out hysterically. Her eyes were flooded with tears.

"I fuckin' loved you. I wanted to marry you, but you turned me down for that fool. What, is it because he got more money?"

"Like you're a fuckin' angel yourself, Eric?" she hissed. "Like you don't have bitches all over you! You think I don't hear the rumors 'cause I don't live in the hood no more?"

"What?"

"So you can honestly stand there and tell me that I'm the only bitch in your life? The only one you're fuckin?" she questioned. "I'm not stupid, Eric. I know what you do! I know who you are. I grew up around dozens of niggas like you."

"You obliviously don't know shit about me," he told her. Eric marched up to her and stared directly into her eyes. Her back was against the wall. She was uncertain about his next action. "You want the truth?"

Tameka remained silent.

"No, I ain't been fuckin' wit' no other bitches, cuz I'm in love wit' you. You were changing me, Tameka. You're my woman… well, was my woman. And I took you places, told you things about me that I never told anyone else. I wanted you to become my wife…but now I see why you ain't accepted my proposal. I see what you really think of me. I'm just some mindless thug to you, huh? That's it? I'm that Brooklyn nigga you called when you need a good fuck and to get high wit'? Huh?"

Tameka remained silent.

"What is it? I'm not classy like him? I don't wear the tailored suits and hold a cooperate position in Manhattan? I'm too rough to have a family of my own, is that what you feel about me? What you lookin' for Tameka?"

Tameka started to speak, but couldn't.

"You know what, I ain't a suit and tie wearing muthafucka, and I'm a drug dealer, a fuckin' gangsta, but I'm real. I've been upfront wit' you from day one. And this is how you do me? I was ready to give up the game for you, girl! I wanted to hold you down, hold us down and try and go legit. I loved you that much, and the only reason why I didn't wild out that night when I saw you in that restaurant with him, is because of that love I got for you. I don't know what I would have done. I love you, Tameka. I really do. But you know what…"

"Eric," Tameka uttered softly, stretching her arm out to grab a hold of him.

But Eric pulled away from her and stared at her in disgust. "Don't fuckin' touch me! Don't ever touch me again."

"I'm sorry," she belted out desperately.

"You sorry! Yeah, you fuckin' sorry a'ight. You sorry I caught ya cheating ass."

Tears streamed down Tameka's soft brown face. Her eyes were filled with pain and anguish. She knew that she loved Eric, and she was desperate for things to not end this way. She had wanted to have her cake and eat it to, and now things had fallen apart. She tried to reach out to him.

Eric stepped back from her, refusing any type of conciliatory gestures from her. The look in his eyes were a clear indication of the anger and hurt inside of him. He had managed to composed himself, and he didn't want to harm her. He turned for the door.

# Boyfriend # 2

"You know what, fuck you. I'm out! You have a good life."

Eric marched toward the door and slammed it with enough brute force to shake the walls.

"Eric!" Tameka called out to him, but he ignored her and kept moving. And just like that, he was gone.

"Baby, I'm sorry," she cried out to him.

The thought of Eric completely out of her life was something she didn't want to contemplate. She wanted Eric, she needed him. She loved being around him. She loved his raspy voice, and his bad boy swag. He was fun to be around, fun to do things with. He was also her friend, in addition to being her lover. And she didn't want to lose him.

"Dammit!" Tameka shouted at the top of her lungs. She had fucked up. She had committed the ultimate sin. Boyfriend number one, had found out about boyfriend number two, and the shit had hit the fan. Her fantasy about being able to keep them both, had just been tossed out the window. And since she now knew that Eric wouldn't accept Caleb, her only hope was that Caleb would accept Eric. Could she marry Eric, and keep Caleb as her sugar daddy? That would be one way to do it. She loved them both, and she was determined to keep them both. Ideally, she would have married Caleb, and crept with Eric, but now things may have to flip. But what about her dreams? What about the life she had dreamed of for so long? What about her Cosby life, and her beautiful family, all living happily in her Harlem brownstone? Eric did say he was willing to give up his bad boy lifestyle. But what could he do? What job could he maintain? What life could they have together if he wasn't balling? Would she have to be the bread winner of the family? What the fuck, man! Fuck! Fuck! Fuck! Tameka dropped to her living room floor and began pounding it with her fist.

Tameka hugged the living room floor in torment with tears pooling beneath her. Still clad in her purple lingerie, she snatched off her clear stilettos, stood up, and threw the pricy shoes into the large, gold leaf mirror that hung over her fireplace mantle. Tameka couldn't stand to look at herself right now. She hated what she saw. She hated the web of lies, deceits and betrayals that she had woven. Eric had truly been good to her, but Caleb was just that man she dreamed of having all her life. Her perfect plan was in ruins.

Tameka walked to the window and peered outside. Eric's truck was gone. Her eyes were transfixed on the dimmed one-way street, and her mind in a haze of confusion. Getting rid of one man to be with the other was something easier said than done. And she was determined to keep them both. She would have to get Eric back on deck. And she would do anything to put her plan back together. She was determined to have her cake, and be able to eat it too.

# Boyfriend # 2

# Chapter Fifteen

Tameka was distraught, and she didn't understand why. Why was she chasing this thug? Why did he mean so much to her? What was it that really got him under her skin? It wasn't dick, because she'd had plenty of that throughout her life. It wasn't the head game, or the sex period. Was it the companionship? She could get that from Caleb. The friendship? She had friends. So what was it, she wondered? What was it about Eric, that had her so desperate to get him back?

Tameka felt like she was a walking contradiction. She told her friends one thing about Eric, but strongly felt another. She recalled the conversation with Bridgette, Tammy and Rosalynn where she called Caleb her *real* boo thang. Had she meant that? Or, was it all a lie? Who really had her heart? For the last two days, she hadn't stopped thinking about Eric. He hadn't called, and whenever she tried to call him, no answer. It worried her profoundly. His well being worried her. She needed to know that he was all right. That was first. And then, she needed to talk to him about their future. Hopefully, they still had one together.

Tameka wandered about her place aimlessly. She had spent her entire weekend locked in her bedroom listening to slow jams, getting high, and slowly draining a bottle of Peach Ciroc. She was fucked up, of that much she was certain. And she didn't know which direction to turn to.

Caleb had been calling her all weekend, but she hadn't answered his calls. She knew he would be concerned, but she wanted to be alone. She *needed* to be alone. Eric now knew about Caleb, so what would happen if Caleb found out about Eric? How would *he* react? Would she lose him too? Her girls were right, she had been taking chances. Stupid chances. She had been juggling these two dudes like she was a clown performing at Ringling Brothers Barnum and Bailey circus. And she was fucking things up.

The television was on, with the sound muted. The movie *Soul Food* was playing. It was dusk out; Sunday evening. Her stereo was blaring, and the soulful sounds of Mary J. Blige spoke out to her. Mary J. Blige was her therapy—her healing companion. Any problems with men, relationships, or life, Tameka always turned to Mary. And no matter what the situation was, Mary always had a track for it. She had heartfelt tracks that could have a bitch crying, laughing, smiling, shouting, and singing along. And Tameka had all of her albums. From her debut *What's the 411* to *My life 11*. Tameka had been a fan for years. And for years Mary had always managed to get her through her drama. She was hoping that Mary would be able to get her through this one.

Tameka laid in her bed curled in the fetal position, clutching one fluffy pillow between her legs, while her head hugged a second pillow. She listened to one Mary track after another. The "*My life*" track was playing, and it was one of her favorite songs. *My life*, Tameka thought, look at my life.

*Life can be only what you make it*
*When you're feelin' down*
*You should never fake it*
*Say what's on your mind*
*And you'll find in time*
*That all the negative energy*
*It would all cease*

The lyrics reverberated in her head, as she sang along. Her bedroom was dark and cold, as she had kept her curtains drawn to block out any light. She hadn't even bothered to get up and dress the last two days, and was clad in a T-shirt and panties. She couldn't stop thinking about Eric. When Mary's song, "Hood Love," began to play, Tameka broke down into tears once again.

*We got hood love*
*I be cussin' I be screaming*
*Like it's over then I'm longing*
*Then I'm feening just to hold ya*
*Cause that's how we do*
*You know that hood love is a good love*
*That's me and you...*

The song reminded her so much of her life and her feelings for Eric. He was definitely that hood love. Tameka rose from her bed, and made the short journey to her window, where she pulled back the curtains and peered outside. She then lit up a cigarette, took another swig out of her bottle of Ciroc, and gazed out her bedroom window. The forecast called for rain all day, and there was a light drizzle cascading off the bedroom window. And the overcast was just how she felt. There was a dark cloud hanging over her. She wanted her light back; she wanted Eric's sunshine smile back.

Tameka took a pull from her Newport, inhaling deeply. She wanted to feel the nicotine seeping into her system. She would have rather smoked a blunt—some spliff, haze, or skunk, but Eric was her supplier and she was dried out. He would always bring by that ooo-wee good shit weed from Washington Heights. It was the type of weed that made her horny and ready to fuck like a porn-star.

# Boyfriend # 2

The knocking at her bedroom door caused Tameka to re-focus her thoughts on what was, and not what had been. She knew it was Rosalynn knocking. She was finally back from hanging out with her man over the weekend and probably wanted to gossip about how well the nigga put it down. It was a conversation she really didn't care to engage in right then.

"Tameka, you okay?" Rosalynn asked from behind the door. "I hear Mary J. playing, what's wrong girl?"

All her friends knew that once they heard Mary J. Blige playing continuously, something was wrong. It was as if Mary J was their sister girl distress signal. And it usually involved man problems.

Tameka took another few drags from her cigarette. "I'm okay."

"Girl, I know you're not," Rosalynn replied. "I hear that *Best of Mary J* playing in there, so I know something's going on. Open the door so we can talk."

Tameka sighed heavily. She knew Rosalynn wasn't going to leave her alone all night. And deep down, maybe that was a good thing, she thought. Maybe she didn't need to be left alone anymore. Maybe it was time to talk.

Tameka put out the cigarette, walked to the door, unlocked it and swung it open. Once she saw Rosalynn standing before her, she couldn't hold back her tears.

"What's wrong, girl? Talk to me," Rosalynn told her.

Tameka exhaled. "I fucked up."

"Is it Eric?"

"He knows about Caleb," Tameka said softly.

"What? How? Oh my god, what did he do to you? Did he put his hands on you? We gonna fuck him up if he did."

"No. He didn't touch me," Tameka lied. "He dumped me."

"Wow. How did he find out about you and Caleb?"

"He saw us together at Isa's in Brooklyn," Tameka told her.

Rosalynn's eyes went wide. "What, he was following you or something?"

Tameka shrugged. "I don't know. He says he went there to surprise me with a meal. But he didn't confront us. He saw Caleb putting a ring on it."

"Ooooh, my god!" Rosalynn hurried into the room and seated herself on Tameka's bed. She placed her hand over her chest. "He proposed to you, Tameka?"

"Not exactly. It was a beautiful, enormous, well-cut promise ring."

"So, one step closer 'til you become his wife," said Rosalynn.

Tameka nodded.

"So, what's the problem?" Rosalynn asked. "Girl, this is what you wanted. You got rid of Eric, and so now it's you and Caleb! Girl, this is a good thing! What are you tripping about?"

Tameka tilted her head to one side and stared at Rosalynn.

"You're in love with Eric," Rosalynn said, upon realization. She shook her head. "Girl, how did you get yourself into this mess?"

"I don't know," Tameka said, shaking her head.

"Damn, that nigga done put that magic stick on you and your ass fell weak."

It made Tameka laughed. And it felt good to laugh. She hadn't even cracked a smile in the last two days.

"You was always complaining that he was high risk, and now he got you going crazy, listening to Mary, eating Bon-Bons and shit. Girl, what's really going on?"

"I fell in love with a gangster."

"Momma, I'm in love with a gangster," Rosalynn said, singing the popular song from back in the day. "Well, then, you know what you gotta do."

"It's not that simple," Tameka told her.

"Why not? You said that you're in love with Eric, so there you go!"

"Yeah, and Eric is sweet. We had fun together, we relate. And the way he looks at me... That man looks at me like I'm his whole world. Like I'm the only thing that matters to him. He treats me with so much respect."

"So, what's the problem?"

"Caleb."

"What about him?" Rosalynn asked, lifting an eyebrow.

"He looks at me that way too. He can give me the world, anything I want. And if he doesn't have it, he'll get it for me. When I'm with him, he puts me first. He's shown me a whole new world. A world that I always wanted to be a part of. When I'm with him, I feel like I'm a celebrity. People look at us like we're Brad and Angelina, or Jay and Bey.

"So what are you going to do?" Rosalynn asked.

Tameka shrugged. "I don't know..."

"Eric is dangerous, Meka. Really dangerous. The lifestyle that he lives... do you really want to be a part of that?" .

Tameka looked at her friend. She knew that Rosalynn was right. But she wasn't ready to let her thug love go. Her heart fluttered whenever she heard his raspy voice She loved the way he would wrap his thick muscular arms around her and hold her. Eric was dangerous, but he made her feel safe when he was around. But Caleb was able to provide that financial security. His money was so long, and deep, that a bitch would look like Scrooge McDuck swimming around in it.

"You know what you need to do," Rosalynn said.

"What, Rosalynn?" Tameka replied, rolling her eyes.

"You need some time for yourself. Shit, look at you. Sitting here in the dark, listening to Mary J, and crying your eyes out. You know the truth was gonna come out sooner or later. You can't keep burning the candles on both ends. You either gonna have to let one go, or let them both go."

It was sound advice, but Tameka wasn't ready to let that happen. Her friend's advice went in one ear and directly out the other. She wanted both Eric and Caleb; she wanted things to go back to the way they were.

# Boyfriend # 2

# Chapter Sixteen

50 Cent's song, *Many Men,* blared throughout the seedy, Brownsville apartment. It was a cool and rainy night. Eric felt he could definitely relate to the raucous lyrics 50 Cent was spitting. He himself felt like many men were after him. Half a million dollars was a lot of money to cough up, and his life was on the line if he didn't come up with it. Eric sat slouched on the couch smoking a cigarette, watching as his young workers seated bagged crack and weed at the dining table. Weed smoke lingered in the apartment from their earlier smoking session of Kush. ESPN was playing on the wall mounted flat screen, while enough guns to take a small country to war, were laid out throughout the sparsely furnished apartment. Eric kept a Mac-10 withing reach, while his 50. Cal Desert Eagle rested in his lap. Semi-automatic shotguns , Uzi's, and AK-47's were also available to them. They were completely ready for anything that came crashing through the apartment door.

Sean sat near Eric smoking. He knew his friend well, and he knew what was on his mind. "Yo E, don't even worry about that bitch."

"How you know I'm thinkin' about her?" Eric asked.

"Cuz I know you, nigga. I see that look in your eyes."

"Man, that bitch done been forgotten."

"A'ight, so you say…but listen, don't get caught slippin' over some pussy. She a sheisty ho…so just move on and let's get this money, and handle this situation ya in."

Eric cut his eyes at his friend. It didn't sit well with him hearing Sean disrespect Tameka even though she was caught creeping with the next man.

"I'm good, man," Eric said with a slick grin.. "I'm ready to handle this shit."

"A'ight…stay that way," Sean told him.

Eric took another pull from the cancer stick. His cold eyes drifted somewhere else for the moment. Sean was talking, but he wasn't quite listening. His mind was wondering through his past. And Eric's past was the streets. He was a foster kid. He never knew his father, and his mother had been a drug addict who lived and died on the streets. She had two sons. And Eric hadn't seen his brother in years. He couldn't even begin to imaging his whereabouts, or even guess if he were still alive.

Eric could have done anything with his life, or at least, that was what his grandmother used to tell him. He had been smart in school, and had always made good grades. He had a 4.0 average and an I.Q of 130. He was considered a genius. But the streets had always called to him, and he was a full blown hustler by the time his junior year in high school rolled around. It was easier to become a gangster than a scholar, his partners would always tell him. But their advice was unnecessary, as the lure of the streets had captivated him. His senior year rolled around, and he found himself trapped in drug dealing and shootings. He had grown up with Sean and others, and over time, they became like brothers. They were his family. And they would always be his family, no matter what. No matter where his future, his brains, or his hustle game took him. And to this day, they remained so.

Eric knew that his world had always been wicked a one. He shot his first gun when he was 12, and caught his first body at the age of 17. He was a survivor of all trades, and he knew how to scheme, read people, plan attacks, and how to run con game. He always stayed at least five or six steps ahead of his opponents, and the majority of the time, he knew what his foes were going to do before they even knew it. It was what he learned playing chess with the old school homeless cats in the park back in the day. It was those same old school cats that helped to foster his love of learning and reading.

Eric read books of all genres. He loved to read. He loved, *The 48 Laws of Power, The Art of Seduction, Behold a Pale Horse., From the Browder File.* He loved to educate himself. He watched educational programs and loved culture. Even though he was a thug, he was a smart man, and there was so much more to him than met the eye. He got his money on the streets, but he also had other avenues for getting money. Of course, some of his avenues were much riskier than others, but at the end of the day, he lived by the motto: *Never put all your eggs into one basket.* grandmother's favorite was: *there was more ways than one to skin a cat.* if nothing else, he had learned to listen to grandma.

"Yo, let's hit the strip club tonight, get twisted and get our dicks suck by a few big booty hoes," Sean suggested.

Eric chuckled. "Nah, I'm good, yo…"

"Nigga, I know this nice spot on Atlantic…bitches in there be lookin' like video vixens and shit Yo, they got body for days," Sean told him.

"I'mma pass on that tonight, my nigga. I got too much business to take care of," Eric replied.

Sean sighed. "Nigga, what's really on ya mind, Tameka or Peon? Because we gonna handle both them bitches…give it time."

"Yo, I ain't worry about either one of them. I'm just tired. It's been a long day."

"A'ight."

Eric stood up, stuffed his gun into its holster and got ready to leave. He gave Sean dap, acknowledged the two young workers seated at the table, and then cautiously made his exit from the apartment. His eyes were alert to everything around him. He knew danger could be lurking anywhere. Peon wasn't his only threat, he had haters in every corner.

Eric jumped into his truck and headed home. It was nearing midnight, he had been taking care of business all day. He felt he needed to go home and get some much needed sleep. He pulled up to his Canarsie apartment and parked. He approached the apartment with extra caution. He had his hand on his gun, ready for anything. It had been a week since Peon's unwanted visit and he wasn't down for another one of those visits. He had been caught slipping once, and had promised himself that it would never happen again.

Eric took the stairs to his second floor apartment, and entered the small foyer to his place with his .50 Cal. in his hand. He wasn't taking any chances. He walked further in his two-bedroom apartment and peered around the apartment, carefully examining the scene. He wanted to make sure that everything was just the way he left it, and that nothing had been disturbed.

Once he was certain the his apartment was free of danger, Eric placed his pistol on his granite kitchen counter top. What was on his mind first and foremost, was hitting his large oval soaking tub, and relaxing in some steaming hot water. He also wanted a nice fat spliff to help relax and ease his mind.

Eric undressed, and put on a comfortable pair of basketball shorts and a T-shirt. He walked into the living room and turned on the plasma screen and changed the channel to ESPN. Being a sports fanatic, and a huge Knicks fan, he wanted to get the latest update on their game against Miami before hitting the tub. He sat back in his Lazy-Boy chair with a blunt to smoke and unwind. He was only a few seconds into his blunt before his doorbell sounded. Eric made a beeline into his kitchen and grabbed his .50 Cal off the counter. He cocked it and headed back into his front door. Why he was tripping like this, was beyond him. Peon and his boys wouldn't have rang the doorbell, that much was certain.

With the gun by his side, Eric peered through the peephole in his door. To his surprise, Tameka was standing outside of his door. What the fuck she want, he wondered?

"What you doin' here, Tameka?" Eric shouted from behind the door.

"I need to talk to you, Eric," Tameka shouted through the door.

"I ain't in the mood to talk."

"I just need five minutes of your time."

"You a scandalous bitch. Why should I trust you?" Eric shouted.

The word scandalous and bitch made Tameka cringe. She wasn't down with being called a bitch, but she kept her cool nevertheless.

"Because you deserve and explanation."

Eric remained silent as he contemplated if he should allow her in. He wasn't sure how much he could trust her. He peered through his peephole once again. She seemed to be alone.

"A'ight, we can talk," Eric said. Slowly, he opened the locks with his free hand, while still gripping the large caliber gun with his other.

Tameka stood in his doorway, looking fly as usual. In fact, it appeared as though she had even gone the extra mile in hooking herself up. Eric could feel a slight stirring between his legs. He nodded at her.

"Come in," he told her.

Tameka stepped into his apartment, and Eric closed the door behind her. When she turned to look at Eric, the Desert Eagle quickly caught her attention.

"How can you live like this?" Tameka said, exhaling. "I mean, I know you're better than this life."

"Don't worry about how I'm living, you ain't in my life

anymore."

"So, it's like that between us?"

"I ain't the one that got caught out there with rich boy."

"His name is Caleb," she informed.

"Caleb, what the fuck kinda name is that?" Eric said with a derisive grin. "But what you here for?"

"I love you, baby…not him," Tameka declared.

Tameka was ready to step forward, to put her arms around him and hug him tightly. His gun prevented her from moving closer to him.

"Can you put the gun down and talk to me without it?" Tameka asked.

"I trust this in my hand more than I trust you right now," Eric replied.

It hurt.

"What do you want from me, Eric?" Tameka asked.

"Besides the truth?"

"About what?"

"This nigga you fuckin'…what he about?" Eric asked. "How long? Why?"

"He's not you…"

"I didn't fuckin' ask you that! I asked what he about?" Eric shouted.

Tameka sighed heavily, and a few tears began to trickle down her face. She didn't know why Eric needed to know this information, and talking to him about Caleb was pure torture for her. But if it was what he needed to hear in order to forgive her and begin the healing process, then she would tell him what he wanted to know.

"He's from Texas, but he lives here now," Tameka said softly. "Yes, he's rich. He's very established. He's a stock broker with Goldman Saks."

"Oh, yeah?" Eric sneered. "Where'd you meet him at?"

"We met in Atlanta, at the airport," Tameka said, lowering her head. "I missed my flight coming from New Orleans, and so we started talking. I met both of y'all around the same time. I liked both of y'all...but I loved you. I fell in love with you, and only you."

"You love me, but you fucking him?" Eric said, staring at her in disgust. "Where they do that at?"

"Eric..."

"You fucked him?" Eric asked, cutting her off.

Tameka lowered her head once again. "You already know the answer to that question."

Eric shook his head and turned his gaze away from Tameka. Tameka stared at him, and she saw pure hurt on his face. It made her feel as if she died a little on the inside.

"It just happened. I didn't mean for this to go as far as it did," Tameka told him.

"Well it did."

"How can we fix this?"

"Sometimes, shit can't be fixed."

Tameka shook her head. "That ain't us."

"Look, I got a lot to deal with right now," Eric told her. "Seeing you with him just made shit even more complicated."

"Baby, just talk to me. I wanna make us better. I want to make us work." Tameka forgot about the gun in his hand and moved closer to him. She attempted to wrap her arms around Eric, to feel his hard, muscular body against hers, but he quickly moved away from her.

"What the fuck you think this is? You think you just gonna come up in here, bat your fuckin' eyes, show off ya sexy figure, and I'm suppose to become putty in your hands? I'm supposed to just forget about everything. I'm supposed to just forget all about that nigga, huh? It ain't that fuckin' easy."

"I'll do whatever it takes to fix us, baby" Tameka pleaded.

Desperation filled her eyes. "Just tell me what to do?"

Eric eyed her with contempt. She said that she would do anything. It was time to put her ass to the test. Eric stepped closer to her and gritted on her. His dark eyes gripped her with a steely, unyielding glare.

"I'm in a crucial bind right now, Tameka," Eric said gruffly. "And I need to get my fuckin' paper up to pay off this debt. So I'm gonna ask you once more, how rich is this nigga, and can he get got?"

Tameka's eyes went from pleading to shock. She shook her head slightly. "What?"

"Since you say you don't really love this nigga, then it is what it is, right?"

Tameka already knew what he was getting at. He wanted her to become a honey trap, which was something she had avoided her entire life. She had resisted doing it for the dope boys in the projects where she grew up, and now that she was grown, she was being asked to do it for love. Could she ever escape her past, she wondered. Could she ever escape the hood?

"If you love me like you say you do, then you gonna help me set this nigga up, so we can both get paid. You understand me, Tameka?" .

Tameka didn't know how to respond. She only nodded gingerly, so as not to upset him. He still held that massive gun in his hand.

Eric took Tameka into his arms and hugged her. He had provided the stick, and now it was time to provide the carrot. He had taken his love away from her, and by hugging her, he was showing her that she could have it again. All she had to do, was co-operate.

Tameka accepted Eric's warm embrace. She didn't know her answer, but at that moment, she knew that it felt good to be in his arms again. She was also certain that she was ready to agree with anything he asked, just to have him back. The two worlds that she had tried desperately to keep separate, were about to cross, and not in a good way. And just like in the movies, when you have two planets about to collide, shit is a total epic disaster. And in those kinds of movies, it's always two outcomes. One, either everyone gets killed, or two, the person in the middle of the two planets gets crushed. And she was the fool in the middle.

Eric was dangerous, Tameka thought. And Caleb was certainly no match for a hood cat like Eric. He was sweet, and innocent, and Eric could possibly put a bullet in his head. Caleb didn't deserve for that to happen. He had done nothing but love her, and show her a great time. But at the end of the day, what choice did she have? She was who she was. She was from the hood, and she loved a nigga from the hood. And her hood nigga needed her. And at the end of the day, they could both come out on top, and they could both get what they wanted. Eric could get the bread he needed, while she would get Eric. And to top it off, they would both have Caleb's money. He had millions in the safe for the taking. She could have a good Cosby lifestyle after all, and still have her gangster boo to boot. Life was about difficult choices. And now the choice came down to her happiness, or Caleb's life. And as always, she chose her.

# Boyfriend # 2

# Chapter Seventeen

Tameka sat quietly just opposite of Bridgette at the exclusive Lava restaurant in midtown Manhattan. She had barely touched her food or drink. Bridgette looked at her friend and knew something was on Tameka's mind. Her conversation was sparse, and she look distant and distracted.

Lava's was one of Tameka's favorite places to eat in the city. She always enjoyed their sweetbread and lobster, along with poached eggs and mushroom duxelle. The elegant restaurant offered fine Greek and Mediterranean cuisine, and combined it with beautiful surroundings and outstanding service. The interior had been decorated with elegant furnishings and boasted several unique architectural features. Original exposed brick covered the walls, while flower-filled urns from Irakilo, handmade Iroko wooden tables from Mykonos, and a chic curved bar made of marble came from the island of Thasos. The restaurant virtually transported it's patrons to the Greek islands

Bridgette was talking, but Tameka was barely listening. So Bridgette decided to test her.

"So, you know I sucked off three strangers the other night, and got fucked in the ass by this convict," Bridgette said matter-of-factly.

"Huh?" Tameka replied.

"Bitch, you ain't even listening to one word I said."

"I'm sorry…I was just somewhere else," said Tameka.

"What's on your mind, girl?"

"Just work," she lied.

"Bullshit. That look you got on your face says it's more than just work. Who are you thinking about? Confess, spill beans."

Tameka sat silently.

Bridgette slightly perched herself over the table and stared at Tameka with an intense gaze. "How long we've been friends, Tameka?"

"Long time…since college," Tameka answered.

"Okay, so why you sitting there looking crazy and acting like I don't know you, or know when something is bothering you. Is it Caleb?"

"We're fine," Tameka replied halfheartedly.

"You're a liar. Whenever you speak about Caleb, you light up. Now, I barely see a spark fly out your ass. Bitch, you forgot that we're both from the same hood. I *know* you, Tameka, you're like a sister to me. What is going on, girl?"

Tameka remained silent.

"Bitch, you just gonna sit there and look stupid?" Bridgette asked, growing more forceful. "I know something is wrong with you, girl. What's up?"

"Damn, why you gotta come at me like that?" Tameka asked.

"Because I need to. You sitting here all distant and quiet and shit. And I know that something is on your mind, but you treating me like a damn stranger. Like we ain't cool like that. Like I ain't down for you or something. That shit pisses me the fuck off!"

"I went to see Eric the other day," Tameka said, finally relenting.

Bridgette looked dumbfounded. "What? I thought you two were on the outs?"

"I thought so too."

"So why did you go see him?"

Tameka remained quiet.

# Boyfriend # 2

Bridgette picked up on Tameka's silence. "Bitch, don't tell me you're still in love with him. You fucked him?"

"No," Tameka quickly uttered.

"But you're ready to. I thought Caleb was your life now? Girl, don't fuck this up with him. He treats you like the queen you are. You deserve so much better than Eric's thug ass."

"You don't even know him like that, Bridgette," Tameka told her.

Bridgette sucked her teeth. "C'mon, Tameka, open your damn eyes and look at shit the right way for once. We grew up around niggas like him. What you think they about? They are all on that same shit, but just using a different fuckin' toilet. He's a thug and a murderer too. And why you're ready to fuck up a good thing with Caleb to be with that nigga, is just crazy."

"It's complicated."

"You make it complicated, Tameka."

Tameka let out a frustrated sigh. She sat back in her seat, nearly in a slouch, and diverted her eyes from Bridgette. She was growing irritated with their conversation, so she took a few sips from her glass of White Russian wine.

"Don't catch an attitude with me, girl," Bridgette continued. "You know I'm gonna always tell you the truth. I ain't gonna tell you what you want to hear, but I'm damn sure gonna tell you what you need to hear. I'm always gonna keep it real with you, Eric is dangerous. He's a high risk. You know I'm a journalist, and I keep my ears to the streets. I have confidential informants all over the city, that are always feeding me stories. And word is out about your boy. I have a friend who is a detective, and quiet as it's kept, Eric is into some deep shit. First off, the nigga is the prime suspect in a double homicide, and second, he's deep in debt to some drug kingpin. Word is, your boy won't be around much longer, *if* he doesn't deliver half a million dollars pretty soon. Now ask yourself, do you want to be in the middle of this?

Do you want to be rolling in the car when they catch up with Eric? Do you? Use your head girl! We are *survivors*. What we do, what we've always done, is survive. Don't let dick, or emotions, or love, or anything else get in the way of that. Do you hear what I'm telling you? It's time to step!"

"I'm not stepping anywhere yet."

"Um huh, okay. You're going to let some dick and that bad boy swag get your ass into some shit you can't get out of. C'mon, Tameka. We're from the same hood, been through the same shit. You should already know better. You already know how niggas like him are already."

Tameka didn't say anything. She only took a sip of wine.

The waitress arrived with the ladies' order on a silver platter. Bridgette had the sea scallops, dressed with an aromatic black truffle condiment and shavings, garnished with artichoke. Tameka ordered her favorite, sweetbread and lobster, along with poached eggs.

The waitress carefully placed their meals in front of them, and then asked, "Will that be all, ladies?"

Tameka and Bridgette both nodded, indicating that they were satisfied.

"Enjoy ladies," the waitress told them, before disappearing into the kitchen once again.

Tameka dug into her lobster first. She closed her eyes and savored the taste of it in her mouth. It was orgasmic to her taste buds. Both of them dined silently for a short moment, before Bridgette downed the last of her wine, and signaled the waitress for another refill. When her glass was refilled, Bridgette took a few deep gulps, placed the glass in front of her, and then peered up at Tameka again.

"Don't get quiet now, we're not done talking about this."

Tameka stared at her in silence.

"So, you're really gonna risk having a beautiful relationship

with Caleb, by constantly opening your legs up to that goon?"
Bridgette asked.

"So, when were you going to tell me about Eric?" Tameka
asked.

"Tell you what?"

"Tell me that he's a murder suspect," Tameka asked. "Tell
me that he's in a lot of trouble with some big time dope dealer?
When were you going to tell me these things, *friend*?"

"I was going to tell you these things, as soon as I had a
chance to," Bridgette said through clenched teeth. "As soon as
you had a free moment. With two boyfriends to satisfy, it's not
like you've had a lot of free time on your hands lately."

"Bullshit!" Tameka sneered.

"Beside, you broke up with him!" Bridgette said, leaning in
closer. "There was no need to jeopardize my sources once you
had broken up. You weren't in danger anymore. As long as you
keep your ass away from him, you were safe. You got that?"

Tameka had enough. She dropped her knife and fork and
shot Bridgette a wicked look.

"Look, I'm a grown damn woman, Bridgette, okay! Who I
choose to be with and fuck, is my damn business. And besides,
when was the last time you *had* and *kept* a man in your life? So
don't you worry about how many boyfriends I have, or how many
men I have to please. That's my business! Besides, you don't
know Eric, like I know him. Back in the day, how many niggas
in the hood were *suspects*? That didn't mean they actually did it!
And if Eric is in debt to some big time dope dealer, then what
makes you think I would abandon him when he needs me the
most? That's the difference between me and you!"

"So, it's like that, Tameka?" Bridgette asked. "All I was
trying to do was look out for your stupid ass! You want to run
out there and get your damn head blown off, then fine, do it! It's
your life. If you want to throw away a millionaire boyfriend, and

a promising career, then go ahead and do it! And as for your little comment about the difference between me and you, that shit is wishful thinking. We're cut from the same cloth, bitch. You and I are exactly the same! But you're even more scandalous. Bitch, I *know* you, so don't start acting like you ain't did dirt, and like your shit don't stink!"

"I don't need you to baby-sit me, Bridgette! I can handle my own. Yes, we're cut from the same cloth, and made the same mistakes. But I know what I'm doing. I've grown up, and I've changed."

"I hope so, Tameka. I really hope so," Bridgette replied.

"Now, can we both just sit and enjoy this wonderful meal without having Caleb or Eric in the conversation? Damn, girl, I got other shit to tell you too," said Tameka.

Bridgette smiled to relieve the tension between the two of them. "Okay. But I will say this. If you wanna keep giving him a piece of your cookie, then that's on you. But when your ass needs bail, don't come calling my phone."

"Whatever."

Tameka didn't want to dwell on her situation with Eric and Caleb. And she damn sure was not about to tell Bridgette about the robbery Eric wanted to implicate her in. If Bridgette had any wind of it, then she would have wigged out and really barked on her. She already had enough on her plate, without Bridgette barking into her ear, and then getting Tammy and Rosalynn involved as well. She just wanted to get through dinner without any more talk of Caleb or Eric. Besides, she was about to go and see Eric anyway. She was sure that she was about to get enough conversation about Caleb, and money, and robbery then.

*****

# Boyfriend # 2

Tameka strutted towards Eric's gleaming Escalade in her wedged heels and form fitting jeans. She moved like a diva on a mission. Her thick hips swayed with each of her steps, matching her fierce walk. The truck was parked on the curb of 126th Street. The cool night air was accentuated by a slight breeze that caused her hair to blow in the wind. The rocky concrete underneath Tameka's shoes was a signature of Harlem's mean streets.

Eric sat behind the wheel of his SUV, puffing on a cigar. It was a change for him. He rarely smoked cigars, but it was Cuban; a gift from a friend. He blew smoke out his mouth and focused on Tameka crossing the street. Her attire, her attitude, her stunning beauty turned heads and stopped traffic in the streets. The men she passed ogled at her beauty and curvaceous figure. Eric could only smile, knowing that what was fantasy for so many men, was the real thing to him. He knew Tameka's body like the back of his hand. He had seen her butt-naked many times. And he knew how his dick curved inside her sweet pussy on the regular. And the way she gave him head and fucked him, was almost criminal. He missed her bedroom ways, and couldn't wait to jump back inside of her again.

Tameka jumped into the passenger seat and stared at him. The cigar was clutched between his fingers, as he blew the sweet thick smoke from his mouth.

"When did you start smoking cigars?" Tameka asked.

"Long time ago...but it's rare for me now," Eric explained.

"You surprise me every time."

"It's always good to keep people intrigued," Eric smiled. "It keeps me on top, gives me that edge."

Tameka didn't reply.

Eric was ready to get down to business. He wanted an answer from Tameka.

177

"So, what's the verdict?" Eric asked.

Tameka sighed. "He's a sweet guy, Eric."

"I don't give a fuck what he is, he could be President Obama, or muthafuckin St. Nick and Mother Theresa all rolled into one. This nigga needs to get got! I need that money, Tameka.! Do you understand this shit?"

"Why him?" she inquired. "There are a million dudes out here that you could jack."

"Why not him? From what you telling me, he's got plenty of it to go around, so he ain't gonna sweat losing like a million or two. So, if you really fuckin' love me, then ya ready to ride wit' me on this then. Ain't no questions about it. Who's ya loyalty to, Tameka? Huh?"

Tameka was quiet.

Eric added in a kicker.

"Cuz I'm ready to step and say fuck you, and go handle this shit on my own. And if I handle this on my own, it's gonna get ugly!"

Tameka finally gave in. Her eyes stared at Eric and were filled with a pang of guilt. She didn't want Caleb to get killed, not behind money. Not over something that was not his fault. He was truly innocent.

"Promise me you won't hurt him," Tameka said softly.

"What, you got feelings for the nigga, or something?" Eric asked angrily.

"He ain't did nothing to nobody!" Tameka told him. "It ain't about feelings, Eric. It's about a square dude who ain't never hurt a fly. He's innocent in all of this."

"Ain't nobody gonna get hurt if we do this right," Eric huffed. "It's gonna be fast, we gonna be in and out. And he ain't even gotta know you was involved. We get this money and we split it, you and me, right down the middle. And baby, we can truly live like a king and queen. We'll leave this fuckin' city and can go anywhere we want. We don't never gotta come back. You feel me?"

Tameka nodded and smiled. And yet, beneath her fake smile lied something much deeper. She was worried sick to her stomach. No matter what life she and Eric would have together, Caleb still didn't deserve to die. She wanted to believe Eric when he said that no one was going to get hurt. But deep down, her gut told her different. She knew Eric, and she knew his type. He wasn't the type to leave witnesses. Tameka could literary feel her stomach twisting in knots.

Eric was in trouble, she thought. She understood that. She understood that he was in some dilemma with a high-ranking drug kingpin, and the last thing she wanted on her conscience, was seeing Eric dead, when she could have helped prevent it. But at the same time, she also didn't want to see Caleb get hurt. The choice between Eric and Caleb was no longer about who she was going to be with, but about which man she wanted to see live. Would she let the drug kingpin kill Eric, or would she let Eric kill Caleb? Her twisted little web of fucking and money, had stopped being fun, and had suddenly become deadly.

"A'ight, this is what's gonna happen. You continue to keep seeing this nigga, and I want a complete layout of this nigga's life. I wanna know where he eats, sleeps, even where he fucks you at. I want a layout of this nigga's crib. Tell me about his security, any codes, dogs or whatnot, you understand this, Tameka?"

She nodded.

"And we hit this nigga when you got him the most vulnerable," said Eric.

"But it's only gotta be just you," Tameka blurted.

"What you mean?"

"I don't want any of your goons coming in on this. I don't want any surprises. I don't want anything to go wrong. And I know your thugs, they can be somewhat trigger happy. It's just you and me, like you said, not Sean or no one. Those are my conditions. Anyone else comes in on this, and I'm walking away."

Eric hesitated for several moments, before finally relenting. "A'ight, just you and me."

Tameka took a deep breath. She couldn't believe that Eric had agreed to do it her way. She felt a slight relief in her stomach, thinking that she may be able to save Caleb's life after all. Taking his money was one thing, taking his life was another. Somehow, someway, somewhere along the line, her life had gone from Cosby Show, to Set It Off. Everything had changed. With Caleb she felt like Jay and Bey. With Eric, she felt like fucking Bonnie and Clyde. There was now an enormous gap between the life she wanted, and the life she was now going to lead. For the first time, in a long time, Tameka felt trapped once again. Leaving the hood and going to college had expanded her options. Now, fucking with Eric, her options had once again been taken away.

# Chapter Eighteen

Jay Z was blasting through the sound system, with the enormous Bang and Olufsen speakers vibrating the walls. A fountain created from champagne glasses was stacked six feet high, and overflowed with Moet. And the room itself, was overflowing with skinny Swedish, and Somali models, and their wealthy stock broker benefactors.

The party was located at The Touraine, a neo classical building with a slight art deco flair. It was this building, which sat on the corners of 65th and Lennox, that housed Caleb's massive Upper East Side, three story penthouse. It was Caleb's home in the city.

Tonight's party was another celebration honoring the host. Caleb had just landed Goldman Sachs a massive Middle Eastern client, and all of his client's oil rich relatives were sure to follow. He had stolen this oil rich, Dubai royal from Barclays of London, and gotten him to move more than a billion in assets over to Goldman's for a trial run. It was an portfolio that Caleb would be running personally, at the investor's request, which meant that his commissions would be through the roof, and that his bosses would now have to kiss his ass even more. He was truly Goldman Sachs golden boy, and all of the banks big wigs were present to celebrate his enormous score.

Tameka walked around the room smiling, and greeting all of the guest. She held a glass of Don P in one hand, while nervously gliding her finger from the other hand around the rim. Parties like

181

this always made her nervous. She didn't want to say the wrong thing, or come across as being stupid, or inadequate. She wanted to impress Caleb, and impress his friends and co-workers. Fitting in with his friends and family was the best way to show that you actually belonged in a man's life. She wanted to play the role of hostess, the role of a dutiful wife to show Caleb that she was ready for him to fulfill his promise. She was ready for the big enchilada, the real deal engagement ring, and not just a damn promise ring. And so she viewed this party as part of her audition for that role.

Eric had told her to act normal, to go back to doing what she was doing, which was fine with her. She didn't mind the champagne, the parties, the Bentley convertible that he let her drive. She didn't mind the clothes, the shopping sprees, and all of the money. And if, at the end of the day, Caleb happened to spring a big fat ass ring on her, then so be it. She would keep that too. Eric had a plan, but she also had a plan. And in her plan, she got to have it all.

Eric needed Caleb's money to pay off his debt. In her plan, Eric would get his damn money, so he could keep his life. Also, in her plan, Caleb wouldn't get killed, nor would he know that she had anything to do with him getting robbed. Caleb would keep his life, Eric would keep his life, and everything would be okay. And what would she get out of it? She would get her life back. She would get to keep her career, she would get to keep her options, and she would get to keep her dream. She loved Eric, no doubt, and she didn't want anything bad to happen to him. And so, she would let him get his money. But what Eric didn't know, was that after he got his money and headed out of town, he would be making that trip alone. She wasn't going. She wasn't going to give up her dream. Being with Caleb reminded her of the life she wanted. Yeah, she was from the hood, but she had also grown up. The objective when you're from the hood, is to get the hell up outta the hood. Why didn't more people understand that, she wondered? Caleb was her ticket to a better life. And she wasn't going to give that ticket up for anyone. Not even for her thug-a-boo.

"Who is *she*?" one of the model chics asked, as Tameka strolled by.

"What's *she* doing here?" another asked under her breath.

"Bitches," Tameka whispered beneath her breath, as she walked by a group of size zero models. She felt as if their eyes were on her, and had been on her since they arrived. They were wondering who she was, and why she was here. To those skinny bitches, her big firm ass made her fat, in their eyes. She hated them. She wanted to pull a Monique on their asses, and tell them to go and eat a damn taco. Skinny bitches!

"How about a dance?"

Tameka turned. It was another middle aged, executive from Goldman. He was tanned, and toned, with perfect teeth, and graying hair on the sides. He also had on a five thousand dollar suit. She exhaled.

It was always the older white guys that were after the black booty. It was they who brought in the majority of the African models with the British accents, while the younger white brokers were the ones with the skinny Swedish and Icelander models on their arms. The older guys knew what the younger ones didn't, Tameka thought. The skinny white bitches could suck a golf ball through a garden hose, but the sisters knew how to work those hips. It was the rich older guys that absolutely loved them some chocolate.

"No, thanks," Tameka told him. "I have to run to the ladies room. Perhaps later?"

"I'll be waiting," he told her.

Tameka strolled into the bathroom, and closed the door. She peered around the room, leaned back against the white Carrera marble sink, and drew in a deep breath. She would be glad when the party was over. She didn't know how long she could put up a front. Sure, she did it all day long at work, but even there, she could relax a little. Omnicom had hired her because of her knowledge of the inner city market. She could use some hood terminology and be a little bit hood at work, because it bolstered her credibility. But here, in front of Caleb's friends, she had to be on guard. She didn't want even the least bit of hood to slip out. She didn't want to say anything out of line, and have Caleb's co-workers laughing at him.

"Relax, girl!" Tameka said, peering at herself in the mirror. "Why are you tripping? Relax!"

Tameka inhaled deeply, and then exhaled and tried to relax. She could hear the Drake pounding through the white Carrera marble walls of the bathroom. She closed her eyes and listened to the lyrics for a minute.

"I'm so proud of you," Tameka repeated, singing some of the lyrics. She was a college graduate. The first in her family. She had made it out of the hood, and she had landed a bomb ass job at the biggest firm on Madison Avenue. She had climbed the ladder, saved, bought her the home of her dreams, and was now dating the man of her dreams. She was checking shit off of her bucket list at a breakneck speed. She was beautiful, fine, and she had her health. On top of that, she wasn't a dumb ass chick. So, what was she so nervous about, she wondered? Stop tripping, girl, she said to herself again. Look, if that man didn't love you, he wouldn't have put a ring on it, to borrow a few lyrics from Beyonce'. So, get your ass out there, and get in the game. Don't hide in the bathroom, show these people that you are ready for prime time!

Tameka examined herself, straightened out her Badgley Mischka dress, and checked her lipstick. She was going to go and find Caleb, and feed off of his strength. Seeing him regularly, would help her get through the evening. It would also give her the strength to see her plan through. Eric would want a report, and she would give him his damn report. She would give him the layout, Caleb's schedule, everything that he needed to pull off the robbery. The quicker it was done, the quicker he could pay off his debt, leave town, and let her get her life back. She had come to far to give it all up now.

Tameka breathed in heavily once again, and then opened the door to go and find her man. The system began pumping out Jay Z's *Where I'm From,* and she heard whoops from the living room.

"What the hell?" Tameka asked with a smile. A party of bankers and stock brokers was getting crunk over Jay Z-s lyrics about life in Marcy Projects. It was too much for her, and she had to laugh. None of them had ever been anywhere near Brooklyn, Bed-Stuy or Marcy in their entire life. And if anyone had accused any of them of listening to rap music, or chasing black pussy, they would deny it until their dying days. They're two faced bastards, Tameka thought.

She made her way down the hall, past a bunch of Middle Easterners. You could tell the guys from Dubai and Saudi, by the ten thousand dollar suits, and hundred thousand dollar Rolex's, even without looking at the color of their skin. They were loaded. Hell, they even smelled like money, Tameka thought. And they liked rap music even more than the white guys.

Tameka made her way to the bedroom, where she found Caleb and Jake standing outside on the balcony. She didn't want to interrupt, so she stood and listened for a moment.

"Caleb, you better get off this balcony," Jake told him. "Those boys over at Barclays may have hired an assassin to take you out."

Caleb laughed. "Yes, I imagine our friends over in London are a little pissed off at me right about now."

"Pissed?" Jake asked lifting an eyebrow. "If they could, they would have you drawn and quartered. You stole a *massive* client from them."

"I did, didn't I?" Caleb laughed.

"How'd you do it, bro?" Jake asked. "You're going to have to tell me your secret."

"Jake, old boy, I could tell you, but then I'd have to kill you."

"These are the types of stories that legends are made from," Jake smiled. "And you are becoming a modern day legend. Your name is ringing in every investment bank in the world right now, you know that? I mean, you could go anywhere, command a seven figure salary, and live like a king."

"Not yet."

"You're still down?" Jake asked.

"Of course I am." Caleb held out his hand, and Jake clasped it. "We're going to do it, man."

"Our own investment firm," Jake said, peering over the Manhattan sky. "It's going to happen. It's really going to happen."

"I just need a couple more big money transactions, and then we'll have the money to do it in style."

"Are they going to move with us?" Jake asked, nodding towards the Middle Easterner in the hallway.

"Of course," Caleb said. "I could talk them into eating a bacon and pork chop sandwich, and washing it down with a bottle of Jack Daniels. I'm the master at this shit, bro."

Jake threw his head back in laughter.

"So, how is Karen coming along?" Caleb continued.

"Beautifully," Jake answered. "She doesn't suspect a thing."

Caleb turned, and spied Tameka in the room. He jumped. "Tameka!"

Jake turned. "Tameka. What's up?"

"Nothing," she said with a smile. "How are you doing,

Jake?"

Caleb and Jake came in from the balcony. Jake kissed Tameka on her cheek.

"I'm good, Sweety," Jake told her. He turned to Caleb. "Going to go mingle, bro."

Caleb nodded.

Jake nodded toward a mound, beneath the covers. "It's all there."

Caleb nodded. "Close the door on your way out."

Jake gave Caleb a half-hearted salute, and then left the room, closing the door behind himself.

"So, what's going on, Sweety?" Tameka asked.

Caleb pulled the covers back on the bed, exposing an enormous pile of money. Tameka swallowed hard. She had to catch herself from blurted out a curse word.

"What the hel... heck?"

Caleb turned, pushed a massive picture to the side, and then pressed the digital keypad on his now exposed safe. The safe door popped open.

Tameka eyeballed the contents of the safe. It was a large metal safe, filled with money. And now, Caleb was adding *more* money to it. The money was all bound together in stacks of one hundred dollar bills, which told her that each stack was either a ten thousand dollar stack, or a twenty thousand dollar stack. Whichever it was, he had an enormous sum inside of his safe. It was so much money, that it actually scared her.

Tameka wondered if she should ask him about the money, or just keep quiet. One day, he would tell her about it, that much was certain. He would have to tell her about it, once she became his wife. But the question was, should she ask him about it before then? If she waited to become his wife, would it be too late then? Tameka shook her head, trying to clear her thoughts. They were ridiculous thoughts. She knew that Caleb wasn't a dope boy, that was for sure. And Jake, his little, White, Harvard buddy wasn't one either. But what the hell were they doing with a million, or a couple of million in cash, in a safe, inside of Caleb's bedroom? Where did it come from? What was it for? She had dozens of questions, but didn't know how to ask, or even if she should. Was it *legal* ? Would it one day get him sent to prison, and her sent to the poorhouse? She was not trying to be another Mrs. Madoff, and go from living lavishly, to visiting a nigga in Federal Prison. That was definitely not in the tea leaves for her.

Caleb finished packing his safe with bands of money, closed it, and then turned back toward her. "Enjoying the party, babe?"

Tameka was taken aback. Did this nigga just turn around and ask me about a fucking party, after loading hundreds of thousands of dollars in a safe that already had a few million in it, like nothing just happened? She could hear her Kat Williams voice about to come out. *Nigga is you crazy; don't you know I can see you?*

"Tameka, the party?" Caleb repeated.

"Huh? Oh, yeah, the party. The party is great."

Caleb walked to where she was standing, wrapped his arms around her, and pulled her close. "What's the matter?"

Tameka shrugged. "Nothing."

"C'mon, now."

"Oh, so you think that you can tell when something is wrong with me?"

Caleb stared at her and lifted an eyebrow.

"Okay, okay," Tameka said, relenting. "I'm just not sure it's my type of vibe."

"What's wrong with the vibe in there?"

"I just don't know anybody."

"It's a party," Caleb told her. "You mingle, you meet people, and you relax and enjoy yourself. C'mon, where's that fun loving Tameka that I know?"

Tameka exhaled. Was she failing the test, she wondered? Caleb would need a good wife to entertain his guest when they threw parties, or held dinners, and she was showing that she couldn't handle herself. Damn-it, she thought. Get your shit together, girl!

"I'm here," Tameka told him. "I was just missing you."

Caleb kissed her on her lips. "I miss you too."

"Well, I'm going to get back out there and mingle," Tameka said, putting on a brave face.

"That's my girl," Caleb said, slapping her behind.

Tameka turned, and walked out of the room. She had to show Caleb that she could play wifey and entertain. She would smile and meet and greet, and even dance with some of those execs who had been eyeballing her ass all night. She would even go over and speak to some of those poofy mouth, skeleton built bitches who thought their shit didn't stink.

Models, Tameka thought, shaking her head. More like broom sticks with extensions. If one of those bitches got out of line, she couldn't promise anything. The Vaseline could come out, the razor blade could find it's way out, and her hair could find itself being tied up in a pony tail. These bitches liked the song, but she would really show them what Marcy was about if one of them got cross with her.

# Boyfriend # 2

# Chapter Nineteen

Tameka leaned back and relaxed in her large, oval jetted bathtub. She adjusted herself, placed the back of her head against the soft pillow cushion behind her, closed her eyes and heaved a sigh. The stillness in her bathroom, and in her home for that matter, made it a place she wanted to remain forever. She wanted to linger in that stress free place of calm coziness.

The bubbles bursting from the jetted tub pulsed against Tameka's wet brown skin, and the complete lower half of her body was submerged in the warm, stimulating waters. She was lathered up in bubbles and soap, and it felt cleansing to her.

A bottle of white wine and a long, stemmed glass was within reach. The lights were dimmed, and Anthony Hamilton's smooth, soulful voice was serenading her. In her mind, she dreamed of her future. And it was a good future. It was a future where she had it all. She was the wife of a powerful stock broker, living in a million dollar apartment on the Upper East Side. She had views of the city, and of Central Park below. Two boys, and one girl, and a nanny to help take care of them. It was her dream life. And Eric was alive and well, and living in Phoenix. A post card here and there to let her know how he was doing, that was all she wanted from him. To know that he was well. And Caleb, well, he was her husband, and the father of her children.

The Sony radio in the bathroom boomed Anthony Hamilton's *The Point Of It All,* Tameka nodded and mouthed the words to the song.

191

# Boyfriend # 2

*I can't stay away from you too long*
*Even if I do I'll always call*
*Checkin' on you make sure you're okay*
*Be the one to brighten up your day*

Tameka sipped from her wine glass, savoring the deep, rich flavor of her favorite grape. Her cell phone was turned off, and she felt a peace that she hadn't felt in weeks. From Anthony Hamilton, to Miki Howard, to Anita Baker, to Patti Labelle, and Mary J. Blige, her MP3 rotation kept her company, and helped to sooth and sedate her troubled mind. And when finally, she decided that it was time to remove herself from the tub, it was almost midnight. Her long relaxing bath had her feeling like a new woman.

Tameka stepped out of her tub dripping wet and reached for one of the towels she had hanging over her towel rack. She slowly dried herself off and gazed at herself in the mirror. She was beautiful, and she knew it. Her long wet hair looked like a gleaming black mane falling down to her shoulders. Her brown eyes looked like beautiful smoked topaz, and her body was so luscious and curvaceous, that no man could resist her. Staring at herself in the mirror, Tameka knew that she could have any man she wanted And having any man she desired was what had put her in the predicament that she was in today.

Tameka tried hard to not think about Eric and his scheme, but the minute she stepped out of the tub and tied the towel around her, it all infiltrated her mind once more. She wondered if they could really pull it off. Could she make it appear as though she weren't involved? Could she somehow convince Caleb she had nothing to do with it? It had to be believable. She would have to act her ass off after the robbery, of that she was certain.

Tameka sighed as she stared at herself in the mirror.

"What to do? What to do?" she mumbled, even though she already knew the answer to that question. She had already made up her mind. She was going to give Eric the 52 fake out, after he robbed Caleb. And then, she was going to be with the man who could provide her with the financial security that she long desired. She just needed to work out a few more kinks in her plan.

The brownstone was quiet. Rosalynn was spending time with her man at his place, which left Tameka plenty of time to contemplate her next moves. She didn't have to worry about conversation, or questions, or any of the other things that Rosalynn would be doing right now. It also meant she had free reign over the television.

Tameka walked into her living room and turned on the television. She changed the channel to MSNBC, and watched the midnight rebroadcast of The Rachel Maddow show. She listened as the liberal pundit discussed Obama's health care plan, and the Republican's defiant measures against bipartisanship. The show then went on to discuss the recession and unemployment rates. It was still bad out there. The rich were getting richer, and the poor continued to get not a damn thing. It only served to remind her even more of how she needed to secure her future. Losing her job, and having her brownstone foreclosed on, was definitely not part of her plan. She needed to lock down Mr. Caleb as quickly as possible, by having him put a ring on it.

The television news only served to depress her. Bad economic news was the order of the day; it seemed like the United States was going into a free fall of depression, unemployment, and debt. And if the Republicans had their way, there was not going to be any help, for anybody, at anytime, under any circumstances. You had to go out there and get yours, by any mean necessary. Which is what she was doing.

Tameka watched a half hour of the show and then turned off the TV. She had heard enough. She walked into her bedroom and strolled up to the window where she gazed outside. Her Harlem block was always quiet. It was especially quiet at this time of the night. Her part of Harlem was free from the roughnecks and hustlers, and scandalous and nasty bitches that plagued other areas of the borough. The brownstones that lined the uptown city street, were all well kept, and all of them had been renovated. Most of the residents on her block were middle class and beyond, with many doctors, lawyers, bankers, entrepreneurs, and business owners as residents. It was a wonderful area to be in.

She removed herself from the window and sat on her bed, where she undid her towel and tossed it into the nearest chair. She picked up the bottle of lotion and began to lotion herself down, working her way up from her feet to her chest. Just as she was about to lotion her breasts and face, her cell phone rang. Tameka reached over and grabbed her phone from the nightstand. It was Eric calling. She hesitated in answering at first, but after second thought, knew that she had to play it cool. She had to maintain the illusion that she was going to leave with him after the robbery.

"Hello," Tameka answered softly.

"What you doin', luv?" Eric asked.

"Getting ready for bed."

"Damn, I wanna join you."

Tameka rolled her eyes. "Not tonight."

"Why not?"

"I got a lot on my mind, Eric."

"You still thinkin' about this shit? Relax, Tameka, it's gonna be cool. Don't stress it."

"I'm not."

"You don't sound like it. Listen, you just do what I tell you to do, and we gonna get paid, and we gonna have a good life together. You feel me, baby?"

"I feel you," she replied halfheartedly.

"This is our time to shine and get this bread."

Tameka remained silent.

"We gonna make it happen for us, baby," Eric continued. "I promise you that. I just wanna leave these streets alone and take care of you. You know you deserve the best, and I'm gonna be that man to give it to you. Let the past be the past, and let's focus on our future. You wit' it, right?"

"Yes," Tameka told him.

A'ight, I know you're tired, so get ya rest and I'll hit you in the A.M. I love you, Tameka."

The three words hit Tameka like a brick to her chest. She no longer knew how she felt about those words, at least not coming from him. Eric was demanding a pretty high price for his love, and love shouldn't cost a thing. It shouldn't hurt, it shouldn't cause you to stress, it shouldn't put you in danger, it shouldn't give you cause for regret. She wondered if Eric knew that. She wondered if he really understood what love was about. She wondered if his love was even real.

"I love you, too," Tameka said softly. She knew her words rang hollow, as soon as she said them.

"Get some sleep, baby. We'll talk later."

Eric hung up, leaving Tameka feeling like she was running on empty. She tossed her phone into the chair next to her towel and continued to get ready for bed. Her mind was swimming with doubt, but she knew that she had to play things through. The cards had been dealt, and it was now time to play the shit out. The only question was, could she freak her hand and come up with a winner? She didn't need all Aces, but a full house damn sure would be nice.

# Boyfriend # 2

*****

Eric sat slouched in the chair grinning from ear to ear. Standing before him was one of the most astonishingly beautiful women he had ever seen. Her long black hair was down, and it framed her face perfectly. Her enticing brown skin was luminescent, and her erect nipples poked through her satin nightgown, accentuating her full breasts. Her long, well-defined legs ended in a pair of clear stilettos, and her body had more curves than a NASCAR race track. She was the epitome of sexy. Utterly breathtaking, Eric thought.

Eric was shirtless, his muscles and tattoos were showing. His jeans were unbuttoned, and the look he gave his ex-girlfriend, Sky, told her that he was more than ready to rock her world. Sky sashayed up to Eric in a way that told him that she was hungry for some dick action.

"You miss me, daddy?" Sky asked, in her seductive voice.

"You know I did, baby," Eric replied.

"How much did you miss me?"

She straddled him, and ran her manicured nails down his chest. Her touch was riveting. Her warm, heated flesh pressed against Eric like the burning sun in the midst of summer. Eric ran his hands across her attractive body and lowered the straps to her gown, revealing her succulent tits. He tasted her nipples, lapping his tongue around each one. She moaned, cupping the back of his head and bringing his face deeper into her chest.

Sky had just come home from doing a four-year bid for drugs and conspiracy at Bedford Hills Correctional facility in Westchester County, New York. It was the same facility that housed Amy Fisher and Jean Harris. Eric had been her boo-thang before she left. In fact, *he* was the reason for her trip up state. She had refused to snitch on him, and as a result, bore the brunt of the full indictment for the heavy weight she had been caught with in the car. She had been carrying five kilos of cocaine and a few pistols, as well as, a couple of assault rifles. She decided to take a plea deal, being that it was her first major offense, and copped out to do seven years instead of going to trial and risk a sentencing of fifteen to twenty. She was eligible for parole in four, which she made the first time up. And now that she was out, the two of them were catching up on lost time.

Sky was a ride or die bitch from the Bronx. She had met Eric when she was just eighteen years old and had fallen in love with him immediately. He was a thug, but was charming and articulate. Sky was naive and trusting. By the time she turned nineteen, he had her. She was completely under his control. Soon, she became his mule. She was running drugs out of state for him on the regular. By the time she was twenty-years old, Eric could do no wrong in her eyes. He lavished her with mind blowing trips, expensive gifts, and hella dick on the regular. She was ready for marriage, kids and everything a woman dreamed of. In her mind, they would become the next Bonnie and Clyde of the game. But the dream came to an abrupt end when she got busted with the merchandise and received her sentence. There was pressure on her from the D.A, the feds, and the state police to give up who she was transporting the drugs for, but Sky remained steadfast, and took her punishment like a thorough bitch. She wanted to show Eric that her love was unconditional; that no matter what the cost was, she was willing to bare it for him, and that she was even willing to go to prison because of her love for him.

Now she was home, and was ready to resume her relationship with Eric. During her stint in prison, Eric wrote her ever so often, and put a few dollars on her books for some prison commissary whenever possible. He kept Sky happy. She did him the ultimate favor, and so he stayed down with her while she did her bid. His staying down, and his letters, led her to believe that everything would be back on again, as soon as she touched down. Eric wanted her to believe that. He *needed* her to believe that. He needed her to stay strong and keep quiet for the entire bid, which she did. And now, she was at a motel room with Eric, claiming the reward for her silence.

"I missed you so much, baby," Sky purred, as her tongue ran across Eric's lips.

"I missed you too," Eric told her.

Her lips tasted like strawberries. Eric's hands roamed freely over her curves. He caressed her small waist and sexy bottom, cupping her juicy ass and passionately tonguing her down.

"I thought when I came home, you weren't goin' to like me anymore. I thought you would forget about me," Sky said with a smile.

"Baby, I can never forget about you. I love you, you know that."

Sky beamed.

"It's just gonna be you and me, always," he promised.

Sky's smile grew wider. She was ready to surrender her body to him once again.

"Who was you on the phone wit' earlier?" she asked.

"Nobody, baby...I was just taking care of much needed business. What I tell you in my letters? When you get out, I was gonna take care of you, and that's a promise I plan on keeping."

"I always knew you were goin' to keep your promise," Sky told him. "That's why I love you, baby."

The two kissed more passionately again. Sky could feel the wetness increasing between her legs. Eric removed his jeans, exposing the hard and long erection that he had developed. Sky took his hard-on in her grip and began stroking him.

"Ooooh, I missed him," she said with a devilish grin.

"You did, huh?"

"Yes, baby. Has he been behaving himself while I was gone?"

Eric smirked. "Somewhat."

"Whatever," Sky said, playfully dismissing him. " I'm back, baby, so don't be sharing my dick wit' anyone else. You tell all them little hoes to back the fuck up, 'cause mamas back."

"You know ya the one and only true bitch in my life," Eric said with a smile.

"That's what I wanna hear."

Sky positioned herself between Eric's knees and continued stroking his hard-on. Sky's raw sensuality was ready to push Eric over the edge. She lowered her glossy lips onto his hard steel pipe and began to polish him off. Her blow jobs were always amazing. Her soft, wet lips had Eric ready to shoot his load instantly. But somehow, he managed to hold his composure. He fucked her mouth like it was a piece of pussy—ramming the mushroom tip of his dick into the back of her throat. Sky's mouth became an erotic vacuum, coaxing Eric's warm cum out of his balls.

"Oh shit, Ooooh, do that shit, baby. Suck that dick!" Eric groaned. "Damn-it, I missed you."

Sky went to work on the dick. It'd been four years since she had something so hard and pulsating between her lips, and she wanted to relish the feeling. Her glossy, full lips enveloped the pulsating flesh nestled in her jaws, as she sucked his dick down to the base, not gagging or missing a beat. Eric continued to groan in disbelief as she sucked his dick like a heated sex slave.

Eric straddled her face and slammed his balls against her chin. The slurping sounds of her wet lips against his dick made him even harder. He didn't want to miss a beat. They took their sexual action toward the bed, where she demanded to be fucked from the back. He flipped Sky over to ravage her pussy. She positioned herself on her hands and knees, curved over, and presented Eric with a view of her glorious ebony flesh. Eric knelt behind her and placed his throbbing dick to her warm, sensual opening.

Sky felt the thick head of Eric's dick penetrate her walls. She moaned and grabbed the bedroom sheets. Eric thrust himself inside of her, clasped her waist, and began banging his nuts against her round ass cheeks, as he fucked her vigorously.

"Ooooh, fuck me," Sky cried out.

Eric got creative inside of Sky, stroking her dripping pussy from all angles, and hitting all her spots. He buried his big dick inside of Sky like a drill boring down into the earth searching for oil. Sky lost complete control of herself.

"Oh shit, it feels so good, baby," she screamed. "Fuck me! Fuck me!"

He fucked her deeper, and harder.

They fucked like crazy, changing positions like a crooked politician. She rode him like a race jockey, and then Eric threw her legs over his shoulder and fucked her that way for a while. They went through every position in the Kama Sutra, before it was all said and done.

Soon, Sky was cumming all over the place. And after a few more deep and passionate strokes inside of her, Eric felt the cum steaming from inside of his nuts right into her.

Moments later, Sky laid snuggled against Eric, feeling satisfied from head to toe. But Eric wasn't really in the mood to lay up and cuddle.

"Baby, won't you get in the shower and I'll join you," he told her.

Sky smiled. "Okay."

She removed herself from Eric's tender embrace and walked into the bathroom butt naked to take a shower. Eric lingered in the bed momentarily. He let out a heavy sigh, and heard the shower running in the bathroom, indicating Sky was doing what he'd asked of her.

Eric rose up out of bed, placed his bare feet onto the thick, blue carpet and peered at the bathroom door. It was ajar. He hunched over, lowered his head while pressing his elbows into his knees and gazed at the door. His mind was swimming with crazy feelings. Sky being home could cause a serious problem with his plans. She could be needy and overbearing. She was straight hood, and ready to continue their relationship from where it had left off. But Eric wasn't so sure about it.

"Baby, I thought you were coming to join me? What's taking you so long? Get ya fine ass in here and let me do you in the shower," Sky called out from the bathroom.

"I'm comin', baby," Eric shouted.

He stood up, still butt naked. He walked over to a small, black bag he brought with him to the room. He unzipped it and eyed the tool inside. He reached into the bag and gripped the Desert Eagle, and then screwed a long silencer onto the end of it. The unthinkable needed to be done. Eric pivoted on his heels and moved toward the bathroom with the silence of a ninja assassin. The huge gun was by his side, and his cold eyes were fixated on the bathroom door.

He entered the steamy bathroom. The shower curtains were drawn, and Sky's curvy silhouette could be seen from where he stood. The mirrors were fogged up, which was good, as it obscured his figure from her.

"Baby, that's you?" Sky's tender voice was heard saying. "I want you to fuck me in here."

Eric neared the running shower. He had no hesitation, as he felt it needed to be done. He'd come too far with Tameka, and was too close to getting a huge payoff, for this bitch to come home and fuck everything up. Eric abruptly pulled back the translucent shower curtains and aimed the gun at Sky. She was caught off guard..

Being wide-eyed with fear, she cried out to him. "Baby, what are you doing…"

*Poot! Poot! Poot! Poot! Poot! Poot! Poot! Poot!*

The slugs ripped through Sky's slender frame like she was paper thin. Each shot slammed into her with tremendous force, putting mountain sized holes from the .50 Cal into her petite frame. Blood, brain matter, and flesh splattered against the walls, and Sky's body crumpled into the tub. Eric stood over the mangled flesh. He didn't flinch or look remorseful in any way. It was only business. He had no more use for Sky. She was collateral damage. She would only get in the way of things. Now, what was left to do was either leave the premises or dispose of the body. Either way, Eric knew that he had to clean up the scene. They should have kept her ass locked up, he thought.

# Chapter Twenty

Tameka nervously paced back and forth inside of her apartment, only stopping to occasionally peer out of her living room window. It was dusk outside, and kids were still outside playing in the streets. Her hands shook nervously, and she found herself continuously wiping her palms on the pants legs of her business suit.

"Girl, what are you doing?" Bridgette asked.

"Nothing," Tameka answered, again peering out the window.

She knew what she was nervous about, but she didn't know why her fears kept her peering out of her living room window. She was scared to do what Eric had talked to her about doing. She was scared that Peon was going to find Eric and hurt him. She was scared that Peon could perhaps even hurt her in order to get even with Eric. Most of all, she was scared that Eric would show up at her brownstone and she would have to face him, or perhaps even worse, revisit their last conversation. That fear, was something that stalked her, like a creepy crawly predator inching its way up behind her. She dreaded having to talk about setting up Caleb again.

Tameka wiped her hands on her pants legs, and she headed into her kitchen to grab a glass of water. Her journey to the kitchen took her past her friends who were sitting on her couch and watching television. Rosalynn slapped her across her ass as she walked past.

"Move that big old butt, girl!" Rosalynn told her.

Tameka made her way into the kitchen, where she bypassed the water, grabbed a wine glass, and then pulled a bottle of Moscato out of the refrigerator. She popped the bottle stopper, and poured herself a hefty glass of wine. Her fears had her wanting more than just water; she needed something to calm her nerves.

"Girl you missing the show!" Tammy shouted.

"Yeah, this bootlegged DVD cost me five dollars!" Bridgette shouted. "You better get your ass in here and watch this!"

Tameka ignored her friends. Her mind was way to occupied to focus on a bootlegged copy of *The Hunger Games*. No, her thoughts were with Eric and Caleb, and what Eric wanted her to do to Caleb. She had never done anything like that, and she was certain that she wouldn't be able to do it now.

Tameka lifted her wine glass and took a big gulp. She needed to get drunk tonight. In fact, she had been leaning on alcohol to get her through the days since Eric first propositioned her with his plan. Of course she had her own plan, but she wasn't too sure if it would work. There were just so many variables. And Eric was leaning on her, day in and day out, about setting Caleb up. That's all their conversations were about now. Money that he owed some nigga name Peon, setting up Caleb, getting out of town. Why couldn't he just say fuck Peon, and leave town without the money? Peon couldn't reach out and touch him in California, or Arizona, or Texas, could he? *Why not just fucking leave?*

Tameka took another big gulp of wine and then leaned back against her kitchen counter. Her mind took her back to her days in the hood, and all of the shit that went on back then. She thought of all the dope boys, the booming systems, life in the projects, and all of the scandalous ass bitches that she grew up with. Including the ones that had turned into set up chicks, who had lured many unsuspecting dope boys to an early death.

Honey traps was what they used to call them, and many jackers from the hood had approached her to become one. Her fat juicy ass would have made her the perfect honey trap to lure a nigga to a motel, so that the homeboys could bust in and kidnap his ass. They promised her a share of whatever they got if she agreed to do it. But she couldn't. And the more she refused, the more they begged. She don't know why she resisted so hard, or even how she was able to resist the temptation. It wasn't like she was loaded with bread back in those days. She could have definitely used the money. But something inside of her wouldn't allow her to do it. Something inside of her wouldn't allow her to cross that dramatic line. Hood bop, yeah she could do. But set a dude up for the killing, was a horse of another color. It reminded her of her friend Jasmine.

Jasmine, or Jazzy, as they called her back then, was known as being the finest chick in the hood. She was Black and Dominican, with long black silky hair, thick sexy lips, and a booty that a nigga could set a forty on. She had no waist, a flat stomach, cantaloupe sized breasts, smooth mellow yellow skin, with an ass like a donkey. The dope boys in every hood fell all over her, and everyone wanted to wife her. It was her looks that earned her the nickname, Jazzy. And it was her looks that ended up getting her a life sentence upstate. And it was that life sentence that made her take her own life in the pen.

Jazzy had fell in with some jackers from the hood, and they got her to start setting up dope boys for motel jackings. And she was good at it, cause plenty of niggas from all over the city wanted to tap that. It wasn't until one of her little motel set ups went bad, that she actually realized what was really happening to the dudes she set up. They weren't just being kidnapped, taken back to their stash houses, and made to give up everything. They were murdered after the fact, and that realization never hit home until one day she had to witness the brutality of the crew she was rolling with. They put a bullet in a dope boy's head right in front of her, after he refused to leave the motel room and take them to his stash. It changed Jazzy's outlook on the whole situation. She quickly went from not being able to sleep, to taking meds to get some sleep, to taking heavier and heavier drugs to take her mind off of what she had been involved in. Eventually, her deeds caught up with her, and she turned state's evidence against her crew, but still ending up getting a life sentence. Absent the drugs, her conscience weighed too heavily on her, and she ended up hanging herself in her cell. It was a cold hard lesson and a cautionary tale that stayed with her. Jasmine had went from being the jazziest chick in the hood, to a junkie, and convict, and then worm food. She was determined not to go that route, Tameka thought. She was determined not to be the next Jazzy.

"Girl, what is wrong with you?" Bridgette asked, strolling into the kitchen. "Why you not watching the movie with us?"

"Huh?" Tameka said turning to face her friend.

"Girl, you've been distracted as hell lately," Bridgette told her. "What's the matter?"

Tameka shook her head, not knowing whether or not to let Bridgette in on her secret. She felt as though she was carrying the weight of the world on her shoulders, and it would be good to get some of it off of her chest. Bridgette was a hood chick, and she knew what the deal was. If there was anyone she could confide in, it would be Bridgette. Tameka's tears began to fall.

"Girl, what's the matter?" Bridgette asked. She hurried to where Tameka was standing and wrapped her arms around her.

"Girl, I don't know," Tameka said, shaking her head.

"You're drunk?" Bridgette asked.

Tameka shook her head.

"What is it? Is it something at work?"

Again, Tameka shook her head.

"Man problems?" Bridgette asked.

This time, Tameka nodded, and began to wipe away her tears.

"What's the deal? Is this about Eric?"

Tameka nodded.

"What?" Bridgette said, exhaling. "Is this about our conversation at lunch last week?"

Tameka shook her head.

"Did he hit you?"

Tameka shook her head and sniffled.

"What is it? Talk to me."

Again, Tameka burst into crying. "Remember, when I told you he caught me with Caleb?"

"Oh my god, girl," Bridgette said, clasping her chest. "He beat you? He threatened you?"

"No," Tameka said, shaking her head.

"Caleb found out?" Bridgette asked.

Tameka shook her head. "No."

"So, Eric is still tripping with you?"

"You remember Jazzy?" Tameka asked.

Bridgette thought long and hard about the name. It was a name that she hadn't heard since her late teens, and it escaped her at first. But like all girls from the hood in the big city, she knew Jazzy's tale.

"You talking about that girl Jasmine from back in the day?" Bridgette asked. She was clearly confused now.

Tameka nodded.

"Girl, what does she have to do with anything?" Bridgette asked. "Didn't she hang herself or something?"

Tameka nodded.

Bridgette threw her hands up in frustration. "Girl, I'm lost."

"You remember what Jazzy went to prison for?" Tameka asked.

Bridgette thought for a few moments. "Didn't she testify on some people. She was running around with a crew of jackers or something."

Tameka pursed her lips, and lifted an eyebrow.

It hit Bridgette like a ton of bricks. "Girl, don't tell me that!"

Tameka nodded, and started sobbing again.

"Eric caught you with Caleb, and now he want's to jack him?" Bridgette asked.

Tameka fell into Bridgette's arms once again. "He wants me to set him up."

"What the hell? Why? For what? Girl, I thought Eric was balling!" Again, it hit her. "Oh my god, girl. This is about that money that he's owes those dealers? Oh my god, girl."

"He *is* balling," Tameka said sniffling. "At least he was. He's in over his head with this. He needs that money or they're going to kill him."

"In trouble! How can he get in trouble? What about his crew? And how the hell did *his* debt become *your* problem?"

"Some guy named Peon," Tameka explained. "You know the story. Hell, you knew it before I did! Supposedly, he owes this guy a lot of money. And if he doesn't pay it back, he's dead. I can't let him get killed."

"Oh my God," Bridgette exhaled. She poured herself a glass of Moscato, and took a long swig. "How did you get yourself into this mess?"

"I didn't do anything!" Tameka shouted. "He caught me, he wanted to know about Caleb. He found out that Caleb is papered up, and he owes all this money, so..."

"Girl, I told you to leave his ass alone, a long time ago!" Bridgette told her.

"I didn't, okay. I couldn't. I love him."

"You *love* him?"

"Yes!"

"So what are you going to do?" Bridgette asked.

Tameka shook her head. "I don't know."

"Are you seriously considering doing this?"

Tameka closed her eyes and leaned back against her kitchen counter once again. "I don't know."

"You can't."

"I can't let him get killed."

"So, you're going to throw away your future with Caleb behind some bullshit?" Bridgette asked. "Eric had *no right* to ask you to do this! He had no right to bring you into this! Girl, you can't throw your life away behind some bullshit like this!"

"I can't let them kill him!"

"And what if he kills Caleb?" Bridgette asked.

"He promised that he won't."

"And you trust him?" Bridgette asked. "What's to keep Caleb from calling the cops on you, you damn fool!"

"Eric's going to set it up so that it doesn't look like I was involved."

"And what if Eric leaves *two* bodies on the floor instead of one?" Bridgette asked. "Ever thought about that?"

Tameka turned, grabbed her bottle of Moscato off of the counter, put it to her lips and turned it up. It was too much for her to think about right now. Bridgette was right in everything that she had said. What if Eric did decide to double cross her? Could she trust him? She loved him, but could she trust him? Did he love her back? Could she let him die? With the bottle in her hand, Tameka headed for her bedroom. She wanted to lie down and think. She had a choice to make. An extremely difficult choice at that. She always knew that it would come down to her choosing between Eric and Caleb, or Caleb and Eric. But she never knew that her decision would cost one of them their life. Caleb or Eric? Eric or Caleb? Tameka found her head spinning. She fell onto her bed, and buried her head into her pillow. Caleb or Eric? Eric or Caleb? The alcohol soon had her snoring. It would be one of the few times she would actually get some rest in the coming days.

.

# Chapter Twenty One

Detective Lane stepped out of the black Dodge Charger under the rapidly graying sky, and began to make his way toward the crime scene. The Days Inn motel was located in upstate New York, about an hour drive from the city. He gazed at the police cars parked near the entrance, and at the chatting uniformed officers that lingered out in front of the two-story motel, who were supposedly securing the area.

Detective Lane was a long serving and much experienced homicide detective, and upon surveying the scene, instantly knew that it was a bad one. He let out a deep sigh, as he maneuvered beneath the yellow crime scene tape and approached the front entrance. He had seen his fair share of homicides during his fifteen years on the force, and eight years as a homicide detective, but each case was different, and the job never got old.

Dressed fashionably in a tailored dark blazer and matching pants, along with polished shoes, and his Glock .23 sitting visible in a paddle holster, he dressed the part of a detective. His looks however, were something completely different; he could pass for an aging male model. The detective stayed in the gym working out and building muscle. He stood six foot in height with a muscular physique, smooth dark skin, chiseled cheekbones, and boasted a pencil-thick mustache and goatee that framed his mouth perfectly. The ladies loved him.

Detective Lane greeted a few uniformed officers with a nod, but no smile. They gave him his respect. Detective Patrick Lane was a skilled veteran, having solved some of the most difficult cold cases in his unit. He was a natural police officer—old school, adept and sharp like a number two pencil.

He walked into the crowded motel room, and was instantly annoyed. The room was flooded with police and other detectives—some dusting for fingerprints, and a few snapping pictures of every minute thing. The room was orderly; no disturbance to the area at all, but the bed-sheets and pillows were missing, which detective Lane found odd. He figured the body was in the bathroom, because of the number of officers gathered near the bathroom door. He walked toward the room and saw his partner, Jonathan Mack, standing by the tub, shaking his head.

"What we got here, Mack?" Lane asked.

"Overkill, that's what we got," detective Mack replied, not bothering to turn to greet his partner. He kept his gaze on Sky's twisted body.

Lane approached the body that was still contorted in the bath tub and shook his head.

"Jesus, what they do… shoot her with a fuckin' cannon?" Lane asked.

"From the big holes in this poor girl, I say it was a Desert Eagle," Mack declared. "It almost tore her in half."

Detective Lane crouched down to get closer to the body. He had a keen eye for spotting the unusual at a crime scene. "Damn, she was young and pretty, too."

"What a waste huh," Mack added.

Detective Lane continued to stare at the body. She had gunshot wounds to her head, face, breasts, stomach and vagina. It was a gruesome murder.

"The maid found her," Mack clued-up his partner. "She's freaked out right now,"

"Whoever did this is a heartless muthafucka," said Lane. "Do we have any I.D on this girl?"

212

"Yeah." Mack nodded. "Her name is Sky Madison, and she just came home a week ago. I found her State Prison I.D on the dresser. We ran her name through the system; she did four years at Bedford Hills for drugs. Apparently she made parole, came here to be with someone, and I guess it didn't really work out. But she's quite away from her home. She's from the Bronx."

"Home on parole for a week, and now we find her dead in upstate New York," detective Lane uttered to himself.

"Yeah, still trying to wrap my finger around it."

"Where are her clothes?" Lane asked.

"We didn't find any. Only thing in the room was her I.D," Mack told him.

Detective Lane stood up from observing the body. It was odd—too odd. Why would her killer shoot her dead, take her clothes and leave her I.D, Lane wondered?

"Was she an informant?" Lane asked.

"We don't know yet. I got James looking into everything right now. We definitely need to know more about this girl," Mack told him.

Detective Lane had a theory. It was the only one that made sense to him. The overkill and the leaving her I.D so she could be identified; It was probably a message to someone.

He looked around the bathroom and nothing seemed out of place, no trinkets, essentials, or anything. In the other room, however, there were common items missing. Detective Lane turned and walked into the other room, with Mack following behind him. Lane peered around the room, trying to take everything in. He stared at the bed with the sheets and pillows missing.

"This killer is smart," he said.

"What you mean?" Detective Mack asked.

"He took the sheets and pillows knowing we would search for any DNA or evidence. They had sex, meaning stains, fluids and semen. I'm thinking that afterward, he made her go take a shower and killed her there. No tussle, just shoot and kill the victim while the shower's running. Probably thinking the running water would clean off any traces of himself from the body. He took her clothes thinking we might find traces of his DNA on them, and then left her I.D. It could be for revenge or maybe even a contract killing. But whoever did this, was close to the victim. She knew him, and knew him well."

Mack nodded. "She's only been out a week."

"Which indicates, she knew this asshole prior to her going in," Lane added.

"Ex-boyfriend?" Mack asked, lifting an eyebrow.

"Almost always is," Lane declared. "Or some asshole pen pal she met while locked up."

"I want this asshole," Mack said.

"I do too. We'll talk to her parole officer, and visit the prison. We need to find out what we can about this Sky Madison. I want to know all of her known associates, inside and outside the prison. I need her letters, her visitation lists, her prison phone records, the works. We get into her circle, know her world, and we'll find her killer"

Detective Mack nodded.

The two detectives exited the crime scene. Detective Lane stood by his vehicle looking stoic. He had the grisly scene running through his head. The image of that young girl's mutilated body was embedded into his mind. He had seen and investigated dozens of murders, but this one was up there as one of his most gruesome. That caliber of the gun used on her petite body, had turned her into a piece of human Swiss cheese. There was something about this case that troubled Lane. He couldn't place his finger on it, but he was determined to work it until he found the answers he was looking for. He was close to retirement and wanted to end his career with a bang. This one, was going to be one for the record books. And he felt like he was up to the task. .

"You hungry?" detective Mack asked his partner.

Lane's thoughts had been interrupted. He turned to look at his partner. "You buying?"

"Of course."

"Then I'm eating," Detective Lane replied.

The two got into their cars and headed for the nearest diner, where they could sit, eat, and go over the case they had just picked up.

\*\*\*\*\*

"New York, New York, big city of dreams, and everything in New York ain't always what is seems. You might get fooled if you come from out of town…" Eric playfully hummed in Tameka's ear, while holding her close to him, as they leaned against the iron railing and peered at the city skyline from Brooklyn Bridge Park.

She laughed. "Everything ain't always what it seems, huh."

"Sometimes," Eric replied with a smile.

"So are you more than meets the eye?" she asked lightheartedly. "Are you everything that you seem to be?"

Eric chuckled. "I'm all me, nothing new, nothing used. What you see, is what you get."

"Um huh. So, what am I getting from you?"

"All this thug loving," Eric said with a smile.

"You so stupid," Tameka told him.

It was a blissful moment for the couple. For a moment, their world was serene, and they seemed to be at a different place. Tameka was nestled in Eric's arms beneath the crown of stars gleaming in the dark sky, with the New York skyline illuminated across the waters of the East River. It felt like the perfect evening. They had toured downtown Brooklyn, had a few drinks in a popular Brooklyn lounge, and now Eric was walking, laughing and snuggling with his sweetheart, in the 85-acre park on Brooklyn's East River Shoreline.

"This is beautiful," Tameka said, gazing at the long spread of downtown Manhattan. The skyline was lit up like a Christmas tree.

"It is," Eric said, gently squeezing Tameka in his arms. "But this ain't even as beautiful as you."

Tameka smiled and blushed.

She was thankful that Eric hadn't brought up Caleb or the robbery all evening. She needed a timeout from the crazy idea, and Eric had showed her a wonderful time on an expensive dime. They continued to gaze at the picturesque view; it was a moment ruined only by the fact that Tameka could feel the butt of Eric's concealed pistol poking against her.

"Why did you bring that thing with you?" she asked.

"I'm just cautious, baby. You know I have enemies out there," Eric replied.

"But here?"

"I'd rather be safe than sorry."

Tameka sighed. Eric was a good lover, a great man, but that gangster side of him truly worried her. She wondered would Eric keep his word and not kill Caleb when the plot went down. She also thought about Bridgette's warning that Eric could leave two bodies in Caleb's apartment, and not just one. Could she trust him, she wondered? The thought of Eric breaking his promise concerned her.

"I just wanna do right by you and protect you, baby....that's all," Eric declared.

"Protect me from what? I can handle myself, Eric."

# Boyfriend # 2

"I know you can. But until we do this shit, and you and me are far away from this city, I gotta make sure that I ain't caught slippin. But I do promise you this, you ain't gotta never worry about me and guns again once we outta here. We gonna live and be in paradise. We gonna have a family, and live like a king and queen from this money we get."

It was a good plan, Tameka thought. It just wasn't a good plan for *her*. She wished Eric the best, and she hoped that he was really able to leave and find some peace in this world. Could he change, she wondered? Could he separate himself from being that dangerous Brooklyn thug into being some sort of decent, hard-working, and lawful human being? She wanted to believe in him. But more than anything, he needed to believe in himself, she thought. He needed to believe that he could change, and that he could be a good person.

Eric began to sway Tameka in his arms. He was too calm, she thought. It made her wonder if he was bi-polar. He was so easy going and soft spoken one minute, and then crazy and foaming at the mouth the next.

"This is what it's about, Tameka," Eric said in his raspy voice. "Look at that city! There's so much fuckin' money on that island right there, it ain't funny. And I'm just tryin' to break myself off wit' a good chunk of what them suited crooks be getting. They got Wall Street and the Stock Market, and I got my pistol and some birds. They on that side of the bridge doing them, and I'm on this side surviving. But you know what's the difference between them and us? Shit, I'm just as smart as any educated white boy, you feel me? I'm supposed to feel inadequate cuz where I'm from? I love Brooklyn, ride or die out here for the longest. Shit, I can cross that bridge and maintain in their world too. I bet you didn't know that. But I guarantee you, none of them muthafuckas can survive in mines."

Tameka listened. He was smart. There were times when she

217

would listen to him speak and almost forget about what he was about. Sometimes he would even use words that were above and beyond what she thought him capable of, and then he would slip back into his bad boy persona. It made her wonder about him sometimes. Was he purposely dumbing himself down in order to maintain a certain image? But right here, right now, he was really in his moment. He was going in on the rich, and his voice had real animosity in it. He sounded as if the world owed him something.

"Where are you going with this, Eric?" she asked softly.

"Nowhere, baby. I'm just ranting, that's all. But I tell you this, fuck that squirrel trying to get a nut theory. I want the whole fuckin' tree, grow my own shit," he told her.

"Damn," Tameka uttered. It was a deep statement. Again, it made her wonder if there was more to him than met the eye. There was something he was hiding within himself, and he wasn't sharing it with anyone.

"So, when is the next time you gonna link up wit' ya millionaire playboy friend?" Eric asked.

The question threw Tameka for a loop. It still felt strange to have Eric bring up boyfriend number two, especially while they were hugged up. It sent a chill through her body.

"This weekend," she reluctantly replied.

"And he's taking you where?"

Tameka sighed. "Why you wanna know?"

"Just entertain me, Tameka."

"Martha's Vineyard, okay?" she said matter-of-factly.

Eric grinned. "Y'all two love birds have fun then. You gonna fuck him there?"

The question definitely made Tameka feel uncomfortable. She pulled away from Eric's embrace, spun on her heels and faced him.

"What is wrong with you? How you gonna come at me like

that?"

"I was just asking a question, that's all."

"Well, you don't ask me those fuckin' kinds of questions. I feel sick just by you knowing about him, and with me going through this shit with you, and then you go and say some dumb shit like that. What is wrong with you?"

"You know I truly love you, Tameka. It's just jealousy, that's all," Eric told her. "I go crazy thinking about you being with that nigga."

"Well, stop it! The only reason I'm still seeing him, is because of this ridiculous scheme you have me involved in! I'm doing this, so that you can get your money and pay off the people who want to kill you! Did you forget that? Do you want me to stop seeing him and step away?"

"Nah, ain't no need to do that, baby. I'm sorry. I just had that quick, vulnerable moment."

Tameka continued to glare at Eric. It was that bi-polar in him again, she thought.

Eric tried to reach for her again, but Tameka took a step back and scowled.

"Just take me home, Eric," she said softly.

"Really?"

"Yes. Really!"

Tameka began walking back to the Escalade. Eric stared at her. He knew she was upset. But kept quiet and followed behind Tameka., as she stormed to the SUV, climbed inside and slammed the door.

Eric climbed behind the wheel. "You know I love you, and didn't mean any harm by what I said. I hope you ain't changing your mind now."

Tameka didn't respond. She allowed her silence to speak volumes.

"Tameka," Eric called to her softly.

"You don't have to worry about me," Tameka snapped. " I'm gonna do my part. You just make sure to keep your promise and make sure nothing happens to Caleb during the process."

"I ain't gonna touch that nigga, Tameka. Gonna scare that nigga a little, but ain't gonna harm a hair on Richie Rich's head. You have my word on that," Eric said with a sly smile.

"As long as we have that understanding," Tameka said, lifting an eyebrow. She was growing more tired of Eric's shit by the day.

Eric started the vehicle, and the two drove off in silence.

# Chapter Twenty Two

Tameka walked around Caleb's Victorian style home on Martha's Vineyard, taking in the ocean's sights, sounds, and smells. She loved the water, and she loved hitting the beach in Jersey whenever she got the opportunity to do so. But this was the first time she had ever been to a real island, especially one out in the middle of the Atlantic, and the sights, and sounds, and smells were all new to her.

Caleb's Victorian style home was a cross between an authentic period home, and a turn of the century lighthouse. It had a captain's crow, a light tower, and even a turn of the century Dutch-style windmill, that made it one of the island's most distinctive and unique properties. It's walking distance to The Inkwell, one of the Vineyard's most famous beaches, also served to make it one of the more expensive residences on the island. The fact that the home was over six thousand square feet didn't hurt either.

Tameka made her way around the house to the rear, where she spotted Caleb lowering the last jet ski into the water. The Wave Runners were mounted on a lift that raised and lowered them in and out of the water for storage or use. It also served as a security feature, as it kept them locked away when not in use.

"Well, what do you think?" Caleb asked, peering up at her.

"I've never been on one before," Tameka said nervously. "I've always wanted to ride one."

"It's like riding a bike," Caleb said with a smile. "It's easy to get the hang of it."

Unconvinced, Tameka folded her arms and shifted her weight to one side. "Yeah, accept when you fall off, you drown?"

"Drown? How can you drown when you know how to swim?"

"Swimming in the pool, or the lake, or wading through water at a beach is different from swimming in the ocean."

"You want to ride on the back of mine?" Caleb asked.

"Not in your life, buster!" Tameka told him. She pulled her bikini from between her butt cheeks, and climbed down onto the jet ski. Caleb gave her a push.

"Remember what I told you!" Caleb told her.

Tameka fired up her jet ski, and took off. She sped through the waters like a speed demon, bouncing over the waves, and crashing back down. The smile on her face was one of pure joy.

Caleb climbed onto his jet ski, backed out, and then hit the throttle. He wanted to catch up to her, but didn't want to get too close. He wanted to give her a wide berth, and freedom to ride and get the hang of the jet ski, before taking a chance and pulling up along side her.

Tameka shouted and screamed out of pure joy. The jet ski ride was what she needed more than anything else. She needed to take her mind off of her conversation with Eric. She needed the freedom of the ocean in order to think. The smell of the waters somehow cleansed a person's insides, she thought. The stinging feel of the salt water hitting her skin was awakening. The wide open ocean vistas gave her a sense of clarity that she hadn't had in a long time. For the last year, she had been trying to decide between Eric, and Caleb. She had been trying to decide who was her future, and who was her past. And it was all so clear to her now. She could perhaps salvage her relationship with Eric, while not damaging her relationship with Caleb. Eric had promised her that she wouldn't be involved. That he would tie her up as well, and that way Caleb wouldn't know that she had set him up. And once it was done, Eric would be safe from Peon, and Caleb would be hers.

Tameka thought about the money in the safe, wondering how much it contained. How bad would it hurt Caleb once Eric took it, was on her mind. She was sure that it wouldn't, because what stockbroker kept their real money inside of a safe in their apartment? No, Caleb had more money; lots more money, she was sure of it. And even if he didn't, he could take her savings and reinvest it. She could take out a loan on her home, and give that to him to reinvest as well. She would help her man get back on his feet if necessary, but she doubted that it would come to that. No, she and Caleb would be fine. They all would.

Caleb spied Tameka in the distance. She was heading flat out south into the ocean. Where was she going, he wondered? Rhode Island? Maryland? D.C.? She was moving away from the island, and away from the reefs and barriers that broke the waves near the island. If she thought the waves were big near the island, she hadn't experience anything yet, he thought. Going full speed in the open ocean was a recipe for disaster. He needed to get her attention and have her turn back.

Tameka's thoughts had her fully distracted. She didn't realize that she had ventured that far away from the island, but she did notice that the waves were getting bigger and that the jet ski was launching itself higher and higher off the surface of the water, and crashing back down jarringly. And then she hit an incredibly big wave.

The monster sized wave sent Tameka and the jet ski soaring twelve feet into the air, before they both came crashing back down onto the surface of the water. The impact sent Tameka flying off of the jet ski and into the frigid waters of the North Atlantic. Her impact against the hard surface of the water revealed that she had not fastened on her life jacket according to the instructions. The buckles and snaps gave way upon impact, separating the jacket from her. And now, her worst nightmare had come true. She was in the middle of the ocean, with enormous waves crashing over her, without a floatation device. She struggled and screamed, and fought for dear life to stay afloat and breathe.

"Oh, fuck!" Caleb shouted. He twisted the throttle all the way on his jet ski, racing to the point of impact. He could see her jet ski bobbing up and down in the middle of the vast ocean, but could not see her because of the waves. He prayed silently that he would catch a break, and then he did. He spotted her arm briefly breaking the surface of the water, before going back under. He willed his jet ski to fly.

Caleb reached the spot where Tameka's arm broke the surface, unsnapped his life jacket, and dove into the cold waters of the North Atlantic. Beneath the surface of the water, he spun, peering around, until he spotted her colorful bikini ten yards away. He swam to the surface of the ocean, drew in a deep breath, and then went back under and swam for her. He swam as fast as he could, as fast as his high school swim instructor had taught him too. He knew that he was about to possibly break some kind of record that could never be verified, but if he reached her in time, and saved her, *that* would be better than ten thousand gold medals.

Caleb grabbed Tameka's arm, pulled her to him, and then swam for the surface despite her panicking and swinging wildly. The two of them broke the surface of the water, where they gasped for air. A waved washed over them just as they had finished inhaling of lung full of sweet oxygen, but it didn't matter. He had her in his arms, and he was not going to let her go. Caleb flipped Tameka around on her back and wrapped his arms around her, to keep her from struggling. He peered around the ocean, searching for his waver runner. He found it twenty yards away.

The swim to the wave runner was a struggle. Although he was extremely fit, swimming in the open ocean, battling current and waves, while pulling another individual in addition to one's own weight, was extremely fatiguing, Caleb could feel every movement, every stroke, deep within his muscles. It was bone aching fatigue, Nevertheless, he made it to his jet ski, boosted Tameka up until she managed to pull herself on board, and then climbed on board himself.

"Can you hold on?" he asked.

Tameka nodded, and coughed. Her lungs felt as though they were on fire.

Caleb started his jet ski, and set a course toward Martha's Vineyard.

*****

Tameka woke to find herself lying in a comfortable bed. She peered around the room, and quickly realized that she was back at Caleb's Victorian home on the island. She remembered all that happened that morning, including Caleb pulling her from the sea. She remembered arriving back at the Vineyard, and being examined by a physician, and then remembered being given a nice warm bath by a pair of Dominican housekeepers. She peered around the room in search of a clock, trying to gauge the hour, so that she could see how long she had been sleeping. She knew that she had been out for a while, as the sun was no longer shining, and her body itself told her that the hour was late.

Tameka threw off her covers and swung her legs out of bed. Every muscle in her body was sore. She felt pain in places she hadn't felt pain in, since she was playing volley ball back in her high school days. Muscles that she forgot she had, were now reminding her of their presence. And on the inside, she still felt bloated, and could taste the sea water in her mouth, and smell the ocean in her nose. Even her red eye gave testimony to the traumatic events of the morning.

Tameka rose, almost tumbling and having to catch her balance, and then made her way across the bedroom, and then down the hall. She found herself in the kitchen, where the thought of a warm cup of coffee danced in her head. But she felt too tired to expend the effort to make any. Her thoughts then turned toward her host.

Where was Caleb, Tameka wondered? She walked through the kitchen into the living room, and then searched the other bedrooms. He was nowhere to be found. She turned her attention toward the back porch. He was seated on a wrought iron chair, staring out at the ocean. A glass of gin and juice was sitting on the wrought iron table next to him.

Tameka stepped out onto the porch, closing the sliding door behind her. The noise from the door sliding close announced her presence.

"You're awake?" Caleb said, without turning to face her.

Tameka strolled up behind him, placed her hands on his shoulders, and stared out at the ocean. The waves were crashing against the beach, and the seagulls were perch on the beams that supported the old wooden peers that jutted out into the water. The moon hung low in the sky, casting it's beams over the ocean toward them.

"I'm up," Tameka said softly.

"How you feeling?"

"Tired."

Caleb patted her hand nestled on his shoulder. "Me too."

"I don't know what happened," Tameka told him. "Everything was so wonderful, and then just like that, it all went so wrong."

Caleb lifted her hand from his shoulder and kissed it gently. "You're safe now, and that's all that matters."

"Thanks to you," Tameka said softly.

"Don't mention it."

"I can't help but mention it. You saved my life. You dove into the ocean, and you pulled me from the waters."

"What else was I going to do?"

"You mean, what else you *could* have done? Well, you *could* gone for help and left me to drown. You *could* have taken off your life jacket and threw it to me. You *could* have just left."

"I couldn't have done any of those things."

Tameka leaned forward and gently kissed Caleb on the top of his head. "You saved my life. You son of a bitch."

Caleb quickly turned toward her. Tameka slapped him.

"What the hell was that about?" Caleb asked, rubbing his cheek.

"How dare you," Tameka said, breaking down into tears. "How dare you..."

Caleb wrapped his arms around her and pulled her close. "It's okay. It's okay."

"It's *not* okay."

"You wanted to drown?"

"No. But I didn't need you to jump into the water and play hero. I didn't need you to risk your life in order to save mine!"

"What man wouldn't?"

"A *lot* of men wouldn't? Don't you understand that? Everyone is not like you! Some people take the easy way out. Some people take the chicken shit route, like me..."

Caleb leaned back and stared at her. A look of confusion covered his face. "What are you talking about, Tameka?"

"I'm talking about *me*," Tameka said crying heavily. "I did something stupid. Something really, really stupid."

# Boyfriend # 2

"What?"

Tameka shook her head.

"You can tell me," Caleb told her. "Whatever it is, we can work through it. No matter what it is, I promise you, we'll get through it... together."

It made Tameka cry even harder.

"I... I haven't done it yet," Tameka said, shaking her head.

"Well, if you haven't done it yet, then what's the problem?"

"The problem is that I even gave it a second thought. The problem is, that I even entertained the idea."

"What?"

"I have something that I have to tell you."

"I'm listening."

# Chapter Twenty Three

*Round of applause, baby make that ass clap*
*Drop it to the floor, make that ass clap*
*Let me see you, bust it, bust it, bust it, bust it, bust it*
*Baby drop it to the floor and bust it…*

Waka Flocka's raunchy lyrics blared throughout the dimly lit Brooklyn strip club. The place was flooded with activity—thick strippers danced butt naked on the stage, while trying to bust it wide open like the lyrics from the song encouraged them to do. The strippers' trimmed pussies and succulent ass cheeks were in full view for the male, and small contingent of female, patrons in the place. A big booty and curvaceous ho clung to the stripper pole and showed off her acrobatic skills for the crowd. She swung around the pole with her legs spread, and contorted her thick physique around the pole like she was a pretzel. Bottles were popping in VIP, and the ladies were looking marvelous in their stilettos and scanty attire, while the atmosphere was festive like the West Indian Day parade.

Eric clutched a huge wad of bills, mostly singles that totaled $500. He wore a maniacal smile on his face as he gawked at the stripper. Smoke, a thick, dark skinned beauty with auburn dreads and a luscious figure, stood butt naked before him in some red pumps. She had Eric's undivided attention, as she moved around the stage seductively, putting on one hell of a show for the audience.

"Shit girl! I'm lovin' you right now," Eric shouted out.

He was flanked by Sean, and the two of them were showing out in the club. They sat drinking, flirting, and enjoying the fruits of their hard labor. For once, the streets weren't on their minds. It was all about the ladies tonight. They came with a pocket full of money, and a hunger to fulfill the flesh. Eric had a wad of bills in one hand, and a huge bottle of Ciroc Peach in the other. He took a swig from the Ciroc and laughed out loud, hugging his boy Sean closely.

"This is what it's about, my nigga...money and bitches!" Eric declared.

Sean laughed.

Smoke was showing out, she was on her back with her legs spread in the air forming a V, a move which put her pussy within Eric's reach. Her body was glistering with sweat and her attitude was all about selling sex. The crowd of males gathered by the stage was a clear indication that she was on point from head to toe— genuine eye candy—and drawing heated attention from everyone. Eric tossed all five hundred dollars up in the air, making it rain down on Smoke. The dollars sprinkled down on Smoke like a rainfall. It was a baller's exploit—showing everyone around him that he had money to blow.

Smoke smiled.

The music continued to blare, and the money and drinks continued to flow. It was party time. He wasn't thinking about Peon, Tameka, or any of his troubles on the streets. His mind was clearly on Smoke, and he was ready to take her into one of the back rooms and have a VIP session with her. The more he watched Smoke dance on stage, the harder his dick grew in his jeans.

"Yo, I'm ready to fuck that bitch, Sean," Eric said.

Sean laughed. "I thought you were in love, my nigga."

# Boyfriend # 2

"And? I can have my fun too, right, my nigga?"

"You crazy wit' it E. But I don't blame you, do ya thang my dude."

Eric tossed more money at Smoke, inundating her with dollar bills.

"But ya in a good mood tonight. What's up wit' you?" asked Sean.

"My nigga, I'm workin' on something big," Eric replied.

"Something big like what?" Sean wanted to know.

"I can't talk about it right now, but believe me, we gonna get paid and shit," Eric told him, holding his cards close.

"You a wild boy, E," Sean stated.

"Nigga's ain't fuckin' wit' me."

Eric signaled for Smoke to come closer. He had another wad of bills clutched in his hand. He already blew through fifteen hundred dollars on strippers and drinks. All eyes were on him and Sean—they were the ballers in the spot. The strippers were craving for the men's attention—but Smoke alone held Eric's interest.

Smoke moved closer to Eric.

"Hey baby, what you lookin' for?" she asked.

"VIP wit' you luv…let's go," Eric said to her.

Smoke smiled. She was ready for it. She knew it was about to be her payday. Eric took the luscious, big booty, chocolate covered stripper by her hand and guided her off the stage. The two of them walked toward the narrowed hallway where the VIP rooms were located. Once inside, Eric pulled out another wad of bills and tossed Smoke two-hundred dollars.

"Damn baby, why you spoiling me?" Smoke said with a smile. "What's ya name anyway, cutie?"

"Bitch, I ain't paying you to talk…just shut the fuck up and bend that phat ass over," Eric said, unbuttoning his jeans.

"A'ight…" Smoke said with a nod. She was already naked.

Eric came out of his jeans, ripped open a condom, rolled it back on his thick dick, and then curved Smoke over a tall chair, spreading her legs. He gripped her swelled, rounded hips and penetrated her soaked walls—dipping his dick into her smooth, chocolate flesh. Her body responded with moans and squirming. Eric quickly became rough with her, as he fucked her from the back, smacking her ass and cupping her tits. He pulled her dreads like they were reins around a horse; he also pulled her ass cheeks apart and drove into her sweet, sex hole like a drill into a wall. Smoke cried out from feeling her inner walls pierced with such power from behind. She started to moan louder, sending erotic vibrations around the room—indicating the sexual gratification she was experiencing.

"Ooooh shit, nigga…fuck me! Damn, just like that…shit, just like that. Damn-it," Smoke cried out.

Eric grunted. He felt Smoke's pussy constricting around his pounding manhood, like a snake squeezing life from its prey.

Dripping with excitement, Smoke felt her body convulse as Eric's dick invaded her pussy walls. He buried himself inside of her, using his muscles to flex his dick. She grabbed the chair tightly, trying to stabilize herself, after feeling her knees wobble.

"Oh shit!" Smoke continued to scream. "Fuck me, nigga! Yes. Got-damn-it!"

Within moments, she came and so did Eric.

Eric collected himself quickly. He got dressed, left Smoke a fifty dollar tip, and exited the VIP room feeling satisfied. He had needed that. Smoke was left in the room pulling herself together. She was $250 richer, and her pussy was still throbbing from the intense fuck.

When Eric stepped back into the dimmed and loud club, he noticed Sean had company.

"Fuck," Eric uttered.

Peon and his goons were standing with Sean, and it didn't

look pretty. Eric had left his gun in the truck, and the two were unarmed and feeling like sitting ducks. Eric walked over to the bar, which is where the action was. Peon turned and saw him coming. The look he gave Eric was poisonous.

"What's going on, Peon?" Eric asked coolly.

"You muthafucka!" Peon exclaimed. "You got the audacity to show your face in this spot! You crazy nigga?"

"I don't know what ya talking about, Peon," Eric said calmly.

"Let's go for a walk then," Peon said gruffly. He wasn't asking.

Eric and Sean were roughly escorted toward the back of the club and into a private back room. It was a storage room for alcohol, and it was filled with boxes and other items. It was concrete, barren, and there was a frightening indication that the room wasn't just used for storage either. The room was eerily quiet, like it was virtually sound proof.

Sean and Eric were defenseless. Four armed goons were glaring at them. Sean looked clueless. He looked to Eric for answers. But Eric remained quiet.

"Is this about the money, Peon? You gave me a month to pay it up," said Eric.

"You fuckin' wit' me, nigga!" Peon screamed. He lifted the . 9mm in his hand, grabbed Eric sharply by his shirt, and pushed the gun into his temple. But Eric didn't flinch. He glared back.

"What the fuck is this about?"

"They found my little cousin dead…shot up in the bathroom in some upstate motel. And the last I heard, you was the last person that seen her," Peon explained through clenched teeth.

Sean looked at Eric. The expression on his face clearly showed that he didn't know anything about it. It was news to him.

"Peon, you think I would be stupid enough to kill your

cousin…fuck is wrong wit' you? I loved that bitch. And besides, I already owe you, so why put myself more in trouble wit' you," Eric told him.

"I don't know…but you're playing games with me, muthafucka, and I ain't in the mood for games," Peon shot back. "But I swear, Eric, if I find out that you had anything to do with Sky's death, I'ma kill you so hard, that I'm gonna make your mamma bleed too."

"Like I said, I don't know shit about her death," Eric lied convincingly. His eyes were locked into Peon's.

Peon lowered the gun from Eric's temple, but he and Sean weren't out the boiling pot yet. The goons still had them surrounded. The door to the storage room was locked. They were vulnerable.

"I'll tell you what, your debt to me is a million now," Peon said. "And I want all cash, by next week."

"What? You crazy, Peon!" Eric protested.

"I might just be…but that should put a little more incentive into your hustle. You're a sneaky muthafucka, Eric…and I don't' like you. You were just always good business," Peon told him.

"You know what; I'll get you your money, don't even worry about it."

"You better…because by this time next week, someone gonna have some serious health issues," Peon declared.

He nodded toward his thugs and they began to exit the storage room. Peon followed behind his men. But he turned to Eric with an afterthought.

"Oh, and get the fuck out my club. I don't wanna see y'all ugly faces in this spot ever again….because if I do, y'all ain't gonna leave this bitch alive."

Peon walked out.

Sean looked at his friend. "Nigga, we need to fuckin' talk."

When the two climbed into Sean's truck, Sean turned to his

friend.

"What's goin' on? Did you do it?"

"Sean, listen…"

"Eric, don't bullshit me!" Sean shouted. "I'm in this shit wit' you no matter what, you my nigga, but don't fuckin' bullshit me."

Eric nodded.

"Yeah, I bodied that bitch," he admitted.

"Nigga, is you crazy? Why?"

"Because, she came home on parole too early and was gonna compromise things for me with Tameka and this plan I got goin' on," Eric explained. "You know how Sky was, she good peoples, but she can be a fuckin' leach sometimes. She finds out about this next bitch, and she gets emotional and starts to act the fuck up. She can get stupid sometimes, my nigga…she don't think before she reacts sometimes."

"But that's Peon's cousin, nigga….you already know how he feels about his family."

"Fuck Peon, my nigga. He bleeds just like everybody else. You think I'm scared of that muthafucka?" Eric asked.

"It ain't about being scared, E…it's about being smart," Sean replied.

"And I am smart. I'm workin' on something big…"

"And if it's so big, why you not letting me on it? Huh, my nigga? You don't trust me anymore?"

"It ain't like that, Sean."

"Then what's it like, E…you tell me? We go way back, and you keepin' shit a secret from me? If I'm gonna follow you into hell, then I wanna know what I'm gettin' into wit' you," Sean told him.

"I feel you, my dude. Just drive me somewhere and I tell you what's up," said Eric.

Sean started the truck and drove away.

Sean drove for a moment, pulling near an alleyway in an industrialize location that Eric directed had him drive to. It was reaching morning, but the sky was still dark and the area was still and quiet like a cemetery.

Sean peered around the deserted area. "What business do you have to take care out here?"

"Something quick," Eric said, stepping out of the truck. "Just wait for me."

Sean nodded.

Eric shut the passenger door, walked toward the driver's side. Sean was focused on the radio.

"I'm sorry, my dude," Eric said softly.

Sean looked up to see Eric's .9mm pointed at him. And before there was any reaction, Eric fired.

*Boom! Boom! Boom! Boom!*

The rounds crashed into Sean's skull, splattering his blood and brain matter all over the front seat. Sean slumped against the steering wheel of his truck with four holes in his head.

"I came too far, Sean…you a good dude, but I can't have any loose ends," Eric said softly.

He walked away, and tossed the gun into a sewer a few blocks away. Eric was moving on, and after the robbery, he was planning on leaving the city.

*****

Tameka sat quietly at her dining room table; her mind busy contemplating the events of the past, as well as the events to come. She took a sip of red wine and looked at Eric. who was seated opposite of her across the dressy table. Two, 12 inch taper candles were lit and allowed for some easy lighting in the room.

# Boyfriend # 2

Kenny G was playing, and the atmosphere had a romantic vibe to it. Tameka had prepared a lovely meal for her man—fried catfish, macaroni, biscuits, collard greens; it was Eric's favorite, a meal fit for her king. She could definitely burn in the kitchen, and Eric loved it.

The two sat and conversed easily for several moments, mostly going over the robbery plan that Eric had put together. He knew security was tight in the building, and Tameka systematically gave him the layout to the whole place—the locations of certain cameras, the on-duty security personal, entrance and exits to the towering building, and most important, the location of the safe. Eric was satisfied with receiving the exact details of everything and was confident that the whole thing would be executed the way he had planned it. He wanted to be in and out, no problems—but simply be a few million dollars richer afterward. And if he had to pistol whip Caleb and take his actions a step further to get what he wanted, he had no problem in doing so.

Tameka's mind seemed to be somewhere else as she dined with Eric.

"You look good, baby," Eric complimented. His eyes were fixated on her welcoming attire. She was wearing a gold colored blouse that came off the shoulder and a rust colored silk skirt that hugged her nicely shaped hips, thighs and phat ass. She crossed her smooth legs underneath the dining room table, revealing a pair of matching high-heels. Tameka's eyes were dramatic and smoky, while her lips were a seductive red.

"Thank you," Tameka replied.

Eric was adamant in going over every inch of Caleb's penthouse suite, knowing about the alarm system, bodyguards and whatnot. The coldness in Eric's heart had temporarily given way while he was around Tameka, and they enjoyed a tasty and wonderful meal together. He didn't think about any of the


237

murders he'd committed in the past month—including his boy Sean. He never gave his vicious actions a second thought. For him, it was about survival and money.

"So we set for everything right?" Eric asked. "There ain't gonna be any surprises once we set this shit into motion?"

"I already told you everything I know about his place, Eric. He trusts me a lot…there's no secret with Caleb," said Tameka.

Eric smiled. "That's what I'm talking about."

The two continued dining.

"How you feel about it?" Eric asked.

"How you think I feel? I just wanna get paid," she replied.

"That's what I'm talking about."

As Eric tore into his fried catfish, Tameka stood up from her seat and excused herself for a moment. "I'll be right back."

She disappeared into the bedroom and came back out with some important papers clutched in her hand. She dropped them in front of Eric as he ate.

"Babe, what the fuck is this?" he asked.

"I need for you to sign them," she asked of him.

"Sign what?"

Eric peered at the papers and was taken aback when he saw that they were life insurance papers. He glared up at Tameka and exclaimed, "Yo what the fuck…I ain't signing this shit."

"Yes, you need two…because one, I'm not going through with the plan unless you do. I need some insurance in my life, and two… I'm pregnant."

"Pregnant?"

She nodded.

"And how I know it's mine. Remember, you were fuckin' both of us," Eric said frankly,

Tameka sighed heavily.

"First off, you were the only nigga that I didn't use protection with, and with Caleb, he always strapped up, and second, he can't have any kids."

"What you mean…?"

"He got a vasectomy a few years ago. Caleb is not too fond on having kids," Tameka explained.

"So you sayin I might be having a son."

"Or a daughter," she interjected.

"And I'm supposed to trust you. He can be telling you anything."

"If you love me like you say you do, then yes. What if something happens to you, I need some insurance in my life, Eric…for our baby," Tameka was adamant.

She stood over Eric with the pen in her hand and demanded that he sign it or she was going to walk away from everything. The paper looked truly legit. Eric was reluctant, but he knew Tameka was serious about it. He took the pen and wrote down his John Hancock across the dotted line. Tameka was pleased.

"Tameka, I swear, if this is some kind of scan you're pulling on me, remember where I'm from and what I'm capable of doing," Eric warned through clenched teeth.

"It's no scam, baby…only just my insurance," she replied coolly.

"A'ight, then let's get this money from this nigga and do us."

# Boyfriend # 2

.

.

# Chapter Twenty Four

Eric entered the building first, and made his way to the elevator and up to the ninth floor. He made sure that he wore his fitted Yankee cap low, along with a hoodie that he wore pulled over it, and a pair of sunglasses to further disguise his appearance. Tameka had scouted the camera locations days before, and so he knew where each and every camera in the building was, where it was aimed, and how to avoid it. He knew how low to keep his head tilted to avoid a good camera angle, and he knew when they panned the room, and at exactly what time the security guard watching the cameras came out of the control room and went down the hall for a restroom break. The entire operation had been planned to precision.

Tameka entered the building ten minutes later, and climbed on board the elevator that would take her to the penthouse floor. Her hands were shaking visibly, and she tried desperately to control her nerves. She fiddled with her long blond wig, adjusting it slightly beneath the hoodie she was wearing, and then pushed her sunglasses up on her nose. She had to make sure that she couldn't be identified as well. Finally, she pressed the button to take her to the penthouse floor, thinking only about what was about to go down.

The elevator door opened on the 9th floor, and Eric climbed on. Tameka stepped to the side, and pulled her purse close. They were both acting for the camera inside of the elevator, because they both figured that the police would get the recording and play it back. So they had to put on their best acting moves. The elevator door opened on the 10th floor, and nobody was standing there. Tameka gave Eric a quick glance, like she was waiting for him to get off. But he didn't. And once the elevator door closed, he made his move.

Eric pulled out his 9mm Glock, grabbed Tameka by her hair, and slammed her against the elevator door. Tameka let out a scream, before growing quiet once Eric placed his weapon against her lips. A look of terror seized her face. Part of it was acting, however, a large amount of it was real. She was terrified that it was actually going down, and she was still uncertain as to whether Eric was going to pull the trigger on her.

The elevator door opened, and Eric flung Tameka out of the elevator and slammed her into the door of the penthouse.

"Open the door!" Eric said, through gritted teeth.

Nervously, Tameka pulled out her key, fumbling the entire time. Finally, she managed to get herself together enough to stick the key inside of the door, and unlock it. Eric twisted the door knob, and shoved her inside of the penthouse. Tameka fell inside.

"Bastard!" Tameka shouted. She was genuinely pissed that he had basically thrown her down. She gathered herself up off the floor, and rose. "Asshole!"

"Shut up, bitch!" Eric shouted. "Where's your little boyfriend at?"

Caleb walked from the bedroom to see Eric standing in his living room holding a weapon.

"What's going on, babe?" he asked calmly.

"This *asshole* just threw me on the floor!" Tameka told him, as she pointed in Eric's direction.

Caleb shook his head. "Now, why'd you have to go and do something like that?"

"What?" Eric shouted. "You think this is a game, nigga? You think this is a muthafucking joke?"

"I think you're the joke," Caleb said calmly.

"What?" Eric cocked his pistol. "I'll blow you're fucking face off, bitch ass nigga! Where's the safe?"

"The safe is where it's always been," Caleb told him. "It's safe."

"You got 'til three, before I start leaving bodies up in here," Eric said gritting. He was growing more and more pissed off by the second.

"Can you even count to three? Caleb said laughing. "Look, let me save you some trouble, *hood boy*. There's not going to be any robbery, or any heist, or any come up, or however you frame it in the hood. It's not happening. Not today, not tomorrow, not ever. You can't tell the weight of a gun when it's empty?"

Eric pulled back the slide on his Glock, and sure enough, there were no bullets inside. He turned toward Tameka.

Tameka smiled, and walked to where Caleb was standing. She kissed him, and then turned toward Eric.

"I heard about your little plot," Caleb continued. "That's why I came up with a little plot of my own."

Eric pointed the gun toward Caleb and squeezed the trigger. He cocked it again, and squeezed the trigger again. He looked toward the front door.

"Don't even think about it," Caleb told him. He pulled out a Glock of his own and pointed it at Eric. "You move, and I'll put a hole in you so big you'll look like a Krispy Kreme. And trust me, hood boy, this one *is* loaded."

Eric shifted his gaze toward Tameka. "What the fuck?"

Tameka shrugged. "I'm sorry."

"Did you really think that she was going to roll with you, hood boy?" Caleb asked with a smile. "Did you really think she was going to give up all of this, for you? If so, you're a lot dumber than you look."

"This how you do me?" Eric asked, shaking his head at

Tameka.

"Apparently so. She handed you an empty gun before you got out the car, didn't she?" Caleb said, and then laughed. "She set you up, so that you would show up here with nothing more than a dick in your hand, didn't she?"

"You're a sorry bitch," Eric said shaking his head.

Tameka smiled.

"This is how it's going to go, hood boy," Caleb told him. "You are going to get shot for breaking into my apartment and trying to rob me. And after I kill you, Tameka is going to file her little insurance claim against you, and she and I will be living it up on your two million dollar life insurance policy, while you'll be pushing up daisies and feeding the worms."

A frown shot across Eric's face. He shifted his gaze toward Tameka again. "That's why you had me sign that policy? That's why? You set me up for *this* nigga? You played me all this time, for this punk ass nigga?"

"You played yourself," Tameka told him.

"Sorry, bitch!" Eric started toward Tameka, but Caleb shook the Glock, reminding him that he was packing. Eric stopped cold and fumed.

"Why would your dumb ass ever sign that policy?" Caleb asked with a smile. "Two million big ones. Life is going to be good."

"You don't look like you need it," Eric told him.

"It's going to help pay for our wedding, and for Tameka's pink Bentley, and for a bigger beach home in the Caymans. Or, we may invest it. Turn that two million into ten. Not sure yet. But I do know one thing. I know that I'm going to spread it all over the bed and fuck her on top of it."

Tameka smiled.

"You don't have the guts to pull that trigger, Wall Street," Eric told him. "It ain't as easy as you think it is."

"I crush people's dreams," Caleb told him. "I take their money. I defraud windows, and old women, pensioners, it doesn't matter. I'll take candy from a fucking baby, if I thought that I could flip it and make a profit. I have many things, but a conscience is not one of them."

"Good for you," Eric said smiling. "But I do think you're forgetting one thing. Ever watch *CSI* or *First 48*?"

Caleb shook his head. "Not my taste. Those are shows for the ghetto set like you."

"Well, you should have caught a few episodes, that way you would have a better understanding of evidence. I didn't break in. There's no damage on the locks. My finger prints aren't anywhere in this place."

"You're wearing gloves, asshole," Caleb told him. "And Tameka is going to damage the outside of the lock before she heads for the elevators. We've already damage them internally, so it'll look like forced entry."

Eric nodded as if he were impressed. He held up his Glock. "And you're going to explain shooting an unarmed man, how? Your bitch took out all my bullets, remember? How you gonna explain that, Wall Street?"

Tameka held out her gloved hand, and one by one, dropped Eric's bullets onto the floor.

"I believe these belong to you?" Caleb asked. They have your fingerprints on them. Of course I'm going to put on some gloves and load them into your gun once I kill you."

Eric nodded and smiled. "Then I guess you *have* thought of everything."

"The best man always wins," Caleb told him. "You shouldn't have bought into that fairy tale shit about the little guy winning sometimes. My kind, will always outsmart, out think, out maneuver, out wit, and supremely fuck over your kind, hood boy."

Caleb turned toward Tameka and kissed her.

Tameka headed for the front door, staring into Eric's eyes as she walked past him. She didn't know how she felt about what she was about to do. But it wasn't her fault, she told herself. She hadn't asked for this shit. Eric had put her into this position, he made her have to chose. And what was she supposed to do? How was she supposed to chose? Was she supposed to chose the hood life? The wifey of a playboy dope man? Who would realistically chose that, when the alternative was the wife of a superstar Wall Street broker? No woman, she told herself. No one!

"Going to call the cops?" Eric asked sarcastically.

"She's leaving, because she can't be here when I pull the trigger," Caleb told him. "She has to be at home, when she gets the phone call informing her that you've been shot. And then she had to play the distraught fiancee, so that she can collect on your policy."

Eric shook his head once again. "Shady, bitch."

Tameka blew Eric a kiss, and then stepped out into the hallway. She closed the door behind her, and peered up at the camera. It was facing the opposite direction. She turned, and scratched up the doorknob with her key, before heading for the elevator. She knew that she had to hurry up and get home, perhaps make a few calls, put on some dinner, and create for herself a verifiable alibi.

The elevator arrived, and Tameka climbed on board. She heard the faint sound of a gunshot, just as the doors closed. Her heart dropped to her knees. Eric was dead. Despite the fact that he had pushed her into making such a drastic choice, she still had deep feelings for him. But in the end, she had a choice to make. And she chose... her.

# Chapter Twenty Five

Tameka grabbed a copy of the New York Times off of the news stand, handed the vendor a couple of dollars, and then headed down the street toward her next stop. She had been rising early the last few days, unable to really get much sleep. Her mind had been restless, her nerves had been bad, and even though she hated to admit it to herself, her conscience had been tugging at her. She couldn't believe what she had been involved in, or what she had been made to do. She thought that she had avoided such entanglements after leaving the hood, and never had she thought for a single millisecond that she would have to make such a deadly decision while working as a white collar ad executive for a Madison Avenue marketing firm. What she was learning was that the higher she climbed socially and economically, the more crooked the people she encountered. At least in the hood you knew what it was, she told herself. But with the people she was around now, they would smile in your face while trying to fuck you, fuck over you, or fuck you off completely. The predators grew more vicious the higher up the ladder she went. And they had the nerves to call people from the hood criminals, she thought.

Tameka made her way down the street toward her second stop. It was morning in Manhattan, and the streets were crowded as usual. She headed into her local Starbucks to order her usual cup of morning Joe, and found a line that was even longer than usual. The line was upsetting, but bearable. Besides, she was

247

early for work anyway, and the line would help kill some time. She would prefer standing amongst the aroma of coffee beans, rather than sitting at an empty desk anyway. Sitting at that desk alone gave her mind time to wonder, time to think, time to reflect, and those were things that she was desperate to avoid. She even found herself taking a hefty amount of Ambien at night, to help her fall fast asleep. Being alone, was something she wanted to avoid at all cost. Alone, was when her mind started to think about what she *did not* want to think about... Eric.

She missed him already. She missed his smiles, she missed his kisses, she missed chilling and smoking a fatty with him. And yeah, she missed making love to him. She missed his head game, and she missed his hood swagger when he walked to the shower after a deep, hot, hard session of passionate love making. She missed their conversation. They had so much in common, as they both grew up in the hood. She had more in common with Eric than with any other man she ever dated, including Caleb. And yet...

Tameka closed her eyes and clinched her teeth. Get in the game, she admonished herself. She had to do, what she had to do, and that was that. There was no turning back now. She made her choice. She had to look out for number one, right? She had to worry about her future, not about Eric, or Peon, or anybody else. It was about her, and about her dreams, and getting what *she* wanted. She deserved to live the good life. She had gone through too much *not* to deserve the good life. She had to put up with too much bullshit, too many sorry ass niggas, too much...

Tameka found her eyes watering up slightly. C'mon, girl, you stronger than that, she told herself. She had come this far. She had her man, she had his trust, and they were deep in this thing together. There was no way he could ever let her go now. They were stuck with one another forever, and that was a good thing. Who better to be stuck to, than a high dollar broker? Okay, she told herself. Calm down, girl. You and Caleb are down like four flat tires, and you got your man. So why are you tripping? Just play your position, bitch, she told herself. Just play your position.

Tameka stepped up to the register, and ordered her Frappuccino with whip cream, and a shot of chocolate. She liked her coffee hot, dark, and sweet. Just like she liked her men. Tameka tossed the clerk a five dollar bill, grabbed her Frappuccino and headed out the door. She was still going to be early, but at least she had her coffee and newspaper to keep her company. She stepped out the door onto the busy streets of Manhattan and peered around.

"You didn't get me one?"

Tameka turned. There was a man standing next to the door, with an open newspaper covering his face. Despite the fact that she couldn't see his face, she instantly recognized his voice and his build.

"Caleb!"

"Shhh!" Caleb said hushing her. "Calm down, and just act normal. We don't know who is watching us. Follow me."

Caleb closed his newspaper and started off, with Tameka following a distance behind.

Tameka couldn't control her emotions. She hadn't seen him since the shooting, and she was happy to see him. Happy to see someone who shared her secret, who she could talk to, who could help her calm her nerves. She was also happy to be able to finally talk to him and ask some of the questions that had been troubling her. *Did Eric say anything else before he killed him? Did he say anything about her? What were his last words? Where did he shoot him? What did the cops say? Are they suspicious?* She needed answers.

Caleb continued down the busy Manhattan street. He wore a long London Fog coat, with a London Fog fedora over his

Armani suit. He looked like a prototypical spy from a bad spy movie. The hat, the overcoat, the newspaper, all brought a bit of comic relief to Tameka as she took in his appearance. For the first time in days, she was able to crack a slight smile.

Caleb turned down an alley, and Tameka followed. She found him standing at the end of the alley behind a large dumpster.

"I miss you!" Tameka declared, practically leaping into his arms.

"I missed you too, baby!" Caleb said, kissing her all over her face passionately. "We don't have much time."

"What's the matter?" Tameka asked.

"I need you to listen and listen carefully," Caleb told her. "I'll explain everything else later. I will find you, just like I did today, and I'll explain everything."

"I have so many questions," Tameka pleaded.

"I know, but they'll have to wait. Tameka I promise, I'll answer your questions in due time, but right now, we still have work to do. This is serious business, okay? I need you to pay attention."

Tameka nodded.

Caleb lifted his briefcase and opened it. He pulled out a manila envelope and handed it to Tameka. "This is Eric's death certificate."

Hesitantly, Tameka took it. She handled the envelope as if he told her it was filled with anthrax. "What? What is this for?"

"It's for the insurance claim," Caleb explained. "The insurance company is going to need it."

"How? How did you get this?"

"I know people," Caleb told her. "I have friends everywhere."

"They won't tell that they gave you this will they?" Tameka asked nervously.

"No. Now don't worry about that. You just take this with you when you go to process the claim. Have you already called to set up the meeting?"

Tameka nodded.

"Good. Inside, is the death certificate, the coroner's report, the police report, the original insurance document, and everything else you're going to need to get the money."

Tameka began to shake her head. "I'm not ready for this. I can't do this."

"You *have* to do this." Caleb pulled out a bank card and handed it to her. "Have them deposit the money to your account, and then transfer to this account. Don't worry, everything is taken care of. We're almost there. I'll contact you again after the funeral."

"*The funeral*?" Tameka asked, lifting an eyebrow.

"Yeah, the funeral," Caleb told her. "You have to go. You have to sit right up front with the family, and you have to cry hard as hell. There's no telling who's going to be watching."

Tameka shook her head frantically. "I can't do that! No, please don't make me do that! I can't go to his funeral!"

"You *have* to go! Tameka, it'll look suspicious if you don't. You're his girlfriend, and you had an insurance policy on him for a lot of money. You have to look like the distraught widow!"

"I *can't*!" Tameka said, shaking her head. "I can't look those people in the eye! *I set him up*! I'm the reason he's in that box! I can't do it!"

Caleb placed his hands on her shoulders. "Tameka! Listen to me! You don't have a *choice*! You don't see this through, we could both go to jail, don't you understand that? You go and you do what you're supposed to do, and you're a millionaire! You have to choose. Prison, or a million dollars? Which on is it?"

Tameka inhaled deeply, and then let her breath out slowly. She nodded.

"Good. Baby, I'll contact you after the funeral. You just stay loose."

"What if I need to talk to you?"

"You can't! At least not yet. Tameka, We can flip this money, and score big. I got a money making investment in the works that is a lock. I can take your half, and flip it ten times over. We do this, and both our troubles are over. We can retire to a beach and sip on coconut beverages all day, and make love on the beach all night. We're almost there, baby. Just a little further. But I'm going to need you to be strong for the both of us. Is that clear?"

Tameka nodded.

"Can you do that?"

"Yes," Tameka said nodding again. "I can do it."

"Good." Caleb leaned forward and kissed Tameka on her forehead. "Count to one hundred, before you leave the alley. Walk west toward your job. I'll be in touch soon, baby."

Tameka embraced Caleb tightly, before allowing him to turn and leave the alley. She began her count to one hundred. It was the longest count she had ever endured. And it was the loneliest. But she knew what she had to do. She had to put on her acting face, go to Eric's funeral, sit with his family, and cry her eyes out. She could do it, she told herself. How many times had she got with some short dick nigga and faked an orgasm? It was the same principal right? She could fake it. For a million dollars that Caleb was going to flip tens times over, she could fake an orgasm on top of the casket. She was almost there. Ten million dollars? Her life was surely about to change.

# Chapter Twenty Six

The 18 gauge stainless steel casket sported gold tone swing out handles, along with gold lugs, and gold trimming. It lay amongst dozen of bereavement flowers and funeral reefs, most of them either white, blue, black, or yellow. The arrangement around the closed casket was immaculate, and Mt. Zion Baptist Church in Brooklyn was filled with mourners—friends, family, and associates' of Eric's. He was a popular man in the hood. The young teens glorified his life and death with pictures on T-shirts, and those closest to him were ready to retaliate something fierce on the murderer responsible for Eric's death.

The streets were buzzing—first Sean was found shot to death in his truck, and now Eric was gone. Their tight knit drug crew was dwindling. The police were telling everyone it was because of a home invasion he committed. The shooter was acting in self defense and shot Eric twice in the head. He was questioned and set free. The family wanted a closed casket funeral; his peoples couldn't bear to see him so deformed—no matter how well the mortician dressed him up and fixed his features, he wasn't going to be the same. The autopsy report said he was shot in the eye and in the frontal lobe, and that he was killed instantly. His brains had been blown out. It was ugly.

Eric was a wild boy, a problem—some say he was becoming a cancer, and that his death was inevitable. He had made too many enemies out in the world, and the walls came crashing down around him.

# Boyfriend # 2

The church organist was playing *Amazing Grace,* and weeping could be heard throughout the church. Eric's family sat in the first two pews, all of them dressed in black, and they were silent. Their tears trickled down their faces, and the anguish that they felt was on full display. Tameka walked into the church flanked by her friends, Bridgette and Rosalynn, and her tears couldn't stop flowing. Clad in a black, form fitting dress and black high-heels, she strutted down the aisle drying her tears. She felt a tiny bit of remorse, and she knew that she would truly miss Eric. Deep down, however, she knew that it was a chess move that she needed to make. But still, it was all a little much for her.

Tameka moved toward the closed casket and began to feel somewhat faint. Her breathing became shallow and it felt as if her knees were about to give out on her. The closer she came toward the casket, the more her body weakened.

"I can't. I can't do it," she cried out.

Tameka suddenly shifted to her right side, almost as if she were a falling tree, but Bridgette managed to catch her before her total collapse. Rosalynn came to her aid as well. They held the grieving Tameka in their arms, and Eric's family made room for her to sit in one of the front pews with them.

"It's okay, chile....be strong," Eric's aunt said to Tameka.

Tameka couldn't stop crying. She didn't know it would hurt so much.

"Get her some water," another family member said.

The family began to comfort Tameka, and she started to do the same. It was a shame that she had to meet Eric's family under such tragic circumstances, as they were a lovely group of people. They hugged each other, and tried to be strong during the duration of the service. Tameka met a few aunts, cousins, uncles, and a ton of close relatives. They accepted Tameka immediately, knowing how much Eric loved her, and the warmth she felt around them, almost made Tameka sick with grief. She felt so fraudulent and ugly. It was hard to look his grandmother in the eye, when she knew that she was the one responsible for setting her grandson up for his demise.

The goons came out in droves to pay their respects to Eric. He was like an icon in Brooklyn. They gave their condolences to the family, and the look on their faces showed they weren't going to let Eric's murder go down in vain.

The pastor of the church stood behind the mahogany podium in his long red and black robe, ready to give his eulogy. Pastor Madison was a handsome Black man in his early fifties and had seen his share of young, Black men gunned down in the streets. He had churned out many eulogies for the fallen—young men and women who'd been victims to the promises of attaining great wealth, respect and/or glory from joining gangs, selling drugs, or living a sinful lifestyle.

Pastor Madison gazed down at the family. They were all new faces in his church, but he felt a connection to them. He and his congregation were doing their best to console the family and make them feel at home, despite the reputation of their lost loved one. Before the pastor could speak, Tameka excused herself and headed to the bathroom. She didn't want to hear Eric's eulogy. It was just too difficult for her to sit through.

Tameka walked into the ladies' room and glanced underneath all the stalls to make sure that she was alone. Once she was certain that she was alone, she walked over to the mirror and stared at herself.

"Get it together, Tameka, you're almost through with this," she said to herself. "You're going to be one rich bitch after all this is done and over with."

She sighed heavily. Everything was going as planned. So far, no one was suspicious of anything. Caleb had made it look like a home invasion and then claimed self-defense. The detectives believed his story, and no one was any wiser. He was rich and his reputation was impeccable, so it had been easy for everyone to believe his story. But it was still hard for Tameka to believe that she had actually gotten Eric to sign the insurance policy. Caleb had arranged it all. He had a connection with a life insurance company where they had it all planned out—an inside source in the company made everything look legit. They needed a signature, and Eric gave her one. The scam made the policy look long-standing, and it designated Tameka as the beneficiary in case of his death. No one in his family was aware of the policy's existence. They were naive to the scam Tameka was pulling off. Caleb had been very thorough and methodical in setting up the insurance part of the set up. He had made sure to dot all his I's and cross all his T's. They chanced nothing. The payout would be quick once all the paperwork was finalized, and she wasn't sure if the agents involved were taking a share of the payout, or if Caleb had simply greased their pockets with some of his own money. It was all so crazy to her, and it had all happened so fast. How Caleb had been able to set up the insurance scam so quickly perplexed her. But like so many things of late, she had learned not to question and to just roll with the punches.

Getting Eric to sign the policy had been easy. After returning from Martha's Vineyard she had lied to him about being sick. She told him that she had thrown up the entire time, and that her and Caleb hadn't had sex. In fact, she told him that she and Caleb had never had unprotected sex. And that was why she was sure that the child she was now carrying inside of her stomach was his. Eric was shocked.

Having a seed to carry on his name meant the world to him. He had promised her that he would do everything in his power to take care of the baby. And that was when Tameka brought up Peon. What would she do if he wasn't around to take care of her and the baby? What if things happened beyond his control, and

Peon left her a widow, and her child a bastard? Would he doom his fatherless child to a life in the streets? Would he make her struggle to raise a child alone? The questions were too much for Eric. If nothing else, he was loyal. And so, it had been easy for Tameka to talk him into getting insurance for her and the baby. Eric signed without hesitation. He wanted to make sure that if anything happened to him, that his son would be all right. He was sure that she was carrying a boy to carry on his name. He was wrong.

Tameka stared at herself in the mirror. She was ashamed of what she had done. So much deceit, so much deception, and too much death. She was ready for all of it to be over with. She was ready to move on with her life and forget. She was ready to leave the church, and never look back.

Tameka took another deep breath, fixed her hair, collected herself, and exited the bathroom. When she reached the church's foyer, she heard some kind of commotion going on inside the church. She walked inside to see many people standing, and there seemed to be some kind of confrontation ensuing up front near the casket.

"That muthafucka owes me a lot of fuckin' money, I want that casket opened," Peon shouted. He was flanked by his goons and didn't care about the disrespect he was showing to the family.

"Sir, this is a church…God's house! How dare you come in here and disrupt this funeral," the pastor shouted.

"I don't give a fuck where I'm at. I'm owed a million dollars from that fool…and I'm collecting either way," Peon growled.

The place was in turmoil. Those loyal to Eric were ready to war and fight with Peon. They guarded the casket with their own lives, creating a wall between Peon and the casket, preventing Peon and his goons from marching forward and demeaning the dead.

"Don't fuck with me!" Peon shouted.

"You need to leave from this place right away, because the cops have already been called," someone shouted.

Peon glared at everyone surrounding him and his men. He was clearly outnumbered and probably outgunned. As a few of the young thugs in the church flashed their guns and were ready to use them.

Tameka watched the uproar from a short distance. She was in awe at what she was witnessing. Even in death, Eric could still stir some shit up. She spun on her heels and hurried toward the exit. It was too much for her. She didn't even tell her friends of her departure.

Once outside and able to get some fresh air, Tameka rummaged through her purse to find her cigarettes. She needed a smoke. But before Tameka could light up, she heard her name being called.

"Tameka," a man shouted.

Tameka turned towards him and he had *cop* written all over him.

"Who's asking?"

"I'm detective Lane, homicide," the man told her.

Tameka's heart fell to her stomach. She was ready to drop her cigarette, but she tried desperately not to panic. What could he want, she asked herself? He was homicide, not fraud. But then again, Eric was dead, and it wasn't because of any fucking break-in. He had been set up to be murdered.

"What you want from me?" Tameka asked.

"I just need some questions answered, if that's okay with you," Detective Lane told her.

Tameka nodded.

"You were the girlfriend to the decease, if I'm correct?"

"Yes."

"And to my understanding, he was shot during a home

invasion he was committing….a robbery."

Tameka nodded.

"What do you want with Eric anyway? He's dead now," Tameka said. "You trying to charge him?"

"Well, to be honest, he's…or was, a person of interest in a murder I'm investigating upstate. The victim was shot several times by a huge gun, and it came to my understanding that your deceased boyfriend was also the boyfriend to my victim. They had quite an interesting history together. Did you know about his other girlfriend, Sky?"

Tameka looked pained. "*His other girlfriend?*"

The look on her spoke volumes, and told the detective much of what he needed to know. Tameka hadn't known about Sky, so she was probably not involved in the homicide. And now that she knew that Eric had another woman, she was probably pissed, and wouldn't cover for him. The fact that Eric was dead, meant little to him, he still needed to tie up his investigation if it turned out that Eric was the killer, or rule Eric out and find the real killer, if it turned out that he wasn't involved. He knew that he could play on Tameka's anger and grief, and finesse the truth out of her.

"They met up after her release on parole from prison, and I'm just trying to put this puzzle together." Detective Lane continued. "But this case seems to have some really long legs on it."

"Well, he's dead now, so I guess your case is open and shut," Tameka said sharply. "I guess we can let the dead rest in peace now."

"I'm sorry for your loss…"

"Fuck you!" Tameka told him. "Be sorry about that." Tameka turned on her heels and marched away.

Detective Lane stood and watched her walk away. Something inside told him that there was more to this case than what it appeared to be. People were dead, and a lot of things didn't add up. Detective Lane felt that there were bigger pieces moving on the chessboard, and that the pawns that were being cast aside were but a mere diversion. There was an unseen hand, a link to all of it, and what that link was, bothered him to no end. Why was a Brooklyn thug like Eric, doing a home invasion in such a posh section of the city? It didn't fit his character. He was a drug dealer on a serious come-up, not a kick door bandit or a stick up kid. It didn't make sense. And why would he kill Sky, and then go and get himself killed in a robbery? What tied those two things together? What was the common thread?

Detective Lane watched as Tameka climbed into her pricey Porsche. She didn't seem too distraught, he thought. The detective lingered in front of the church for a moment, and then made his way back to his vehicle. The truth would soon unravel itself, but it was going to take *him* to start the peeling.

# Chapter Twenty Seven

Tameka stared at the numerous zeros on the check and couldn't believe she was actually holding such a crazy amount of cash in her hands. Two million dollars was a lot of money. She felt that her life was set. Now all she had to do was follow Caleb's instructions on how to deposit the check. She took a seat in the chair and stared at the check for a long moment. Everything in her life was about to change, from her home and wardrobe, to taking exotic vacations across the globe. It was real to her. She had hell getting there, but finally, she was that paid bitch!

Tameka took a moment to breathe. After the funeral, she had met up with her girls and got pissy drunk at a nearby bar. She needed to escape, to get away from the madness. With her being around Eric's family, and then the drama unfolding at his funeral, along with the cop questioning her, it had all taken a toll on her. If it wasn't for the two-million dollar check in her hand, she would have gone crazy by now, she thought. But now, it seemed like it was all worth it.

Tameka was alone in her brownstone. The afternoon sun was shining high at its peek. The Harlem traffic could be heard outside. But inside, she felt calm. She was ready to do the Dave Chappelle and shout out, *"I'm rich, bitch!"* She was ready to do cartwheels inside of her living room. She was ready to go jump on her bed like a five-year old. She was ready to do *her*, and that meant shopping sprees, trips, and quitting her job, *finally*.

261

# Boyfriend # 2

But first, she needed to call Caleb and let him know that the check came. Tameka reached for her cell-phone and excitedly dialed Caleb's number, but there was no answer. She dialed a second time, and still, no answer.

"Why isn't he picking up?" she wondered.

She didn't stress it. She put the check in a secure location and went into the kitchen. It was still hard to believe that the insurance scam actually worked. Caleb had resources and clout everywhere. He really did have friends in all places. He was the man. He was her boo, and she was ready to love him forever and fuck him nightly, like they were in a porno.

But the scary part was still ahead, she thought. She still had to deposit the huge check into her account. Just thinking about it sent nervous shivers throughout her body. What if the check brought up red flags with the bank teller? What if they were ready to arrest her when she stepped into the bank? There could be people watching her. A huge windfall like this was sure to alert the IRS, maybe the feds, and other unknown branches of government. The thought of being caught and tried for murder, fraud, and all of the other bullshit she had done to make this payday happen, truly frightened her.

Tameka opened the kitchen cabinet and pulled out a bottle of red wine. She needed a drink. She poured a good amount into a glass and threw it back like it was water. She poured herself another glass, and then another, and drunk herself into serenity. She took a seat in the living room and the only thing on her mind was money, and making more money with the money she had already attained.

Hours went by, and Tameka remained secluded in her home like a mouse in a hole. She didn't want to make any moves until she contacted Caleb, but he wasn't picking up his phone. It was going straight to voice mail. Soon it was evening outside, and Tameka made up her mind to risk it; she would deposit the check into her account, first thing in the morning. She was sure it would clear and everything would be okay. Caleb was smart. He had brought her this far, and she trusted him. She knew that all of his shit was on point.

The next morning, Tameka strutted into the Wells Fargo bank in midtown Manhattan with a giant smile on her face. Her smile belied the nervousness she felt inside. Today she chose to wear a business ensemble so that she looked like a person who should be depositing a two million dollar check. She was clad in a Grey pinstripe two button jacket suit, along with a pair of matching heels, and had her hair styled in a bun. She strolled up to the teller to deposit the check. The bank wasn't crowded today, so she was able to move through the line rather quickly. When finally, it was her turn, she approached the bank teller and handed her the check.

The young bank teller smiled. "I'm gonna have to get my manager for an amount this huge."

"It's not a problem, right?" Tameka asked.

"No Ma'am," the teller told her. She quickly disappeared into the back.

Tameka sighed and waited patiently for that bank manager to arrive. She tried not to look nervous, but she was becoming more so with each passing moment.

*Please don't let this become a problem,* she thought to herself. A moment later, a pale and portly middle-aged male following behind the teller walked up to the counter and greeted Tameka.

"Is there a problem with the check?" Tameka asked.

"No Ma'am. We just have to verify everything, and it may take a little time," the manager told her.

"Okay."

Tameka had nothing but time. She wanted to do everything

right. This was huge for her. She followed the manager into his office and waited patiently while he made the necessary phone calls. A half hour later, Tameka walked out the bank with a huge smile on her face. Everything had went well. The money was in her account, and it was going to take a few days to clear, but she was ready. The paperwork was in her hands, and Tameka was officially a millionaire. Now, all she had to do was wait for further instructions from Caleb about the wire transfers. She paused and tried to call him again, but like before, there was no answer. Tameka didn't want to worry, but there was some concern that maybe something was wrong.

She hailed a cab in Midtown and climbed inside. Feeling like the hard part was finally over, Tameka wanted to celebrate a little.

"Where to?" the cabbie asked,

"Take me to the nearest fuckin' bar." Tameka told him. "I need a damn drink."

The cabby smiled and drove off.

Tameka slouched down in the backseat, and for the first time in a long time, genuinely felt like she could relax a little. The stress of setting Caleb up, and then of double crossing Eric, of having to attend Eric's funeral, and then of having to cash a two million dollar insurance check, bled from her body. The only thing she needed now, was for Caleb to call her back.

The cab moved through Midtown and after a while, Tameka couldn't contain herself. She gazed at the high-end stores and boutiques lining 5th Avenue, and thought about returning to them with virtually unlimited resources to shop.

She couldn't help the smile that spread across her face. *"I'm rich, Bitch!"*

# Chapter Twenty Eight

Tameka made her way down Frank Sinatra Drive in Hoboken, trying to drive as inconspicuous as possible. She nervously peered into her rear view mirror at least once every three seconds to make sure that she wasn't being followed. She didn't know why Caleb had chosen this place anyway. Going across the bridge into Jersey and driving along the Hudson was always a traffic nightmare.

Caleb's message had been delivered to her in a bouquet of flowers with no name on it, by a suspicious looking delivery guy in a unmarked delivery van. The card that came with the bouquet expressed sympathy for her loss, but the cellophane papers that were wrapped around the flowers gave a different message. They had instructed her to drive to her favorite Starbucks in Manhattan, which she did. Upon arriving there, she received another note telling her that the coffee she was looking for could only be found in one place. The old Maxwell House coffee plant across the bridge in Jersey. And so here she was, parking at Castle Point Skateboard Park, so that she could run across the street to the luxury apartment and condo's that the old coffee plant had been converted into.

Maxwell House on the Hudson was an exercise in sheer luxury. They boasted not only a rooftop courtyard, but a large rooftop pool with a spa, a fully equipped gym and exercise studio, along with a private club, and concierge services for it residents. The location itself was a shoppers wet dream, as it was near all of the newest, latest, and greatest shops and trendy restaurants in the area. The fact that it was situated near a subway station, was next to the Hudson, was surrounded by parks, and had an unobstructed view of the Manhattan skyline didn't hurt either. Town homes in the building started at three million.

Tameka climbed out of her toffee brown, convertible Porsche Boxster S and peered around. She absolutely loved this part of Hoboken, and had actually looked at another building just down the road. But as the area was now happening and trendy, with upscale shops and hot restaurants popping up all over, she found that the asking prices were ridiculous.

Tameka exhaled, grabbed her purse, and turned to start her walk across the street. She was startled by a young skateboarder skidding up next to her, and flipping his skateboard high into the air. She actually panicked and ducked.

"Hey!" Tameka shouted. "Watch it!"

The skateboarder could be no more than seventeen. He looked young, and even a little out of place. He looked rich and clean cut, with yellow blond hair, and ocean blue eyes, although his clothing was that of a skater.

"Hey, babe, I saw you," the kid told her.

"Babe? That's no way to address women," Tameka told him.

The skater twirled his skateboard around, and placed it back on the ground. "Cool, whatever. You're going to the top floor. He's waiting for you by the pool."

The skater hurried off.

"Hey, wait!" Tameka called to him, but it was too late. He was away just as fast as he appeared. She turned her attention back to the building.

Tameka hurried across the street as fast as she could in heels. She was still in her work clothes, and that meant heels and a business suit. Both of which she couldn't wait to get out of, and even more importantly, she couldn't wait to free herself of the tight ass bra she was wearing. She hated that thing with a passion.

Tameka headed into the building and strutted across it's luscious marble floors to the elevator. Once inside, she selected the button that would take her to the rooftop pavilion. The elevator opened up on the rooftop to reveal a world that few even knew existed, and even fewer had the privilege of experiencing. They had built a lush tropical paradise on top of a roof in the middle of Jersey. It was as if she had been magically transported to Negril Bay, Jamaica.

Caleb was seated next to the swimming pool in nothing but swim trunks. He had two tropical drinks sitting at the table next to his lounge chair. Tameka smiled, and made a bee line in his direction.

"You look comfy," Tameka told him.

"Life is good," Caleb told her. He lowered his sunglasses and peered over them at her.

"Isn't a little cool to be swimming today?" Tameka asked.

Caleb nodded toward the lounge chair next to his. "I'm getting in some practice. You should too."

"I don't have the luxury of being so calm," Tameka declared. "I had to do a funeral, remember?"

"And you did it well, my dear."

Tameka took the seat next to him. "We do have a problem."

"And what is that?" Caleb asked, sitting up.

Tameka reached into her purse and pulled out an envelope. "They didn't direct deposit the check into the overseas account like you wanted them too. Instead, they cut me a check."

"They cut you a check?" Caleb asked, lifting an eyebrow. "You're carrying around a two million dollar check in your purse?"

Tameka shook her head. "No, this is the paperwork for the

check. I didn't know what to do, so I deposited it."

"Where?"

"Into my account?" she told him.

"Your personal bank account?"

Tameka nodded. "Is that bad? Did I mess up?"

Caleb shook his head. "Naw. That's what they expected you to do."

"So what do I do now?" Tameka asked. "I don't know what to do."

"Easy, babe," Caleb said, waving his hands and motioning for her to calm down. "All you have to do, is transfer the money overseas."

"Won't they get suspicious?"

"Who? The insurance company has already paid the money out. It's part of doing business. It may raise some eyebrows, but hell, you're not being implicated in his death. He was a street thug! The police asked me some questions, but my reputation is stellar. I'm a millionaire, a rising star on Wall Street, and this street punk came to rob me. It's an open and shut case. As long as they can't tie me to you, then we're all good."

"And you don't think anyone will tell them?"

"That's why we're going to send the money overseas," Caleb told her. "We're going to send it overseas, play a shell game, and then bring it back over here through various investments."

"I don't know how to do any of that!"

"Don't worry about it. I'll handle everything. You just write down your account numbers, your passwords, and I'll take care of the rest. This is what I do, baby. Relax."

Tameka exhaled, and allowed herself to do just that. She had no doubt that Caleb knew exactly what he was doing when it came to investing, and moving money around.

"Okay, so you transfer the money, and then what?" Tameka asked.

"Then, we fly down, sign some papers, and have a relaxing vacation away from prying eyes. We'll go down to the islands and relax, take a much needed vacation, and just be us."

Caleb rose from his lounge chair, walked behind Tameka, and began to massage her shoulders. "You could use a vacation, babe. You've been through a lot, and you could definitely unwind."

Tameka closed her eyes and relaxed. "I could," she purred. "I really need to unwind."

"I'll have a ticket waiting for you at JFK this weekend," Caleb whispered into her ear. "Don't worry about packing, you can buy clothes once you get to the island. We can make love all night, sip champagne and relax in the hot tub all day. Maybe a little scuba diving, some para sailing, some long moon lit walks along the beach."

"Mmmmm, sound wonderful," Tameka told him. "I need that. I really really need that. But no jet skis."

Caleb laughed. "No jet skis."

"What time should I pick up the ticket?"

"It'll be waiting for you whenever you're ready."

"I can't wait. I want a deep massage with a lava rock treatment, and an warm oatmeal bath."

"You can have all of that and more," Caleb said, kissing her ear lobe.

"I love you," Tameka whispered.

"I love you too, babe," Caleb told her.

# Boyfriend # 2

# Chapter Twenty Nine

Tameka had grown accustomed to luxury. Caleb had opened her eyes up to a different lifestyle, a completely different level of luxury and service, a completely different world. And yet, she still could not find the words to describe the view she was experiencing from her balcony.

Caleb had booked them the presidential suite on the top level of the Ritz-Carlton, Grand Cayman. And the balcony attached to the suite overlooked not only the beautiful Greg Norman designed golf course, but beyond that, provided a stunning panoramic ocean view that stretched across the horizon. The water itself, was a hue of blue that she had never before witnessed. She knew that if there existed Heaven on Earth, then surely it must look like this.

Caleb stepped up behind her and placed his arms on her hips. She leaned her head back against his chest. She felt a feeling that she hadn't felt in a long long time. She felt safe, she felt as if she had finally found what she had been searching for her entire life. She felt connected, like she was finally home.

"It's so beautiful here," she sighed.

"It is."

"How many times have you been here?"

"Many," Caleb told her. "You know, the Cayman's is a big financial transaction hub."

"Where you hide all your rich clients money to keep it from getting taxed?" Tameka asked with a smile.

Caleb laughed. "Exactly."

"Must be nice," Tameka said. "I think I majored in the wrong subject. Should have went to school for finance."

"You can always go back."

"You're going to help me?"

"Of course."

"Hmmm, my own personal tutor. I think I like the sound of that. And if I'm a naughty student, are you going to paddle me?"

"I'm going to spank you right on your behind," Caleb told her, slapping her butt.

"Ooooh, you're going to make me into a really naughty student," Tameka said with a laugh.

A knock came to the door.

Caleb turned. "Must be room service."

Caleb released Tameka's hips and headed for the door. He opened the door and was greeted by a uniformed servant pushing a silver cart, with sterling silver serving ware.

"You can just place the cart in the living room," Caleb told him. He pulled out a twenty, and handed it to the servant.

"Would you like me to serve, sir?"

"No, that'll be all. Thanks."

The servant left the room, and Caleb closed the door behind him. He turned to Tameka.

"Dinner is served," Caleb declared.

"In a moment," Tameka told him. "I'm still enjoying this view."

"Did you already sign those papers I left on the coffee table?"

"I did," Tameka told him. "I placed them on the credenza."

Caleb walked up behind her and pulled her close once again.

"I can't get over how beautiful this place is," Tameka told him again. "I could live here forever."

"We could."

"Yeah, right."

"No, really. We could."

"How?" Tameka turned and faced him.

"I can do everything that I need to do from the island," Caleb explained. "I could fly into New York every once in a while when necessary."

"And your bosses are going to go for that?"

"Sure," Caleb shrugged. "We have offices all over the globe. We have a pretty big one here. I can just transfer to this office. This is the Grand Caymans after all. Like I said, it's a major financial hub. Working from here would be no problem at all."

"Living here would be a dream come true," Tameka told him.

"Then let's do it."

"Just like that?"

Caleb nodded. "Just like that."

"And my home? And what about my job?"

"We can rent it out, and as far as your job goes, you don't have to work anymore. Just retire. You're a millionaire now. Besides, we can live off of my money."

Tameka was doing cartwheels on the inside. Living off of Caleb's money in the Grand Caymans would definitely be a dream come true.

"Caleb, tell me you're not just playing with me?" Tameka said staring into his eyes. "Tell me you're not just pulling my leg."

"I'm not." Caleb said, staring back into her eyes. "If this is what you want, we can do this."

Tameka exhaled. She didn't even know if she wanted to go back to New York any time soon. She could just call Bridgette, and Rosalynn, and have them take care of things for her. She could submit her resignation by fax. She could go shopping and get a new wardrobe tomorrow. That would be a great way to explore the island. Everything that she had worked so hard for, was now coming to fruition. Her lifetime of struggling, and scratching and clawing, and begging borrowing, stealing, and fucking her way to the top, was now coming to an end. She had finally reached her destination.

"Are you happy?" Caleb asked.

Tameka nodded. And she truly was. She was the happiest that she had ever been.

Caleb placed his hand on the side of her face and leaned forward and kissed her passionately. Tameka closed her eyes and moaned. Caleb lifted her up off the ground, while kissing her all over her face, and carried her through the suite to the master bedroom. He sat her down on the edge of the bed, still kissing her, and then pulled off her robe.

Tameka was still fresh from the shower she had just taken, her hair was slightly damp, and she had the faint scent of Shower to Shower powder all over her body. Caleb worked his way down her neck, onto her chest, where he engulfed her erect nipple. She moaned passionately.

Caleb was wearing only boxer briefs, and a fitted wife beater, and she could see that he was clearly standing at attention. In fact, it appeared as though he had placed a giant cucumber inside of his briefs. The sight of it startled her for a brief moment.

Caleb gently pressed his hand against Tameka's shoulder, imploring her to recline onto the bed, which she did willingly. She climbed back onto the giant king sized bed and opened her legs, showing him her prize. She had dried it off when she left the shower, but it was once again soaking wet.

Caleb started at Tameka's lips, kissing one, and then the other with soft gentle pecks. He took her top lip into his mouth, and then her bottom one, sucking on them gently and savoring them as if they were pieces of forbidden fruit, of which he had long been deprived.

274

# Boyfriend # 2

Caleb made his way down her face, kissing her chin, sucking on her neck, engulfing her ear lobe. Her sucked at her ear lobe foretelling the pleasure that her clitoris was soon about to experience. Tameka moaned. She couldn't wait for him to make his way south.

Caleb's tongue ran down Tameka's neck to her shoulder, and then down her chest to her breast. Once again, he took her erect nipple into his warm mouth and sucked gently. Slowly, he moved from one breast to the other, from one nipple to the other, giving each of them equal attention. She felt as if she were about to burst.

Tameka placed her hands on Caleb's shoulders, pressing down, guiding him, practically begging him to continue on to her vagina. She wanted to feel his tongue gliding over her clitoris. She was desperate to feel his tongue wiggling around inside of her body, she wanted his tongue to lick her pussy until she had tears in her eyes.

Caleb kissed Tameka on her stomach, running his tongue over her navel, and then down to her vagina. She arched her back and moaned at the first stroke of his tongue across her southern lips. Her hand immediately shot to the back of his head.

Caleb's tongue parted Tameka lips with deep lashing strokes. He wrapped his lips around her labia and sucked intensely. But he knew what she was waiting for. He knew what she loved the most. He took his hand and placed it and the top of her vagina, and gently elongated her pussy, completely exposing her pearl tongue. He then took it into his mouth, and sucked. The suction he applied was gentle at first, and then it built slowly, until he found himself sucking nearly as hard as he could. It was this move that always got her. It was this move that made her cum, and curse, and clutch the bed sheets.

"Ooooooh!" Tameka let out a watery cry, and she orgasm fiercely. She could feel the liquid flowing from inside of her. Her body shivered with ecstasy.

Caleb's tongue tickled her clit for a while longer, before he began to work his way back up her body. Again he kissed her stomach with tiny gentle pecks, and again his tongue played with her navel. Soon, Tameka found her breast inside of his warm mouth once again.

Caleb sucked her nipples, again giving equal time to each, before continuing on to her neck, and then finally, her lips. He kissed her with a passion that took her breath away. Tameka felt a way that she had never felt before. The way his hands glided over her body, the way he took her lips into his, the way he handled her body. He was treating her as if she were fine china, but also as if that china contained the last meal on Earth. He was delicate, yet passionate. His warm breaths against her ear, the side of her face, against her neck, heightened all of her senses. And then he placed himself inside of her.

Tameka arched her back and cried out. Although he entered into her gently, it felt as though he just kept going deeper and deeper inside of her. The first thing that came to mind was a train entering into a tunnel. But it was as if this train was never going to end. And that's how she felt. She wondered when he was going to run out of dick to put inside of her. She could feel his long, thick rod, deep inside of her body. He was stretching her out so much that he was pushing her cervix apart. Where all of this dick came from, she did not know. Was it the island, the ambiance, the money that was making his dick so thick and hard, she wondered. She had never felt him like this before. But it felt good to her. In fact, she had been exploding continuously on the inside since he went inside of her. The pressure on her G spot was enormous and unyielding. And the crazy thing was, the only thing he had done thus far, was put his gigantic dick all the way inside of her. He hadn't even moved yet. And then he did.

Caleb slid out and then back down into her, and the

sensation of his large thickly veined manhood rubbing against her inner walls caused her to shake and shiver. She could feel everything, including the large mushroom shaped tip deep inside of her stomach. Tameka buried her nails into his back and let out a watery scream.

Slowly, Caleb slid in and out of her, and each time he pushed deep inside of her again, she came. Tameka wrapped her arms around him tightly and whined. She was wet, and growing wetter with each of his strokes, but her wetness wasn't making a bit of difference. His dick was so big and she felt her pussy moving in and out with each of his strokes.

Why was he so hard, Tameka wondered? What the fuck was going on?

Caleb wrapped his arms around her, and rolled over so that she was now on top of him. What she felt when he did that, was something she had never felt before in her life. He punched her insides so deep that she damn near jumped up off of the bed.

"Oooooh!" Tameka cried out. She quickly placed her hands on his ripped stomach so that she could lift herself off of him just a little bit. Never in her life had she thought there was such a thing as too much dick. And now, she found herself trying to keep some out of her. But Caleb wasn't having it.

Caleb clasped Tameka's hands, taking it away from his chiseled stomach, causing her to once again slide all the way back down onto his fully erect bullet train. Tameka clinched her ass and quickly tried to jump up off of him again. At least a little bit.

"Ooooh, shit!" she screamed.

Caleb pulled her forward, so that her body was laying on top of his. Her face rested near his, and they were chest to chest. He then placed his hands on her ass so that she couldn't flee, and began to thrust upwards. And flee was exactly what she tried to do.

"Oh god!" Tameka shouted. "Oh shit! Oh shit! Oh! Oh!"

Caleb continued to hold her ass with one hand, and her back with the other, while thrusting his thick, long, dinosaur dick deep up into her. Tameka slammed her hands against the headboard and tried desperately to raise up to escape the punishment she was taking.

"Oh fuck!" Tameka shouted. "Fuck! Fuck! Got damn, nigga! What the fuck? Oh, help me! Help me! I'm sorry! I'm sorry!"

A smile crept across Caleb's face. He had her apologizing and she hadn't even done shit. Tears poured down Tameka's face. She was thick ass hell, with a body built like it could take some punishment. But the way Caleb was fucking her, and the amount of meat he was putting inside of her had went beyond punishment. It was now considered torture. The way he was fucking her, would have been against the Geneva Convention.

"Fuck!" Tameka screamed. "I quit! I quit! I'm sorry! Please! Please!"

Tameka banged the walls of the suite, and screamed for dear life.

"Make me cum!" Caleb told her. "You better hurry up and make me fucking cum!"

"How?" Tameka shouted. She tried to squeeze the muscles in her vagina, but her pussy was already tight, already full, and already being stretched beyond capacity. "Please! Get it! Get it, babe! Get it! I'm sorry!"

Caleb thrust so hard that his dick lifted Tameka into the air off of him. He quickly slid from beneath her and stood next to the bed. Tameka collapsed on the bed, breathing heavily, thinking that she was about to get some rest, or at least a little bit of relief. Caleb had other things in mind. He grabbed her waist and lifted her butt up.

"No!" Tameka pleaded.

Caleb grabbed Tameka's hair with one hand, and stuck his

dick inside of her using his other hand.

"Ahhhhh!" Tameka shouted. She tried to escaped by moving forward, but Caleb had her by her weave.

"Uh-un!" Caleb told her. "Bring that pussy back here!"

Caleb began to pound Tameka's pussy from the back. And hitting it doggy style, meant that he was hitting nothing but pure pussy. He was going in deep. Tameka's screams were constant, and loud. She grabbed the cover with both hands and squeezed.

"Ahhhhhh!" Tameka screamed. "Got dammit! Help me! Help me! Please! I'm sorry! I'm sorry, Daddy!"

Caleb pulled her hair harder, and then slapped her as hard as he could across her fat juicy ass. "You better make me cum!"

"Got damn, nigga!" Tameka shouted. There was no way she could maintain her little miss proper vocabulary. He was getting abused, and her pussy was on fire, her vagina was hurting, and she had at least twelve inches of thick dick deep inside of her stomach. She started pounding her fist against the bed and against the headboard.

"Ain't nobody coming to save you!" Caleb said, while stroking. "The only way out, is to make me cum. So, make me cum!"

Tameka knew what she had to do. If she was going to get fucked to death, she at least had to go out like a soldier. She couldn't cum anymore herself, and the only way to save her pussy was to go all out on a pussy suicide mission. She had to squeeze and throw that ass back into him.

"Got damn, nigga!" Tameka screamed, as she threw her ass back into Caleb's oncoming dick. The collision of her giant firm ass, against his enormous dick was like two Mack trucks colliding. "Ooooooh!"

"Here it comes, baby!" Caleb told her.

"Hurry up!" Tameka shouted. "Please! Please!"

"Who's pussy is this?" Caleb asked.

"Got damn! It's yours, nigga! It's yours!" Tameka shouted.

Caleb pulled his dick out, and shot his hot cum all over Tameka's big juicy ass. Some of it even shot across her back. Tameka collapsed onto the bed. She couldn't move, and she could barely talk. She knew that she couldn't walk. At least for the next twenty minutes.

Caleb turned toward the shower. "Weak ass."

Tameka shook her head and peered down at his dick, which was still huge, and still throbbing. "Get that thing away from me."

"That was just round one," Caleb said with a smile. "Wait until tonight."

"Un-un," Tameka said, shaking her head. "That was it. Damn, boy. You owe me a new pussy."

Caleb laughed.

Tameka rolled over on her back and stared up at the ceiling. "You broke my pussy."

Caleb nodded at her. "And don't you forget it."

"I'll never be able to forget that," Tameka said, trying to catch her breath.

Caleb turned and headed for the shower.

Tameka placed her hands between her legs and rubbed herself. She was sore and aching. "That nigga broke my pussy."

# Chapter Thirty

Tameka was still walking funny the next day. She almost stumbled and fell when she stepped onto Caleb's 100 ft luxury sailing yacht.

"Whoa, be careful!" Caleb said, catching her. "You okay?"

"Lost my footing," Tameka smiled. She peered around the boat. Everything was meticulous. It was all extremely high quality, and hand crafted. "Wow."

"You didn't ask me for permission to come aboard," Caleb told her.

Tameka snapped to attention and saluted him. "Permission to come aboard, sir."

Caleb returned her salute. "Permission granted."

"So, since you're the captain of this vessel, does that make me the First Mate?"

Caleb shook his head. "You can't just jump onto a boat and declare yourself First Mate. You have to earn that rank."

"I thought I earned it last night."

Caleb stared at her and pursed his lips. "You couldn't even let a brother get a part two."

"Ahhh, that's because part one fucked me up," Tameka said with a smile. "What got into you yesterday? I'm starting to second think this move. Especially if you're going to fuck my brains out like that. I wouldn't last a month down here."

Caleb laughed. "Just wanted to get one really good one in."

Tameka nodded. "Well, you definitely did that."

# Boyfriend # 2

Caleb cast off, and using the motor, powered the sail boat out of the harbor and charted a course for the open sea. Tameka leaned back in the co-pilot's chair next to him and put on her sunglasses. It was beautiful out today, she thought. The Sun was out, there was only the slightest and gentlest of breezes blowing off the ocean. She was sitting by her man on his multi-million dollar yacht, striking her best Jackie Kennedy pose. This was definitely the life. She could get used to this. She wondered if she could even get him to run for political office in the future. After he made them a ton of money of course. The money came first, then the political power and fame. She could even see herself being the next Michelle Obama.

Tameka adjusted the Chanel head scarf around her head and neck, trying to emulate the glamorous photos of Jackie O cruising on one of the Kennedy's yachts. Her Cosby dreams had fallen by the wayside of late. She was too big for those now. She had surpassed that wealth, and now she was after even bigger bread and even more power. She had thoughts of being called The Senator's wife, or the Governor's wife. Yeah, she thought, those titles fit her perfectly. She and Caleb could build a political dynasty together.

Caleb put the yacht on full power, quickly losing the Cayman Islands in the background. Tameka rose, climbed over the deck of the yacht and headed to the comfortable weather proof lounge bed built into the front hull of the yacht. She had seen many a picture over the years of skinny white bitches in itty bitty bikinis lying on the decks at the front of their husband's or boyfriend's or sugar daddy's yacht, and she wanted to strike a similar pose. Of course, she would have Caleb snap some photos of her while she did it. These are the photos she would send back home to show everyone, so all of those bitches could eat their hearts out, she thought. Eat their fucking hearts out, she repeated in her head.

Tameka reclined, relaxed, and began taking in the morning sun. Soon, she found herself dozing off into a nice and much needed siesta.

\*\*\*\*\*

Tameka woke and stretched and yawned. She peered around, taking in her surroundings. She was surrounded by nothing but ocean as far as the eye could see. She realized that she was on the deck on Caleb's yacht, but that the yacht was now just drifting leisurely with the current. She turned to look for her love, and found him still at the stern sitting in his captain's chair. He winked at her, and sipped from an ice cold drink.

Tameka yawned and stretched once again, and then rose. She had needed the nap, as her body was completely fatigued. And sore. Tameka climbed over the deck and headed for the stern. She climbed back into the seat next to Caleb's.

"You know you snore as loud as a diesel engine?" Caleb asked.

"Get out of here!" Tameka said, hitting him playfully. "I do not snore!"

"Loud!" Caleb said with a smile. "Sounded like someone was ripping sheets up there."

"Stop it!" Tameka laughed.

Caleb took another sip.

"What are you drinking?" Tameka asked. Lying in the Sun all morning had parched her throat.

"A hard lemonade."

"Sounds good," Tameka told him. "I could sure go for one."

"A pitcher in the kitchen," Caleb said with a smile.

Tameka rose, and headed down the stairs to the luxurious cabin below. The boat not only had a nice sized master bedroom, but also two guest rooms, a dining area, and a fully equipped kitchen, along with a nicely equipped living room with a state of the art entertainment system. It was in this living room, where Tameka almost suffered a heart attack. She screamed for dear life, when she saw Eric sitting on the couch watching television.

"What's up, Baby?" Eric said with a smile.

Tameka ran out of the living area, back up the stairs to where Caleb was.

"Eric is downstairs!" Tameka shouted. Her heart was racing a million miles an hour.

Eric walked up the stairs and joined them. He placed his hand over his face to shield the sun. "Damn, it's bright out here today."

Tameka stumbled backwards. Her gaze shifted from Eric to Caleb, and from Caleb to Eric. "What the fuck is going on here!"

Eric placed his arm around Caleb and both of them laughed.

"Tameka, I want you to meet my boy, Caleb," Eric told her.

"I went to your fucking funeral!" Tameka screamed.

"You went to a closed casket funeral," Eric told her.

"I met your family!" Tameka shouted. "I sat with them. I hugged them. I comforted them!"

Eric shook his head. "All actors, all paid."

Caleb laughed. "You can see those same idiots off Broadway, three nights a week."

"What the fuck is going on?" Tameka asked angrily.

"Eric and I are boys from way back," Caleb told her.

"Actually, we attended Harvard together," Eric told her.

"What the fuck happened to your voice, your accent, what's going on here?"

"Simple," Eric explained. "Like all bitches, you wanted your cake and you wanted to eat it too. Instead of being faithful, you tried to play both of us."

"And instead, you got played," Caleb told her.

"Like all greedy, scandalous bitches who try to fuck their way to the top, you got fucked," Eric said laughing.

"You planned this?" Tameka asked. She couldn't believe her ears. Her face went from shock, to horror, to anger once the realization set in that she had been played. "You two mutha fucka's planned this? You faked his death! You both been fucking me, and playing me the whole time?"

"You played yourself," Eric told her. "Like all bitches blinded by greed and money, you saw what you wanted to see, and believed what you wanted to believe. You saw a Brooklyn thug, so I gave you one."

"You sick son of a bitches!" Tameka shouted. "I'm going to kill you! I'm going to kill both of you!"

"Here's where you got that wrong, sweetie," Caleb told her. "You are about to be shark dinner. And me and Eric are about to be back in Grand Cayman in time for dinner. And from there, we plan on catching a plane to the Bahamas, where we've transferred the money."

"Money?" Tameka shouted. "This whole set up was about the money? You'll never get away with this. Never!"

"We already have," Eric told her. "You're the one who got the insurance on me."

"And filed the claim," Caleb added. "With a bullshit death certificate it would seem."

"You gave it to me!" Tameka shouted.

Caleb shrugged. "And you placed the check into your account."

"And then transferred the money out of the country," Eric added.

"I didn't transfer shit!" Tameka said angrily. She stared at Caleb. "You did!"

"Who else has your password, your bank account information, routing numbers, etc..." Eric asked. "Only you."

"Caleb has them."

"You gave out your banking info?" Eric asked sarcastically. "How stupid can you be?"

"And for what reason?" Caleb asked.

"To transfer money from her illegal insurance fraud scheme," Eric answered.

"That she got from?" Caleb asked.

"From setting me up to be murdered," Eric answered. "Which sounds like Capital Murder to me."

Tameka's mouth fell open. She realized that they had her. They had her cold. She had took out the insurance policy. She had cashed the check. It would look like she transferred the money out of the country. And to top it off, it would look like she was part of the scam all along. *If* they didn't charge her with capital murder for setting Eric up for the kill. They had made sure that she couldn't go to the cops.

"You son of a bitches," Tameka repeated softly, while shaking her head.

"We knew you were a greedy bitch the moment we picked you out of the crowd in New Orleans," Caleb told her. "And you proved us right the whole time. Playing both of us. Agreeing to set me up, and then betraying Eric and setting him up. You were the most scandalous bitch we ever came across."

"Fuck you!" Tameka told him.

"No, I fucked you," Caleb told her. "I got a really good one last fuck last night. And now, it's time for you to exit stage right."

Tameka peered over her shoulder at the water. She began shaking her head. "Please, don't do this. Please don't do this to me! You know what happened to me in Martha's Vineyard. Please, I'll do anything. I won't go to the cops, I promise."

"You can't go to the cops," Eric told her. "Not unless you

want a capital murder charge."

"And then a fed charge for insurance fraud," Caleb added.

"Please, don't do this to me!" Tameka pleaded.

"I'll tell you what," Caleb told her. "I'll give you half a fighting chance."

Caleb lifted a life preserve jacket and tossed it overboard.

"Please, no!" Tameka told them.

"Hey, you better jump in and go after it before it floats away," Eric told her. "Man, that must have been some fuck. He's never given a chick that much of a chance before."

Caleb and Eric shared a laugh.

"Time to go, ma!" Caleb told her.

"Noooooo!" Tameka screamed.

Caleb and Eric grabbed her, and lifted her into the air. Tameka struggled and fought and tried desperately to find something to grab onto, something, anything to cling to. Caleb and Eric carried her the the edge of the boat and tossed her into the water. Tameka screamed.

"Silly bitch!" Caleb said staring down into the water at her.

"Don't do this!" Tameka shouted, while peering up at them from the ocean.

Eric knelt and peered down at her. He pointed. "You should start swimming *that* way!"

Caleb laughed. "And If I were you, I would hurry. Tiger sharks and blue tips like to feed at dusk and at dawn. If you back stroke, you can probably make it back tomorrow in the wee hours of the morning."

"Don't lie to her," Eric laughed. "She's shark food."

Caleb jumped behind the wheel, started up the boat, and turned it around. They could hear Tameka's screams for them to come back. Eric patted Caleb on his shoulder.

"Dude, I've been thinking," Eric told him.

"What's up?" Caleb asked.

"You've played the rich guy for the last three chicks," Eric told him. "It's my turn to play the rich broker. I want to drive a Lamborghini too."

"And you want me to play the hood cat?" Caleb asked with a smile..

"You're better at playing the hood cat than I am," Eric told him.

"But I like playing the rich dude." Caleb told him. "Besides, my Brooklyn accent is rusty."

"As a matter of fact, now that I've thought about it, you've played the rich guy the last five times!" Eric told him.

"Okay, okay," Caleb said holding up his hand in surrender. "You play the rich dude the next time."

Eric thought about it for a few seconds. "Naw. I'm just fucking wit ya. I love being me and showing my rough and ready BK upbringing."

"I knew you did," Caleb told him.

"So where to?" Eric asked.

"When do you have to be back at the office?"

Eric peered down at the date on his Presidential Rolex. "I still have a couple of days."

"Then how about a quick stop in Jamaica to pick us out a new target?" Caleb asked.

"Sounds good to me, bro," Eric said smiling, and slapping Caleb across his back.

Caleb accelerated the boat to full speed. He peered off into the distance, placed his sunglasses over his eyes and shook his head. "When will these bitches ever learn?"

He and Eric shared a good hard laugh.

# Epilogue

Tameka clawed her way onto the beach, pulling herself the last few yards by her fingers, and nothing more than sheer will. Her lungs and eyes were burning from the salt water of the ocean, and her insides felt as if they were on fire. Despite her best efforts to keep the putrid ocean water out of her system, she had swallowed much of it on her desperate six hour swim to shore. And she had paid the price for it.

Tameka inside convulsed violently, as her stomach worked overtime to expelled what it had already expelled. The salt water had given her diarrhea, and she had shitted several times during her long journey toward the shore. And now, her stomach was paying the price. And so was the rest of her body.

Swimming through the ocean for that length of time, had taken everything from her. She had expended her all on her journey to the shore. Her muscles hurt so bad, it felt as if the pain was emanating from her bones. She bore a constant body wide cramp, and her skin was chaff and raw, and pruned up because of the length of time she had been in the water. Toenails had fallen off, her weave was long gone, and she was bleeding across her thigh. Sometime during the wee hours of the morning, on the last leg of her journey, a tiger shark has risen from the depths to take an investigative bite. Salt water had poured into her womb, and her thigh burned like fire. And yet, she continued to swim.

Tameka didn't know what time it was, or exactly where she was at. What she did know, was that she had finally made it to a

289

beach. The waves and kind ocean current had pushed her into shore the last leg of her journey, and she had expended the last few ounces of her energy clawing her way the last few meters onto the beach. Her blood loss, along with her fatigue, was now in the critical stages. She had been determined to live, during her swim. And she even thought at one time, that she might actually have a fifty-fifty chance of making it. After the shark bite, she reduced her chances to ten percent. Now, laying on the beach and clinging to life, she reduced her chances once again. At least until she saw a set of headlights coming toward her.

Tameka was too weak, and too thirsty to scream for help. Fortunately, the vehicle was headed right at her. She now entertained the possibility that she might even live. She had been determined to live. She was too stubborn and too vengeful to die. Caleb and Eric had fucked over her, and Caleb and Eric had to pay for what they had done. She was a vengeful bitch from the hood, and if it took until her dying breath to wreak that revenge upon them, then so be it. So fucking be it.

The vehicle stopped just in front of Tameka and she heard voices, and saw figures rushing toward her. Those were the last images she recalled, as she lowered her head into the sand and passed out. The last thoughts that passed through her mind before losing consciousness? She was going to kill Caleb and Eric. She was going to kill them, if it was the last thing on Earth she got to do.

# Boyfriend # 2

# Tameka's Revenge

# coming soon

35682666R10165

Made in the USA
Lexington, KY
20 September 2014